Will thought dandelion wishes were a waste of time.

Will thought dandelion wishes spread weeds into the world. Will thought–

Emma spun around and plucked the dandelion from the side of the road. She didn't care what Will thought. She and Tracy had been making dandelion wishes since they were kids.

She turned toward home, stopping in the middle of the bridge over Harmony River. She tried to catch her breath. She tried to be as calm as the water flowing beneath her.

It wasn't possible. Not even with a dandelion wish at the ready.

What would she wish for?

Dear Reader,

Welcome to Harmony Valley!

Things aren't as harmonious here as they once were. Jobs have dried up and almost everyone under the age of sixty has moved away in the past ten years, leaving the population…well…rather gray-haired and peaceful.

Enter Will Jackson, newly minted millionaire and hometown success story. He's been on the fast track too long and is looking for a break. But then his sister, Tracy, and her friend Emma get in a car crash, and he realizes Harmony Valley would be a perfect place for Tracy to stay permanently. If he could just create a business for his sister and keep her away from Emma's spur-of-the-moment adventurous tendencies, everything would be fine.

Emma may look as if she walked away from the accident unscathed, but she bears emotional scars. She wants to rebuild her friendship with Tracy and heal. But nothing in life ever comes when you want it, especially not love and healing.

I hope you enjoy Will and Emma's journey, as well as the romances in the works for friends Flynn and Slade as they get their winery in Harmony Valley off the ground. I love to hear from readers and you can always check on the progress of Harmony Valley on my website, www.MelindaCurtis.com.

Melinda Curtis

HARLEQUIN HEARTWARMING

Melinda Curtis

Dandelion Wishes

A Harmony Valley Novel

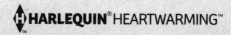
HARLEQUIN® HEARTWARMING™

Recycling programs
for this product may
not exist in your area.

ISBN-13: 978-0-373-36644-6

DANDELION WISHES

Copyright © 2013 by Melinda Wooten

Printed in U.S.A.

MELINDA CURTIS

grew up on an isolated sheep ranch, where mountain lions had been seen, and yet she roamed unaccompanied. Being a rather optimistic, clueless of danger sort, she took to playing "what if" games, which led her to become an author. She spends her days trying to figure out new ways to say "he made her heart pound." That might sound boring, but the challenge keeps her mentally ahead of her three kids and college-sweetheart husband.

Nothing in my life would be possible without the love and support of my immediate family, extended family and close friends. This past year was a roller coaster and you helped keep me strapped in.

With special thanks and hugs to A. J. Stewart, Cari Lynn Web and Anna Adams for holding my hand and kicking my butt throughout the writing of this book.

And to Carrie Knudson, thank you for the laughter, the love and the memories.

CHAPTER ONE

TODAY WAS THE day.

There'd be hugs and smiles, reminiscences and laughter.

And apologies. Of course there'd be apologies. But they'd be accepted and waved aside because best friends stood by each other. Always.

Today was the day.

If Emma Willoughby repeated it to herself often enough, this time it might come true.

Standing in the parking lot next to clumps of cheery daffodils, she checked her purse to make sure Tracy's gift was inside. She silenced her cell phone. She pasted a friendly smile on her face, passed under the grand portico and headed toward the massive glass doors of Greenhaven Rehabilitation Center.

The doors slid open as she neared. On previous visits, she'd recognized people in the lobby—elderly actors recovering from strokes, aging politicians recovering from hip surgeries, elite athletes recovering from injuries. But in nearly six months, she'd never caught a glimpse of Tracy.

The Sunday receptionist, Francie, looked up to greet her, recognition stealing the beginnings of a smile from her face.

Today, Emma silently prayed.

Francie pushed her rhinestone glasses up the bridge of her nose, tugged the lapels of her aquamarine polyester jacket tightly together and sent an icy glance toward a tall, aging security guard, who stepped forward to block Emma's path. In all the months Emma had been coming here, this was the first time Francie, Greenhaven's gatekeeper, had set a guard on her.

"Young lady, I'm terribly sorry."

Emma's smile weakened. She would not give up. She would keep coming every Sunday until someone let her in. Tracy's family couldn't keep her out forever.

"I know I can't go inside, Francie." Emma reached into her purse for her gift—a Carina Career doll. She'd been handing the receptionist a doll every Sunday for months. This week Carina was an astronaut. The dolls were meant as a reminder of their friendship and to let her best friend know Emma believed she still had plenty of choices ahead of her. "Could you please give this to Tracy?"

Francie blanched. "I can't take that. Tracy Jackson is no longer a patient in this facility."

Emma felt a moment's panic. "What do you mean?"

"Tracy Jackson is no longer a patient in this facility," Francie repeated. She glanced at the security guard once more, a disapproving line deepening her already furrowed brow. "I must ask you to leave."

Tracy was dead.

Emma tried to form a word—any word—that would refute that possibility. But the air in the lobby had become thick and heavy—suffocating—until Emma knew she was going to collapse if she didn't move.

On a gasp of air, she spun and ran to her car parked at the far edge of the visitors' section. The chilly bay breeze clawed at the hem of her dress, buffeted her hair. By the time she reached the new Subaru, she was shaking so badly she dropped her purse to the ground and leaned against the car door as memories assailed her.

She and Tracy on the bank of the Harmony River building a mud fort for frogs. She and Tracy dreaming about different futures in the

Carina Career section of the toy store. Tracy bursting into their dorm room doing an uncoordinated victory dance after landing an internship at an ad agency. And then the most painful memory—Tracy's near-lifeless body, head smashed against the passenger window of Emma's car. And everywhere…blood.

They'd known each other since they were three, and yet Tracy's family hadn't let her say goodbye, hadn't let Emma know she had died.

But why would they?

Emma had been driving the car that caused the accident, the accident that had put Tracy in the hospital, the accident with killing complications.

A violent, shuddering sob threatened to break her into sharp, tiny pieces. Tremors shot to her fingertips. Useless fingers that had been unable to draw or paint since the accident. Emma ached to create from a blank page or canvas again, but if an empty, soulless existence was her penance for the accident, so be it.

Francie appeared at the Subaru's fender, huffing and clutching a shoebox under her arm. "She's not dead."

Emma's limbs turned to liquid and she slid to the ground, landing on her tailbone, asphalt scraping her legs. She ignored the pain. Tracy was alive.

"There, there." Francie knelt beside Emma, smelling of breath mints and garlic. "Company policy forbids me from telling you what happened, but you came every Sunday for more than five months. It broke my heart to turn you away."

"Thank you for telling me," Emma choked out.

"Are you okay to drive? Want me to call someone?"

Granny Rose. Her grandmother had practically raised Emma while her mother established a career as a cutthroat trial attorney. After Tracy, it was Granny Rose that Emma turned to with her problems. She had always looked up to her grandmother's wisdom, wit and courage. But Granny Rose was eighty and lived hours away in Harmony Valley, in the northernmost corner of Sonoma County.

"Fine. I'm fine." Or she would be when she could catch her breath. Emma scrubbed at her eyes. "Do you...do you know where Tracy is?" It would be exactly like Tracy's self-made millionaire brother, Will, to have found a specialist in Switzerland and moved her there.

"Francie!" a male voice rumbled from beneath the portico. "I hear you talking to that girl. Don't make trouble for yourself."

Francie frowned and pressed the shoebox into Emma's hands. "I can't say more, but I wanted you to have this." Using the car for balance, the receptionist stood. "You take care."

Emma lifted the shoebox lid. More than twenty thumb-size Carina Career dolls stared vacantly up at her, one for every week Emma had tried to come and visit Tracy.

A slip of paper was tucked in the corner of the box.

Had Tracy written her a note?

Emma reached for the paper with trembling fingers.

An invitation to visit? Or a request to stay away?

An address was scrawled in thin, spidery handwriting on Greenhaven stationery, too neat to have been written by her friend. Emma made out a familiar address in Harmony Valley.

Tracy's.

"This is going to be good." The false enthusiasm left a sour taste in Will Jackson's mouth. He opened the front door of his childhood home. "Dad's been lonely with both of us gone. And now he'll have a full house. You and me, just like old times."

Tracy walked in, looking to all appearances like any other twenty-six-year-old in blue jeans, a beige T-shirt and short, tousled blond hair. Until she spoke. "I want. To…to go. To—"

"I know you want to go back to your own apartment," Will interrupted. There was no way he'd let his little sister return to San Francisco, to the place she shared in the city with Emma. Tracy was still fragile. Oh, she got around all right, her broken ribs and broken leg having healed. But when her skull smashed into the car window it caused damage, resulting in aphasia, a language disorder. Her speech would probably always be halting, although specialists promised it would get better as long as Tracy fought.

But Tracy had given up fighting to improve.

"You'll go back after your next round of speech therapy." If Will could persuade, bribe or exhort her to return for a new form of transcranial direct-current stimulation—brain shock therapy. He had two months to convince her before the test trials started. "Here's your cell phone." Miraculously, Tracy's iPhone had survived the crash. Will had waited until now to give it to her. Harmony Valley was surrounded by several mountains that prohibited more than an occasional bar of cell-phone service. He didn't want her texting Emma, the so-called friend who'd nearly killed her.

Controlling and overprotective? Maybe he was. But his sister had brain damage and couldn't be trusted to understand what her friend had done, let alone make appropriate decisions right now.

Tracy scowled at the phone. She scowled at the saggy green microfiber couch and worn brown leather recliner. She scowled at the stuffed trout on the wall and the orange burlap curtains. She'd scowled at everything in the past month to the point where her doctor at the rehabilitation hospital thought she might make more progress at home.

"You've got a way to go until you can live on your own again." Much as it worried Will to think about Tracy living alone, odds were against him being able to protect her forever. But if things worked out the way he wanted here in Harmony Valley, those odds evened out.

Her scowl intensified. "My. Car."

Will shook his head. "Doctor's orders. No driving."

Tracy opened her mouth, presumably to argue, but closed it again and stomped off toward her room. A door slammed, shaking the entire house. Shaking Will's resolve.

The family portrait over the fireplace tilted. His mother, immortalized at age thirty-nine, gave him a lopsided, infectious smile. He set the family photo to rights, wishing it was as easy to right the rifts in the family and keep everyone safe.

Will's father Ben came in through the kitchen door carrying a large duffel bag with Tracy's belongings. His boots and faded jeans showed the wear and tear of years working on the farm. "Where's Tracy?"

"In her room."

Ben put the duffel on the scarred kitchen table. He grabbed a glass from the cupboard and filled it with water from the sink. "Give her time. She went from being an independent, healthy woman to someone who's had to depend on others for everything."

"She shouldn't have gone to that conference in Las Vegas with Emma." Just the thought of Emma Willoughby induced chest-tightening resentment. She'd walked away from the car accident unscathed.

"Son, I know you want to protect your sister, but people have got to make their own choices." Ben rubbed a hand back and forth over his thinning blond-gray hair. "I was wrong to let you shut Emma out. I was afraid of losing Tracy. But now—"

"There's only one choice here, Dad." There would be no repeat mistakes. No playing with fire. "Aren't you even the least bit angry at Emma for what's happened to Tracy?"

"Of course I'm angry. It isn't fair, what Tracy's going through. But those girls have been friends since they were toddlers." His father leaned against the sink, watching Will sit at the head of the kitchen table. "Where one went, the other followed. And oftentimes, they followed you."

"Tracy's not following Emma anymore." The first thing Will had done upon learning the details of the accident was ban Emma from the hospital. The road had been clear, the day sunny, Tracy dozing in the passenger seat. There were no drugs or alcohol in Emma's system. She hadn't been on the phone or texting. And yet, Emma had crashed the car. She was to blame, the same as he knew

Harmony Valley Grain was at fault for his mother's death. "Emma's too much like her grandmother. Too irresponsible."

"I like Rose. Nobody can say that old girl doesn't live life to the fullest. Tracy and Emma have always done the same." Ben arched faded eyebrows. "Maybe you ought to try it."

"Yes, because look where it got Tracy. Responsibility comes before fun." That was how Will had become a millionaire so quickly. And now he was determined to help revitalize his hometown before he increased his fortune further. If only Rose could be made to see that change wasn't a four-letter word. "Rose may be on the town council, but she doesn't understand her responsibilities. She won't even consider our proposal to rezone the Henderson property for a winery."

"Sometimes it takes more subtlety than a hammer, son. You and your friends tried to ram change on Rose like an unexpected enema."

That was an image Will didn't want to contemplate. "Two members of the town council asked us to develop a business and jump-start the local economy. They should have told Rose they wanted to bring some life to this town. How is this my fault?"

Will, Flynn Harris and Slade Jennings had struck gold a few months ago when they'd sold their popular farming app for millions. They'd returned to their childhood home to decompress before coming up with their next big idea. But life in the one-gas-station town moved slower than the Harmony River. If cell-phone service was spotty, internet connections were an urban myth. The population was almost solely comprised of retirees who lacked skill and comfort with technology. Withdrawal from work and the world left Will and his friends sleepless, jittery and irritable. And most concerning? They hadn't come up with a new app idea.

The winery was a solution to everything—their burnout and boredom, the town's nearly nonexistent economy and Will's dilemma about a way to protect Tracy in case her brain damage was permanent.

"I don't see why you can't take over here and make a living being a real farmer. Generations of our people have worked this land. You should be proud of your roots."

"Dad, for the hundredth time, I don't want to be a farmer." Will lived for the chaos of programming and development. He thrived on long days and longer nights challenging his brain to wrestle down code that would accomplish the impossible. Will, Flynn and Slade had spent five years living their work, programming and troubleshooting, working out of a crappy apartment in San Jose as they scraped by on the most pitiful amount of venture capitalist funding on record.

Ben scoffed. "If you start a winery, you'll be a farmer. Or will this winery be a hobby?"

What Will hoped was for Tracy to run the winery. Using her business degree would give her purpose and keep her from being judged by anyone who assumed her IQ was tied to her halting speech. Will had to convince Tracy it was best to move home permanently. He was waiting for the right nonscowling moment to tell her.

"It's an investment, Dad. My passion is programming."

"A hobby, then." His father crossed the living room to restraighten the picture over the fireplace. He didn't turn around when he'd finished, but stared at the family portrait and the love he'd lost.

Will communicated better with his sister these days than he did with his father. The two men were never on the same wavelength and things had only become worse since the accident, when Will had taken charge of Tracy's care. "I'm headed over to see Rose and then I'll be at Flynn's house."

Ben gave a wry chuckle. "The old girl can see your agenda a mile away. You'll never get her vote."

"It's Sunday." Will shrugged, forcing an enthusiasm he didn't feel. "Rose likes me on Sundays."

CHAPTER TWO

HOURS AFTER LEARNING of Tracy's release, Emma parked her car behind Granny Rose's sea-foam-green-and-white Victorian home in Harmony Valley and climbed the creaky planked steps to the front door. As a freelance graphic artist working mostly on print advertising for magazines, Emma could work on her laptop wherever she chose, uploading her completed work when she found an internet connection. She could design in Harmony Valley for a few days, hoping she might see Tracy, and upload her work before the weekend.

After the accident, the Jacksons had been guarded, not only with who visited Tracy, but with details of Tracy's condition. Granny Rose had learned that Tracy suffered from aphasia, but had never gotten a straight answer from Tracy's father as to why Emma was being kept away. She'd know how best to approach the Jacksons about visiting now that her friend was home. Well, home to their hometown anyway. Next best thing to their apartment.

The welcoming aroma of pot roast and the familiar canned sound of Gene Kelly on vinyl drifted out an open window. Granny Rose didn't have an answering machine or a cell phone. She hadn't answered her house phone earlier and didn't know Emma was coming.

"I'm singing in the rain. Just singing in the rain…." Gene Kelly's voice floated beneath her grandmother's breathless vibrato and above the shuffle of her shoes on the wooden floor. It was Sunday night and Granny Rose was reenacting one of her favorite musicals.

Emma opened the stained glass door, stepped inside and froze.

The last time she'd seen Granny Rose dance was a month ago. She'd been wearing a white silk button-down and a black pencil skirt. Fred Astaire had been spinning on the ancient phonograph.

"I'm laughing at clouds. So dark up above…." Her back to Emma, Granny Rose tipped an Elvis umbrella over her shoulder. She was wearing a pair of faded red long johns that drooped from her skinny butt. They probably would have bagged even more if her waist hadn't been cinched into a white tutu.

Rose, in yellow duck boots, tripped and nearly fell onto the antique coffee table, sending the wood-trimmed settee skittering into the wall.

"Granny!" Emma dropped her purse and ran to steady her grandmother.

Granny Rose shrieked. She elbowed Emma in the ribs, stomped on her foot and stumbled free. Turning, she hit Emma on the head with the Elvis umbrella.

Emma crumpled beneath one of the best Sedona landscapes she'd ever painted. The orchestra swelled.

"Granny Rose." She lifted her head. "It's me. Emma. Your granddaughter?"

Gene Kelly closed the song softly. Granny Rose lowered the umbrella and stared in bewilderment. "Emma?"

Emma nodded. Blood pounded in her foot and at her temple. "Is that the tutu from my dance recital when I was twelve?"

Granny Rose's gaze dropped to the stiff white tulle. She looked around the cluttered living room, taking in the phonograph needle butting against the record label. "My raincoat is at the dry cleaners." Her breathless voice lacked its usual confidence. "Is it time for cocktails?"

"Yes." Emma could use a stiff drink.

"I didn't expect you." Granny Rose steadied Emma as she stood, although the eighty-year-old needed a bit of shoring up herself. Her huffing as she caught her breath seemed to bow her shoulders. "If you stay until next weekend you can come to the Grand Marshal Selection Ceremony."

"I'd like that," Emma said, studying her grandmother cautiously. "Tracy moved back home today," she added. "I was hoping—"

Someone knocked on the door.

Granny Rose straightened instantly. "I bet it's that computer nerd again. He should know it'll be a daisy-wilting day in winter before he gets my vote."

"Who?"

"You know, what's-his-name." Rose in her duck boots headed toward the door, thrusting the Elvis umbrella ahead of her like a sword.

"No, no, no." Emma didn't know how a computer nerd could set Granny Rose off, but she hooked Rose's bony elbow and spun her around. "You can't answer the door like that."

"It would be rude of me not to answer the door." She spoke in a tone one could only learn from a semester at Vassar.

"I may not have been a debutant," Emma

protested, "but even I know you can't greet guests in Grandpa's underwear."

Granny Rose looked at herself. Her hands flitted over the tutu. And then she handed Emma the umbrella. "Don't be fooled by the way he looks. He's got an agenda and he's not above charming you out of your pants to get to me."

IN THE TIME he and his partners had been trying to get their property rezoned for the winery, Will had encountered both support and opposition in Harmony Valley. But the real wild card was Rose Cascia. Most days, she was a hellion on wheels, running roughshod over Will's efforts to garner support for their winery. But on Sundays...

Her Sunday-afternoon hobby involved dressing up and performing musicals in her antique-filled living room. And on Sundays, Rose was usually in a good mood and seemed happy to see him. Will always made a point to stop by.

But this Sunday, as he powered off his music and removed his iPhone earbuds, it wasn't Rose who answered the door. It was a disheveled woman in a red dress leaning on an umbrella as if it was a cane. As soon as she saw him, she seemed to do a double take.

A warning bell went off in his head, urging him to pay attention, access his memory banks.

"I'm so glad you stopped by." She gave him a tentative smile. "I was going to come over to your house tomorrow. So I could apologize to Tracy and your family in person."

Memory clicked into place. He hadn't seen her in four years. Her cheekbones were more prominent, her makeup more subtle, but her dark eyes were the same.

Emma Willoughby.

Will's ears rang. He couldn't help himself; he clambered for something his father disapproved of.

Retribution.

He'd waited six months to rip into Emma for nearly killing his sister. The first two weeks he'd sat at Tracy's bedside, wondering if she was going to die from the injuries Emma's careless driving had inflicted. And after Tracy had turned the corner to recovery, he'd spent more than five months trying to imagine every excuse Emma might give for the accident.

And yet Will stood on the porch, staring at the woman, unable to speak.

"Are you all right?" she asked.

Was he all right?

"Are you kidding me?" he exploded. "No one in my family will ever be all right. Tracy came this close to dying." Will thrust his hand in front of Emma's face, his thumb and forefinger almost touching.

"I'm sorry," she whispered, her face pale. "It was an accident."

He drew a deep, shuddering breath and stared over Emma's shoulder.

In the living room, the tiny wood-trimmed love seat sat cockeyed in a corner. The delicately carved walnut coffee table tilted on two legs against a bookshelf.

"Is Rose hurt?" Will pushed past her and called, "Rose? Rose, where are you?"

Rose's voice warbled a show tune from somewhere in the back. *Thank God.*

"Granny's changing." Emma released her ribs to brush her dark bangs off her forehead with one hand, flinching. Her fingers came away bloody.

What on earth had happened in here?

Will's conscience warred with his need for retribution. Emma would live. But she needed something to stop the bleeding and possibly an ice pack. Without asking what had happened, in two strides he was at the narrow hall table. He reached into a porcelain vase for a bandage, which Rose kept close at hand, he knew, for emergencies.

Emma stared up at him as he lifted her bangs out of the way and bandaged her wound. Her hair smelled like flowers and felt like silk. "Is Rose getting ready to perform?"

"No more performances today." Guarded dark eyes caught his skeptical glance. She backed away to thread the umbrella carefully into the stand on one side of the door. And then she gave him a small, apologetic smile. "I'd like to visit Tracy."

Will didn't hesitate. "She doesn't want to see you."

"She...she said that?"

He looked away and didn't say anything.

"You haven't asked her," Emma said. It wasn't a question. Color returned to her face in a slow creep of pink that seemed to fortify her. "You haven't asked her, but I will."

Will crossed to stand very close to Emma, so close he registered a green fleck in her dark chocolate eyes. "Let me be clear. My sister trusted you with her life. An apology isn't enough, could never be enough."

Rose swept into the room in low-heeled pumps and a black skirt that fell just below

MELINDA CURTIS

her knobby knees. Her white hair was in a tight bun. Her hard gaze landed on Will.

"I don't think I've had time to tell you, Emma," the older woman said. "But this man wants to convert Harmony Valley from a peaceful small town into a soulless tourist destination."

So much for being welcome on Sundays.

CHAPTER THREE

WILL JACKSON KNEW how to push Emma's buttons.

He hadn't always. When she was a kid, he'd been her and Tracy's reluctant rescuer. When she was a teenager, he'd been like a nosy, overprotective older brother, one who'd had the potential to be attractive, if he'd removed his braces and learned how to use hair product. And then he'd gone away to college and transformed himself into a serious hunk, determined that Tracy never have any fun.

Today, authority exuded from Will like heat waves off a summer sidewalk. He didn't need a power suit. His navy polo and faded blue jeans couldn't disguise the stench of carefully managed success. He had the lean, lanky body of a surfer. Only his sun-kissed gold locks were conservatively trimmed and his fierce blue eyes didn't miss a thing. The man was well put together, handsome and heartless.

The last time Emma had seen Will was four

years ago. He'd been waiting for Tracy outside their apartment. She and Tracy had just returned from a hot road trip to Tijuana for a friend's bachelorette party. *Hot* being the operative word since Tracy's air conditioner had died in Bakersfield, and the California valley was having a record heat wave. Despite short shorts, a tank top and cornrowed hair courtesy of a beach vendor, Emma's deodorant had given out hours before and she was sweltering. She didn't look, smell or feel like entertaining a man who was far from being her biggest fan.

Will had taken Emma in with one quick, disapproving glance, then ignored her, preferring to ream out Tracy for taking off without letting him know where she was. They'd been twenty-two, for crying out loud.

Emma understood that Will probably hated her for causing the accident, but what she'd never been able to understand was why Will had seemed to hate her in the first place. It didn't help that she'd been a mess when he came to the door today. Since she was a teen, he'd treated her like she had the Congo Cooties.

Emma fingered the bandage beneath her bangs and sighed.

And now, according to Granny Rose, Will wanted to remake Harmony Valley. He probably planned to cancel everything that gave the small town its character, like the annual Beer Belly Serenade and pumpkin bowling for the Harvest Queen crown.

Emma sagged uncomfortably on her grandmother's thinly padded, red-velvet settee as the strains of *South Pacific*'s chorus built. Even Granny Rose's pot roast at dinner hadn't cheered her up. There were too many unanswered questions banging about in her head: whether Granny Rose's long-johns performance was anything to worry about; how much of a threat Will posed to Harmony Valley's cherished way of life; if she'd ever be able to paint or sketch again; whether or not Tracy could forgive Emma for the accident.

Granny Rose sat in her rocking chair by the window, moving in time to one of her favorite musical numbers. She didn't own a television. And she didn't look as if she was up to answering questions. Her lids were heavy and her lined features slack.

"I bet Tracy's happy to be home. There's no place like Harmony Valley," Granny Rose mused.

"No, there isn't."

"I hope Will didn't fill your head with nonsense about his winery while I was changing. We adopted a no-growth policy for a reason. We don't want change. After the grain-escalator explosion, we wanted peace and quiet." Her grandmother spoke slowly, as if stringing together a sentence tired her.

Was this malaise a sign that she was finally slowing down? Or was something more serious affecting Granny Rose's ability to think?

Glass-half-empty pessimism had never been Emma's style. She preferred to look on the bright side. Maybe her grandmother was tired after a busy day. Maybe Emma was misreading Rose's mental state. Emma used to get fuzzy after a long day of painting. If Granny Rose was worried about Harmony Valley, it might account for her being distracted. "When was the last time you went to the doctor?"

Her grandmother replied in the same measured cadence. "Didn't I tell you? Dr. Mayhew died last winter. His replacement is in Cloverdale and wetter behind the ears than a baby duck in a rain shower. He told me I needed to slow down and take up yoga." Granny Rose harrumphed. "I was a highflier in the circus, not a contortionist."

Her grandmother had been many things

before settling down, including a brief stint as a Rockette and a transatlantic-cruise-ship cocktail waitress, where she'd met the man of her dreams.

"You sound worn out, Granny."

"Worry will do that to you." She stopped rocking. "When I first came here, I thought this town was a cultural wasteland, a place with blinders on as to what was happening in the rest of the world. It had never hosted a speech from a candidate for president or governor. There was no opera or a cultural museum. But do you know..." Rose leaned forward, eyes suddenly bright. "My attitude changed. The mix of people here is unlike anyplace else on earth. And I learned to love it." She pointed at Emma with one slender finger. "We like Harmony Valley the way it is."

Here was the familiar, determined Granny Rose. Emma sat up with a roll of her shoulders. "I like it, too."

Granny Rose laughed. "Kathryn, you hated growing up here. We didn't have television and there weren't enough boys. You couldn't get out of here fast enough."

Emma's breath hitched. Kathryn was her mother. For the second time that day Emma reintroduced herself. "Granny, it's me. Emma."

Rose blinked. "Emma?" She smoothed her white hair back with fingers that trembled. Emma didn't know if the shaking came from age, illness or stress. "Emma. You've always loved Harmony Valley." And just like that, Granny Rose was herself again.

It was like losing the car-radio signal when you went beneath an overpass. Only this tuner required a doctor to fix it.

"I do love it here." Emma loved it so much that more than half of her freelance portfolio and some of her bestselling works were based on the unspoiled views. Not that she couldn't sketch or paint elsewhere. She had. Sedona, Yosemite, Yellowstone. But Harmony Valley was different. Not as grand. Not as colorful. But infinitely more peaceful.

If... *When* Emma painted again, it would be in this place. With all of Granny Rose's love and support. And hopefully Tracy's, too.

"Well, I have a busy day tomorrow. I like to be fresh in the morning." Rose stood, wobbling a smidge. If Emma hadn't been watching, she would have missed it.

Emma rushed to her grandmother's side, offering an arm to lean on. She'd call her mother in the morning and tell her she was getting in touch with Granny's doctor. "Let me walk you back."

"My room is just down the hall, not across the continent," her grandmother snapped with all the pepper Emma knew so well.

Emma chuckled, breathing in the familiar scent of rose water. "Humor me. I've missed you."

After a moment's hesitation, Granny Rose accepted Emma's support with a wry laugh. "Isn't it lovely to have someone to lean on?"

"You miss Grandpa, don't you?"

"Every day. But he's going to be waiting for me when my time comes, the same as he waited for me under the oak tree in the town square when we were courting."

Emma loved to hear how much her grandparents had loved each other, probably because her lawyer parents had barely survived a messy divorce when she was a toddler. That was when she and her mother had come to live with Granny Rose.

The floorboards creaked more than usual, almost as much as her grandmother's knees. "You know he wants to cut down the oak tree in the town square. He doesn't care that half the town received marriage proposals under that tree."

"Who doesn't care?" Emma turned on the hall light. It flickered, then burned bright.

"That computer nerd. He's a pain in my tuckus."

"Mine, too."

Emma bid Granny Rose good-night, and then lugged her bags upstairs, depositing the shoebox full of Carina Career dolls next to her bed. Her room at Granny's was small with a single bed covered in a green-and-gold star quilt and an old walnut dresser that didn't take up much floor space. Emma loved the room. The southern exposure let in the most wonderful natural light.

When Emma was ten, she and Granny Rose had painted the walls the palest of blues and taken all the permanent pictures down so Emma could hang her works. She'd filled the walls last summer, but sold all those paintings to contribute to the cost of Tracy's care.

Tonight, the empty walls spurned her.

Tomorrow she hoped Tracy wouldn't do the same.

AFTER WILL LEFT Rose's house, he walked along the fragrant bank of the meandering Harmony River, dodging blackberry vines and the occasional tendril of a wild yellow rose. The sun had dipped behind one of the hills surrounding Harmony Valley, creating a humid, hazy twilight.

When Emma realized he hadn't asked Tracy if she wanted to see her, she'd glared up at him, the bandaged bump pushing through her dark brown bangs as stubbornly as she pushed up her chin. He'd seen that headstrong look of hers before—when she was seven and had been convinced that she and Tracy deserved a chance to play baseball with the older boys; when she'd found him and his fourteen-year-old friends skinny-dipping in the Harmony River and wanted to jump in; when he'd answered an SOS call from Tracy after the pair had sought refuge in a strip club when they'd realized they were in San Francisco's Tenderloin district after-hours.

Emma Willoughby was trouble.

His sister was at a critical juncture in her recovery. She'd hit a plateau and was emotionally beaten. The last thing Tracy needed was a reminder of the accident or some ill-conceived adventure of Emma's. He had to keep her away.

A figure stepped onto the path ahead of him, immediately recognizable. Her jeans and beige T-shirt bagged on her too-slim, too-frail frame.

"What are you doing here?" Will asked his sister with forceful cheer.

Tracy's mouth worked in a halting cadence. "You. Took. Too. Long."

Sorrow clung to Will like a lingering hangover. His sister used to talk high-speed and nonstop. Doctors told them these next few months were critical for Tracy's recovery. Somehow he had to get her back on track. Tracy needed a goal to work toward, something more concrete than smoother speech.

Sorrow became anger, directed at Emma and her carelessness. "I visited Rose. I need all the votes I can get."

"Suck. Up."

"Come look." Will leaned against a eucalyptus tree, breathing in its minty scent. The trees here bordered the property he and his business partners had purchased. Neat rows of chardonnay and cabernet sauvignon grapes filled forty acres like ranks of green soldiers. The farmer in him appreciated the effort required to build the vineyard and keep it healthy. The businessman looked at the farm buildings the town council threatened to condemn and shuddered.

Tracy leaned against the trunk next to him. "Pretty."

Now was the time to plant the seed. "How would you like to run our winery when it's done?" Tracy struggled with speech, but she was as sharp as ever. This could be the goal she needed to push herself further in her recovery.

She thrust away from him, scowling. "You... I... No. Why?"

"It was just a thought. You have a business degree." Will backed down. It was too soon. He'd wait a few more days before mentioning it again.

"Minor," she corrected with a shake of her head. "English major."

He ruffled her short blond hair, careful not to touch the sensitive scars on the right side.

She swatted him away and grinned, the expression so rare of late that Will froze, afraid any movement might startle Tracy into remembering she had little to smile about.

There was no way he was risking that smile disappearing forever. "Did Flynn pick up pizza?"

Tracy nodded.

"Come on."

They walked along the river to Flynn's

grandfather's house. Crickets sang a gentle chorus as they passed. Shadows lengthened and began blending with the night.

Flynn and Slade waited for them on the wraparound porch, watching the river go by and drinking beer. After days trying to generate enthusiasm for the winery in Harmony Valley, Will and his friends took refuge in the weathered white rattan chairs on the outdoor porch.

The *Jeopardy!* jingle drifted out the screen door. Moths fluttered around the porch light.

Tracy perched on a redwood bench and looked out toward the river, but she wasn't watching the calm waters. Her gaze was unfocused.

"Pizza's in the kitchen. Italian sausage or pepperoni." Flynn pulled a beer out of a small cooler and handed it to Will as he came up the steps. His Rolling Stones T-shirt was wrinkled, as usual. Reddish-brown hair hung to his shoulders beneath a Giants baseball cap, as usual. "Which musical did Rose perform tonight?"

Will opened his beer and leaned against the porch railing. "I'm not sure." Two months ago, Will would've been hard-pressed to name any show tunes. Oh, how the mighty had fallen.

Flynn readjusted his Giants cap and grinned at Tracy. "Do you remember when Rose did a one-woman rendition of *Chitty Chitty Bang Bang* for elementary school?" He waited until she nodded. She, Emma and Flynn had been in the same grade in school. After Emma, Flynn was Tracy's closest friend. "It was so funny, I thought I was going to wet my pants. And then Rose picked me and a couple other kids for the finale. I got to sit in this cardboard car she'd made. I thought I'd died and gone to heaven. Didn't matter that I only knew the chorus. For a moment, I was a man of the world." Flynn sighed. He'd been dreaming of visiting all the places his grandfather had served overseas ever since he was a kid.

Tracy's laughter was soft and all too brief. They knew Flynn wanted to take his grandfather around the world with him, but Edwin's heart was failing.

The river sidled past and crickets chirped. Inside the house, the *Jeopardy!* buzzer did its off-tone double beep.

Will wished Tracy would say something, start a conversation, bring up a positive childhood memory.

"Why don't you know which production Rose put on?" Slade stretched his long legs across the porch, clasping his hands over the ends of his tie. As their financial guru, Slade believed in living the leader look 24/7. According to him, you never knew who might be willing to invest in their next big idea, so he had to look legit. "What happened?"

Will didn't want to answer, not in front of Tracy, but it would be a bigger issue if he didn't. "Rose's granddaughter showed up."

"Emma?" Tracy sat up so quickly the bench she was on nearly tipped over.

Will couldn't tell if Tracy wanted to say more or not. She wrinkled her slim blond eyebrows when she struggled for a word, the same way she did when she was unhappy. They all waited for her to say more, but she went mute.

Slade smoothed an imaginary wrinkle in his slacks and then fiddled with his tie. Will had a theory about those ties. They were a gauge of Slade's mood—a bold, bright color meant he was content and focused on results, an artistic pattern signaled something stormy or melancholy and on black-tie days Will made sure to avoid asking Slade for anything. Today's tie was a bright orange diagonal strip. That boded well for the winery. "Was this a planned visit? Or does Emma know Tracy's home?"

"She knows." Will continued to study his sister. "She wants to visit Tracy."

Tracy blew out a breath. "I don't…don't."

"You don't want to see her," Will finished, greatly relieved.

"No." Her brows furrowed. "I. Don't. Want. You. To—"

"You don't want me to let her visit." Will tried again.

"No!" Tracy stood, growling in frustration.

"Let her get it out." Flynn leaned forward.

She shook her head. "I don't. Want you. To…to…" Tracy glanced up and to the left. The doctors had told them when she looked in that direction she was trying to access memory for the words she needed. Her hands circled like upside-down eggbeaters. "Stop. Emma."

"Are you sure?" Will set his beer down and moved closer to capture Tracy's hands. Her delicate hands. "She's the reason you're like this." Broken. Fragile.

Tracy blinked back tears. "Let me. Decide." She tore free of his grip and ran down the steps, across the verdant grass.

"She needs space." Flynn held Will back when he started off after her. "It's got to be frustrating."

Will shrugged off his friend's hand, grasping his beer by the neck to keep a hold on the resentment churning in his gut. If only Emma hadn't come back. If only Emma hadn't talked Tracy into going to Las Vegas six months ago. "Tracy doesn't like me telling her what to do." Wanting to follow his sister but knowing she needed space, Will anchored his beer on the porch railing.

"I'm going to make an unpopular suggestion," Slade said. "You're worried about Tracy, and Flynn's worried about Edwin's recovery from his heart attack. This project has gotten too complicated. In addition to the winery we're opening a restaurant, a tasting room and a gift shop? Maybe we should—"

"We're ten miles east of Cloverdale," Will cut in, trying to hammer out his frustration. "No one will drive forty miles north of the heart of Sonoma wine country on a twisting, narrow road simply for a glass of our wine. It's too much trouble. We need to make Harmony Valley a destination. Build something out here besides our winery. I'd love for someone in town to open a day spa or a bed-and-breakfast."

"A gelato parlor or a bakery. Maybe even a coffee shop." Flynn had a huge sweet tooth.

"What I wouldn't give for a latte every morning."

"Why don't we stick to what we know and design a new app?" Slade fiddled with his tie.

"Take off your tie," Will snapped, his frustration finding a new target. "It represents everything we aren't. We're supposed to be a lean, independent, creative firm, able to turn our talents toward a new opportunity on a dime. Not a suited-up, slow-moving corporation."

Slade leaned forward. The old wicker chair groaned in protest. "It sounds like you're saying you don't want to be responsible for employees and buildings and a harvest. I agree. Let's move on."

"I can't move on." Will passed his beer bottle from one hand to the other. He hadn't told either of them that he wanted Tracy to run the winery. Slade would argue that a junior advertising executive wasn't qualified to manage their business. Flynn would argue Tracy didn't drink wine. It didn't matter. He needed to tell them. But when Will opened his mouth, he said, "You're the one who said we needed a tax shelter."

"And you're the one who said it would be simple to start a business here." Slade got to his feet. He might not have been as tall as Will, but he was broader. "All we've found are roadblocks and complications."

Will's temper flared and his words came out angrier than he'd intended. "Flynn and I, we need a break from the creative side of things. We promised ourselves we wouldn't be one of those one-hit wonders, remember? We promised ourselves the freedom to focus on what we do best—out-of-the-box design. I don't have any ideas to work on. Do you?" Will rounded on Flynn.

"Nope. My mind's as blank as a new hard drive." Flynn tipped his baseball hat toward Slade, seemingly unconcerned by his creative block. "I'm a wealthy man, not that anyone around here cares, and not that my grandfather will let me spend any money on him or this property." The same as Will's father wouldn't allow him to pay for improvements on the family farm. "But I'd like to enjoy being a wealthy man before I burn through another five years of my life becoming wealthier."

"Amen," Will said grimly.

"Try to understand where we're coming from," Flynn said, ever the peacemaker. "Tracy needs Will right now, and our winery is the best thing that's happened to my grandfather in a long time. He needed to feel useful after his heart attack. I won't back away from this deal for that reason alone."

"But if you need any further convincing," Will said. "Think about this—it's next to impossible for us to come up with any new ideas when we're worried about our families."

Slade's long features turned as hard as the granite face of Parish Hill. He was an only child. His mother had always been fragile and had died of a heart virus when he was a teenager. His father had committed suicide soon after Slade graduated from college. Divorced, Slade had no family left.

"I'm sorry," Will began, knowing the words wouldn't be enough.

But Slade had already left, heading for his family's empty house.

CHAPTER FOUR

EMMA WAS BACK in Harmony Valley.

Tracy closed her bedroom door and scowled at the princess bedroom set she'd picked out when she was eight.

On days when she was scared, Tracy wished she'd died in that car accident.

She had no memory of the crash itself, but she did remember what had happened afterward in flashes. Emma taking off her white bra and using its padding to staunch the bleeding on Tracy's head, her voice high and thin as she told Tracy everything was going to be all right. Emma asking a passing motorist for a blanket to keep Tracy warm. Emma begging Mediflight to let her ride along, and after they refused, squeezing Tracy's hand with one last bit of reassurance before she'd left on the high-flying roller coaster that had had her throwing up on herself.

Emma had lied. Everything wasn't all right. Tracy hadn't woken up again until a week

after the accident. The doctors had put her
into a coma until the swelling in her brain
decreased. And when she'd come out of it,
Emma hadn't been there. Tracy had been unable to ask about her friend, not with a tube
down her throat and a morphine drip cloud-
ing reality. It wasn't until a highway patrolman
had shown up to ask her about the accident
and they'd lowered her morphine dose that
she'd found she could scribble out words. He'd
told her Emma had survived. The bigger question: *Where was Emma?*

Tracy sat on her full-size bed next to the
window and stared out at the moonlit night,
at the acres of chest-high corn her father took
such pride in growing.

After she'd stabilized, they'd moved her to
a rehabilitation hospital, where they had a no-
cell-phone policy.

Still no Emma.

Her father and Will alternated their visits.

Still no Emma.

Tracy grew tired of bedpans and flash cards,
well-meaning therapists who sang goofy kids'
songs and wanted her to sing along. Emma
would have understood, would have busted
Tracy out for a much-needed afternoon of
playing hooky. They'd have hit the mall or

found one of those small shops that made their own ice cream. They'd have gotten a scoop of something fattening and decadent, like coconut cream cheese or turtle truffle.

Still no Emma.

And nothing seemed right.

Oh, it was right in Tracy's head. She had mental conversations with herself as quickly and smoothly as before the accident. She'd surprised her doctors by being able to silently read and write fluently. And her broken bones had healed. She could walk and run and, although she hadn't tried, she suspected she could dance.

But resuming her job at an ad agency was out of the question. Tracy couldn't sit with her peers and shout out ideas. She couldn't contribute to a fast-paced conference call. And she could no longer smoothly present storyboards to advertising clients.

But that wasn't the worst of it. The worst of Tracy's situation was that everyone treated her like an invalid. Her father wanted her to rest more. Her brother finished her sentences. Doctors, nurses and specialists patted her knee and told her things would get better if she just obeyed every request they made and tried to speak. Again and again and again. Until Tracy hated the sound of her own faltering voice.

She pressed her forehead against the cool window and fingered the cell phone that had no network. Maybe that wasn't even the worst of it. The worst of it was that the doctor had recommended shock therapy as a next step in her treatment, which in laboratory experiments had increased blood flow to the brain and helped reconnect synapses so that speech was smoother.

Attach electrodes to her brain and start zapping her?

No flippin' way!

She'd stopped cooperating with her therapist. A few weeks later she'd been discharged, which annoyed the heck out of Will. He kept talking about her needing more therapy. Didn't he realize what they wanted to do to her?

And now Emma wanted to see her? Tracy was so upset she could scream. Only her scream would probably come out like a trebly Tarzan wail and upset her father.

Tracy both wanted and didn't want to see Emma.

Truth was, she didn't want to see anyone, not like this. Maybe she'd cloister herself away in her room, with its pink ruffled bedspread and pink flowered walls and only have conversations with herself. For the rest of her life.

"YOU THINK WILL took it upon himself to protect Tracy from you? I had hoped it was doctor's orders. I never could get Ben to say exactly." Granny Rose poured a cup of coffee and carried it over to the breakfast nook where Emma sat.

It was barely six in the morning and Granny was already dressed in olive slacks, a faded blue denim shirt and scuffed work boots. Her snowy hair was caught up in an intricate chignon. She paused before setting down Emma's coffee, taking in her bike shorts, tank top and messy ponytail. "Going for a bike ride?"

"Up Parish Hill." The main road through Harmony Valley wound along the river and then at the northern tip of town ribboned its way up the hill.

Her grandmother nodded approvingly, straightening the morning paper. "But why keep you away? It's not like you're the devil." Granny sighed. "Well, piffle. We'll just see about that today, won't we?"

"It's been so long. Tracy probably thinks I've abandoned her." She hadn't. She hadn't been able to get past Will. But Harmony Valley didn't have security guards. "I'm going over there later in the morning and hopefully Will won't have her locked up in the attic."

"Now I wish I'd never let that computer nerd into my house on Sundays, although he did like show tunes. I caught him singing along once." Granny Rose slid into a chair across from Emma, so clear and normal that last night's long-john dance and fatigue seemed like nothing to worry about. "No matter. Tracy's here and Harmony Valley is a small town. You're bound to bump into her sometime and then you can have a nice long talk." Granny Rose reached across the table and touched Emma's hand. "Speaking of talking, let's talk about your fears regarding your art. No one ever got through an artistic block by ignoring it."

The beginnings of a dull rumble filled Emma's ears. She clutched her warm coffee mug. "I'm not—"

"You're not blocked? Or you're not ignoring being blocked?" Granny Rose's faded blue gaze was gentle. "It takes more than talent to fill a canvas or a sketchbook. You need drive and passion."

"And courage," Emma added over the intensifying noise of the car accident replaying in her head. She willed herself to shut it out and her hands to stay steady on the mug. "It's impossible to be creative without courage."

Granny Rose's white eyebrows arched. "Since when did you lack courage or passion? I can't count the number of times I've had to force you to stop painting or sketching to eat. Sometimes you get so lost in a project you lose all sense of place and time."

Fear shuddered through Emma's veins, threatening to sweep her away. Being lost in a project was precisely what had made her crash and nearly kill Tracy. Her mind had been more focused on an idea for a painting than on the road.

Emma planted her coffee mug on the table with only slightly trembling hands and peered more closely at her grandmother's to-do list. "This is for today?"

"No, dear. It's my morning to-do list. Don't change the subject."

Emma did anyway. "Mow lawn, weed vegetable garden, make cupcakes, visit Cloverdale Elementary, bring easel down from attic." Forget that most people younger than her grandmother wouldn't accomplish that much in one day, let alone one morning. Granny Rose was going to bring down the easel. She expected Emma to paint while she was here.

The dull roar in Emma's head increased, reverberating down her arms into her fingertips until she had to sit on her hands to stop their shaking. It was nothing—nothing—compared to what Tracy had to go through every day. Emma forced her lips into what she hoped was a smile. "Just looking at your list tires me out. When was the last time you relaxed and had a cup of coffee with your friends?" The last thing she needed was Granny Rose tired and slightly out of it two days in a row.

"Pish. My friends drink wine at the end of the day. We're too busy living life to dawdle over coffee every morning." There was nothing out of the ordinary about Granny Rose today. She had all her usual bounce and energy, more at eighty than Emma had at twenty-six.

"How about if I do the yard work after I go for a bike ride?" Exhaustion was just what Emma needed to clear her head, which had begun to throb.

"That would be lovely. I'll start on the cupcakes. I'm staging a production of *The Music Man* with the fourth graders in Cloverdale.

My cast needs to keep their strength up."
With no mention of the easel, Granny Rose
stood and bent to kiss the top of Emma's head.
"Don't forget in all your rushing to stop and
see the world."

"I might say the same to you" Emma
smiled, more easily this time as the pounding
at her temples receded slightly. She finished
her coffee and went in search of her old ten-
speed bicycle in the garage. A few swipes of a
rag took care of the bike's cobwebs and Emma
was on her way.

The sun hadn't risen high enough to chase
away the morning fog. It clung to the grapevines and blanketed the river. The bicycle tires
glided over the pavement with only a whisper
of sound. She crossed the bridge into town
slowly, taking in the way the first bright rays
of light snuck through the trees, admiring the
varying shades of silver green on the eucalyptus bark. An image flashed in her mind's
eye of a canvas filled with the scene before
her, but it was quickly followed by a ripple of
panic-driven, leg-pumping adrenaline.

"Be aware of your surroundings," Emma
mumbled. "Stay in the moment."

The road took her behind the few businesses

on Main Street. Soon she was at the beginning of the loop that wended its way up Parish Hill and down on the other side of town. The first switchbacks were soft grades. Emma managed them easily. Then the hillside steepened, and fog and eucalyptus trees gave way to the occasional oak and sunshine. Poppies and dandelions thrust optimistically upward from the gravelly soil.

Emma rounded a bend and saw a jogger ahead.

Buff, blond and bossy. Will Jackson.

A photographer would have snapped the image. Everything about him was golden, from his hair to his tan skin to the way the early morning light illuminated him.

The sight of Will set her teeth on edge.

He'd kept her away from Tracy for six months.

Emma considered turning around, but he'd most likely see her retreat. That stubborn Willoughby pride, the one she could have sworn she didn't have, egged her on. She shifted gears and pumped the pedals like she meant business, which meant she nearly fell over.

Emma righted the bike and shifted gears again. She wouldn't let Will beat her to the top.

WILL'S IPHONE SHUFFLED to a Blink-182 song
that had a fast beat his feet didn't want to keep
time to. He was sucking in air like a clogged
air filter on a '57 Chevy. But he kept pushing up this hill. Each time Will took on Parish Hill, he made it a little farther. There were
ten switchbacks. He'd managed six the other
day before slowing to a walk. Someday, he'd
run all the way to the top.

The town council meeting was tonight and
Will had a lot of people to see beforehand.
It had been a month since their permit and
rezoning requests had been put on hold. A
month of pulling together facts, drawing up
blueprints and kissing up to residents who
might support them. Tonight, he hoped he
and his friends weren't going to stand alone.

A sound behind Will had him spinning on
the defensive. It wasn't unheard of—if you believed local myth—for a mountain lion to attack out here. He cocked his arm back, ready
to launch his only weapon besides his signal-
less iPhone—a water bottle.

But it wasn't a mountain lion behind him.
It was Emma, legs churning pedals as she
rounded the turn below. She wore black bike
shorts and a tight blue flowered tank top, ex-

posing most of her lithe limbs. Emma might have pulled off the professional racer look, if not for the uneven back and forth, near-tumbling way she worked the bike. And the way that she was smiling beneath a pink helmet decorated with daffodils and ladybugs.

Laughter filled the air—warm, unbidden and unexpected.

His, Will realized with a start, watching Emma close the gap between them.

He frowned, put his hands on his hips and told himself Emma hadn't heard him laugh. He waited for her and what would certainly be another argument about visiting Tracy.

Instead of stopping at his side, Emma kept going. "See you at the top." And then she laughed. To be sure, it was a ragged, I'm-breathing-hard kind of laugh. But she delivered it with an I'm-gonna-kick-your-butt jab.

Will spun and put his body through the motions of a jog. But the hill was steep and he'd lost momentum. His overheated muscles and aching joints responded to his commands in agonizing slow motion. Emma started to pull away, even though she couldn't have been going much faster than he was. The next switchback seemed miles off.

Will refused to give up even as the distance

between him and Emma stretched. Adrenaline blazed through his muscles until they shook and threatened to collapse. His lungs burned, each breath a fiery agony. One switchback.

Two.

This was as far as he'd ever gone without reducing the pace to a walk.

Emma was moving slower. She'd changed gears a few times, but Will was betting money she didn't have any options left.

Switchback number seven loomed above. Emma was about fifteen feet ahead. She glanced over her shoulder at Will, never losing that hitching, awkward rhythm.

Emma was going to win. He could stop. He should stop. But to do so meant to surrender. To Emma? *Never.*

And then she fiddled with her gearshift and her chain clicked in loud, stuttering protest. It clicked and clacked and then dropped to the pavement.

Emma's feet did a quick once around the pedals before the bike tilted toward the ground. She hopped out of the way as it crashed.

Leaving the road clear for Will to reach the next switchback first.

The thrill of victory propelled him to the elbow in the road. There was no sense going any farther. They were both spent. Will walked in small circles, attempting to fill his lungs with much-needed oxygen, trying to keep his muscles from convulsing him into a permanent fetal position. He'd been clutching his bottle of water and now drained it. After a few moments, he rasped, "You suck."

She'd righted the bike and was walking it up the hill, feet digging in to build enough energy to reach him. "I had you all the way."

"Doesn't matter. I won."

"Nobody won. We didn't make it to the top." Emma popped out the kickstand and removed her helmet. Her hair was plastered to her head and sweat trickled down the sides of her splotchy red face.

And yet, there was something about her that wasn't unattractive to look at. Her inviting curves. Her challenging grin. Her warrior attitude that dared any man to take her on.

A memory surfaced. Emma wearing a red backless prom dress that clung to every dangerous contour, her dark tresses woven in a bride-like style threaded with delicate white flowers. Also not unattractive.

Emma wiped at her temples with her forearms, and directed her frustration at an inanimate target. "Stupid chain."

Will took a second, more assessing look at her. His system was in cool-off mode. Rivulets of sweat dripped off the ends of his hair. Most of the rest of his body was just as soggy and droopy. Emma looked about as sexy as he felt.

Which was great. That moment of attraction must have been due to oxygen deprivation. The prom memory was a fluke. It wasn't like he'd taken her to the event. He'd only made a preprom appearance to intimidate Tracy's date. "Did you lose track of what gear you were in? You had me until that last gear change."

"I did, didn't I?" She grinned as if she'd won the Tour de France.

That smile somehow managed to trap the air in Will's lungs. Something about Emma burrowed under his skin in a way he vehemently rejected, and had been rejecting since he was in high school. She never played it safe. She never obeyed the rules. She was like a predinner chocolate—temptation you couldn't resist, even when you knew it was wrong.

He exhaled forcefully. "As soon as I catch my breath, I'll fix your chain."

Where had that offer come from?

Emma's mouth puckered as if she was going to refuse him, but then she laughed and nodded.

They looked out over what they could see of the valley and the hills that bordered it, an uncomfortable silence settling between them as if they were both remembering they were at odds. Not that this was unfamiliar territory. Will's most vivid memories were of Emma opposing him. Convincing Tracy to go tubing down the Harmony River when it was still raging from spring rains. Dragging Tracy to a New Year's Eve celebration in Union Square when the girls were naive freshmen in college. Driving with Tracy to that bachelorette party in Tijuana despite the fact that a young woman had been abducted in that city a few weeks earlier.

Oh, Emma was good at flashing a "forgive me, I know I've been bad" smile and a good excuse: *We knew what we were doing. It was all innocent. Everything turned out fine.* Only that time, everything hadn't turned out fine. Tracy had almost been killed.

Emma plucked a dandelion from her feet, studied it for a moment and then blew its white parachute seeds into the wind. She knelt to pick another one, closed the distance between them and held it up to Will. "How about a dandelion truce?"

Generations of farming blood had him warding her off with one arm. "It's a weed."

"It's a dandelion." Emma twirled the stem back and forth. "Kids make wishes on them all the time."

"And blow the seeds of a weed out into the world." If wishes could make Tracy whole, he'd blow an entire crop of dandelions into the wind. But chances were those dandelions wouldn't result in wishes. They'd sprout up in his vineyard. "Farmers kill dandelions."

"Suit yourself." Emma studied the white puff, drew a deep breath and blew another handful of delicate white parachutes on to the breeze.

Will knew he shouldn't ask, but he couldn't help himself. "What did you wish for?"

"If I told you," she said in a solemn voice, as if she truly believed in dandelion wishes, "it wouldn't come true."

Will felt a chasm open between them, shored up by differences like belief in fairy tales, Santa Claus and happy ever afters. He stood with the realists. She danced with the dreamers. It had nearly cost his sister her life.

He was right to bar her from seeing Tracy. Wishes couldn't make his sister well.

Emma knelt by her bike and fiddled with the chain. Apparently she'd decided she didn't need his help. "What's a good time to come by and see Tracy?"

"Don't. I talked to Tracy last night and she doesn't want to see you."

"You're lying." Her hands, splotched with grease, shook.

"I'm not," Will lied. He'd do anything to protect Tracy. "Flynn and Slade were there. Ask them." He was betting she'd never do it.

"You can bring a thousand friends to testify she doesn't want to see me and I still won't believe you." Emma's face was as closed off as the latest firewall software to a cyber attack.

"Don't come by, Emma. You'll be the one to get hurt this time."

"I don't care." She pushed her chin in the air, but her lip trembled.

And he was twelve all over again, bending to her will. "At least wait until tomorrow. The trip home tired her out."

She nodded stiffly. "All right. But I don't need your permission. And I wouldn't try to keep her locked up in that house forever. She'll resent you for it." The chain dropped onto the sprocket. Emma jammed her helmet on, hopped on the bike and left, her rear brake squealing at him as she returned the way they'd come.

"I don't have to keep Tracy in the house forever," Will muttered to himself, catching sight of a drifting dandelion seed floating on the breeze. "Just until you leave."

CHAPTER FIVE

THERE WAS NOTHING Emma disliked more than being made to feel she was a shrew. And that was what arguing with Will did to her.

She'd apologized to him twice, but he still treated her as if she'd pointed a gun at Tracy and pulled the trigger. It left a bleak, bottomless sensation in her belly. Oh, she'd like to blame Will for that feeling, but her guilt was the cause, not Mr. Perfect's lack of forgiveness. She shouldn't care that he'd refused her attempt to apologize twice. The only absolution that should matter was Tracy's.

Emma outran the emptiness as best she could. She'd biked back to Granny Rose's, driven the riding mower over the half-acre lawn and pulled some stubborn weeds out of the small vegetable garden. She'd called her mom and left a voice mail about Granny Rose, requesting a callback that probably wouldn't come for days. In the middle of a murder trial, her defense-attorney mother only dealt with life-threatening emergencies. Granny Rose being Granny Rose didn't qualify.

Emma didn't want the easel but she couldn't stand the thought of Granny Rose climbing up the rickety attic stairs and wrestling it down, either, so she carried it to her room. And just to punish herself, she put a fresh canvas on it, got out her sketching pencil and stood like a statue, left hand hovering unsteadily over the canvas.

Since she was a little girl, she'd loved to color, draw and paint. She lost herself in the process of creation, her senses taking in the scene she was trying to capture to an internal soundtrack that was sometimes soothing, sometimes lively and always passionate. But now all she heard was the repercussion of a diesel engine bearing down on her, the trumpet of brakes locking. She was aware of sliding, losing control and the uneven rasp of Tracy's struggle to live.

She couldn't imagine Will losing himself in a moment. He noticed everything, as he held himself with a rigid grace the Renaissance masters would have loved to paint. If Will was naked.

Not that Emma wanted to imagine him without clothes. She didn't sketch or paint people and she certainly shouldn't be imagining her best friend's brother in his birthday suit. But the seed had taken flight, just like her dandelion wish. And instead of mentally planning out the foggy-morning image of Harmony Valley's bridge before moving her pencil, she found herself dwelling on the golden glimmer of his hair in the sunlight, the elegant taper of tan shoulders to his waist, the bunch and release of his quads as he ran uphill. But even those vivid images didn't liberate her talent, or free her hand, or quiet the internal wail of frustration when the canvas remained blank.

Granny Rose believed Emma could overcome this block. Emma wasn't so sure. Even as she stood there, her breath came in labored, near-panicked gasps, and not just because her art had deserted her.

What if Tracy never forgave her?

"WE USED TO eat ice cream with girls on that bench under the oak tree." Slade stood at the northern corner of the town square, fiddling with a solemn black tie. He hadn't looked at Will all morning as they'd called on various residents and discussed the benefits the winery would bring the town. "I haven't seen anyone under there since we've been back."

The midmorning sun warmed what had been a brisk spring breeze, bringing with it the smell of chicken grilling at El Rosal, the one restaurant left in town.

Tracy wandered over to the wrought-iron bench beneath the town square's lone oak tree.

In his memory, Will saw Tracy as she'd been a year ago—a glow to her cheeks and clothes that didn't hang off her petite frame.

He thought of Emma's determination to see his sister, regardless of who got hurt; all the ways Slade couldn't hide his despair at being alone; Tracy's resentment; the town's resistance. His worries stacked on each other until the possibility of failure weighed down his shoulders and dragged at his heels.

Will hadn't found an opportunity all morning to mend his rift with either his sister or Slade. They had a bit of time to kill before their next appointment. He opened his mouth to apologize.

And Flynn interrupted. "The ice cream parlor closed when I was in high school." Flynn gazed wistfully into the window of the empty corner shop as he adjusted his Giants cap over his tangle of reddish-brown hair. "Maybe we should open an ice cream parlor instead of a winery. It'd make Rose happier."

Will rolled his shoulders back and crossed his arms over his chest. When the stakes involved his sister, he stood firm. The winery would succeed. "Harmony Valley is at the end of the road. Who's going to drive this far for ice cream?"

"How about gelato?" Flynn grinned. "I'd bring a date out here for gelato."

"You aren't very discerning in your women or the places you take them." A hint of a smile slipped past Slade's bad mood.

"We need to focus on the winery and related businesses. That's the only way to attract significant outside revenue when Harmony Valley is about as convenient to the rest of the county as the sun is to Uranus."

"Ouch. Okay, I give." Flynn held up his hands, exchanging a look with Slade that seemed to say Will needed to be humored.

"A lot of people are going to come to the council meeting tonight." Will forced himself to uncross his arms and draw a breath. "If enough of them speak on our behalf, we might sway Mayor Larry or Rose."

"*If* people speak positively." Slade fingered his tie, the movement taunting Will like a red flag in front of a bull. "You've lost your perspective. Admit it. This isn't about saving the town. It's about you overcoming another challenge, proving something to us or your dad or someone."

"Prove?" Will sputtered. "I love the smell of success the same as the next guy, but this has nothing to do with my ego. We made a commitment to—"

"You committed!" Slade's words burst out as if he'd been holding them in too long. "I've been crunching numbers and waiting to see how this plays out. But I've said all along that wineries are a money suck. I'm all for a tax shelter, but not this one. If I had my way, Harmony Valley would be a ghost town." Slade stopped and turned away, as if he'd said too much. But then he added in a muted voice, "You should feel the same way after losing your mom here."

Will followed Slade's gaze to the skeleton of a grain silo visible over the treetops. The Harmony Valley Grain Company had been the primary employer in the small town until the grain elevator had exploded, killing Will's mother and three others. The company had closed before the embers were cold, forcing the workforce to move, other businesses to fold, schools to shut down and leaving nothing behind but cash settlements to grieving families.

The Jackson family's settlement had paid for Will's and Tracy's college tuitions. But nothing could replace the fact that they were motherless. Or erase the fear that life could be lost at a moment's notice.

"You'd abandon this place?" Flynn looked perplexed. "But it's home."

"Not to me." Slade cast a sidelong glance up the north end of Main Street toward the house he'd grown up in.

And then both he and Flynn turned their attention to Will.

Did Will want the town to die?

He shook his head. "There are painful memories here, but more good ones than bad. And as corny as it sounds, residents don't look at us and tally our net worth. I don't feel the pressure to add to our resume of work while I'm here." Although the lack of a new program to code against made him restless.

"That doesn't bode well for the future of our company." Slade started to smooth his tie, then seemed to think better of it and set his hand on his waist.

"We are not one-hit wonders." Certainty

rang through Will's words, despite the whisper of doubt, the one that slipped into his thoughts on nights when he couldn't sleep. But he'd heard that chorus before and proved it wrong. "Maybe this break and this winery are what we need to reboot that creative spark."

Will's gaze drifted to Tracy, whose head tilted up to watch clouds pass by. "This isn't about my pride. I want to open this winery so Harmony Valley will thrive and my dad won't be so isolated. I want there to be emergency services here in town rather than thirty minutes away. But mostly, I want this winery to provide a job for Tracy." Now was the time to say it. He drew a deep breath. "I want her to manage the businesses once we're up and running."

"Is that all?" Flynn looked from Will to Slade. "That's okay with me."

For one brief moment, Will experienced the lightness of relief.

Then Slade's voice came down with trust-me-on-this negativity. "We talked about hiring someone with experience. Tracy has none. This makes the risk even greater."

Will was used to overcoming obstacles and opposition. But for five years, Slade had been on his side. He'd known Slade wouldn't approve of his choice. He'd known, and yet he'd hoped. "My sister needs a job in a place where people know and understand her. She gets tongue-tied under stress." He stared down the road toward Slade's house, realizing how helpless Slade must have felt when his father died. At least with Tracy, Will could keep trying. Slade had no second chances.

The dread Will had been holding back for six months broke free, spilling into his words until he could no longer hide how the weight of responsibility threatened to crush him.

"I worry about Tracy all the time. Can I hope for something close to normal in her speech? What if she has an emergency and can't get the words out quickly enough? Are people going to judge her intelligence by the way she talks? Tracy's doctors tell me what to do and I feel hope. And then I try to help her and nothing works." He clenched and unclenched his fists, trying to expunge the helplessness. "If we can perform CPR on this town and Tracy has a role in our organization, I'd be happy. She doesn't have to run everything. Maybe just the gift shop. Or the tasting room."

Slade cleared his throat.

But the flood of Will's frustration wasn't finished. "It's the doubts that drive me insane.

Will Tracy be like this forever? Speaking in broken English and with pain so deep in her eyes that I can't find the bottom? I know Tracy doesn't want any handouts from me. But if you don't approve of hiring her, I'll pay her salary out of my own pocket.

"Last night Slade said Tracy was a distraction. But he's wrong. Carving out a place in the world for her is my life's work right now. And these businesses we're proposing can give her that place." If only he could make Tracy see. "If I can't fix Tracy so she can return to her old life, I need to help her create a new one. Everything else, including our next multimillion dollar sale, is a distraction."

Will hadn't realized an empty street could be so silent.

Slade stared at Will with fathomless black eyes that neither condemned nor supported.

"Slade," Will began, "what I said last night… I was a jerk."

"You get a pass," Slade said gruffly.

"I need you standing by me. You and Flynn." Together, the three friends could do anything—if they all concurred.

"We're doing this, then?" Flynn asked Slade.

Their financial partner nodded curtly.

"Since I'm in charge of our investments, I'll agree to pursue rezoning if you both agree that at each step in development we review our options. If this winery ever becomes a losing proposition, we cut our losses."

Flynn and Will agreed.

Will was determined he'd never let the winery come to that. His tension slipped away, loosening his limbs. He scanned the town square, tensing when he noticed it was empty. "Where's Tracy?"

Flynn pointed. "She headed back along the river toward your house."

The river path would take Tracy past Rose's home. Where Emma, Tracy's Pied Piper, was staying.

Will stepped off the curb, but Flynn held him back. "You have to let Tracy deal with Emma in her own way."

Will pulled his arm free. "She's not strong enough yet."

"Emma!" Granny Rose returned from her visit to the elementary school in the next town around eleven-thirty, her booted feet echoing throughout the old house. "Come here."

Emma saved the print ad she'd been revising for one of her clients on her laptop before going downstairs.

She found Granny Rose on the porch, reaching through an open window to start the record player. "Schoolchildren make me want to dance for joy."

After her bike ride, Emma's legs felt as if they were in plaster casts, stiff and cumbersome. Dancing would be impossible.

The Andrews Sisters began singing about a bugle boy. What little booty Granny Rose had started shaking. Her arms stretched out midair, fingers snapping. And then she held out her hand to Emma. "Let's dance, sister. I'll lead."

With a slump to her shoulders, Emma shuffled forward. "Do I have to?"

"It's either that or color!" Pointing to a coloring book on the table, Granny Rose laughed, the sound rippling above the music, cresting over Emma's sour mood and washing away most of her reluctance.

At first, Emma stumbled through the steps of the swing like a zombie with two left feet. But then, miraculously, her muscles warmed and loosened and her spirits lifted. She and Granny cut a rug back and forth across the porch as if competing in their own dance competition.

TRACY HAD SLIPPED the noose of Will's leash and was heading back to the house like a schoolgirl playing hooky.

Her body and spirit needed a lift. Life here didn't feel much different than in the rehabilitation hospital. Banned from driving, she still couldn't go where she wanted when she wanted. Harmony Valley was another cage and Will her jailer. It was hard to believe, but being a shock-therapy lab rat might allow her more freedom.

And then she heard music.

Although it was a tune from a different generation, it was the music of Tracy's youth. The music she'd learned to dance to—big-band swing. Just listening to the song as she walked down the narrow path by Harmony River buoyed Tracy's steps.

The Andrews Sisters beckoned her closer, inviting her to set aside her worries, if only for a few minutes. She couldn't see Rose's house through the trees, but with the volume up this loud, the older woman had to be outdoors, dancing on the wraparound porch as if her shoes had wings.

Tracy and Emma had danced many a summer night away on that porch. Tracy had danced away her grief after her mother died.

Taking the path around a blackberry bush, she stopped in the shade of the eucalyptus grove.

She and Emma—

Emma was dancing with Rose.

Emma.

Dancing. As if she didn't have a care in the world. As if the crash hadn't permanently destroyed her dreams.

Had Emma been dancing the entire time Tracy was in the hospital?

Her pulse quickened until it felt like her heart would hammer its way out of her chest if she didn't do something. She took a step out of the shadows, but a hand on her arm held her back.

"Don't," Will said.

Tracy snapped her arm free and turned toward Rose's house, fueled by anger at both Emma and Will.

Will yanked her back again. "Don't."

Emma had been here all this time? Dancing?

"What are you going to do?" Will's contempt was palpable. "Dance with them?"

That was the furthest thing from her mind. Tracy wanted to yell at Emma, wanted to make her listen to all her frustrations. She wanted to shout and scream and howl in pain. She wanted to accuse and blame. She wanted to finally have someone understand the anger and uncertainty that beat a pounding staccato in her chest.

Tracy opened her mouth to tell Will what she had in mind, but all that came out was, "I…"

Her pulse dragged to a sluggish near halt.

Who was she kidding? It would take hours to get everything off her chest.

Will must have sensed her defeat because he pulled her deeper into the trees, farther down the winding path toward the river.

And she let him.

"TRACY?" EMMA STEPPED out of Granny Rose's arms. She thought she'd seen Tracy in the trees, her blond hair catching a ray of soft sunlight. Emma ran down the front stairs and into the eucalyptus grove bordering the river. "Tracy!"

But it wasn't Tracy who awaited her. It was Will.

Beneath the trees, he exuded none of the golden-boy aura she'd admired on Parish Hill. He was breathing heavily, as if he'd been running. But his blond hair didn't glisten, his skin didn't radiate vitality and there wasn't a fleeting shout of laughter as when he'd first seen her this morning.

"How can you dance?" The anger in Will's voice thrust barbed points at Emma, bringing her to a halt. "You were dancing like you were happy."

The emptiness that never receded completely expanded inside of Emma, filling her with a bleakness that welled into her eyes and threatened to overflow. But she wouldn't cry. Not in front of Will. "I wish I could make you understand. Part of me cringes every time I feel a hint of happiness because I caused the accident that nearly killed Tracy. Me." She tapped her chest. "I carry that with me every day and I always will. But I was trying to make my grandmother happy just now. I owe it to her."

Glaciers were warmer than Will's expression.

"So if I was smiling, if I looked happy, I'll admit, there may have been a moment when the music swelled and I felt hope. Hope that I'd finally see for myself that Tracy is okay." She searched the area again for any sign of her friend, but she was gone. "I'd switch places with Tracy and take on all her suffering if I could. It would mean the world to me if she forgave me, but she doesn't have to. Whatever she thinks, whatever she feels, I'll honor that, but she has to tell me herself. Please," she added, feeling suddenly weary.

Will's gaze cast about as if searching for his arguments. Finally, he said, "Tracy was crushed when she saw you."

"She was here?" Emma clung to hope.

"You upset her. She went home." Will looked along the river toward his family's property. "She's hit a plateau in her recovery. She needs rest before her next round of therapy. Once her communication improves, she'll be better equipped to handle the stress of the everyday world." He cast her a sidelong glance. "And people like you."

"Me?" Emma stepped back.

The edge returned to his voice. "People like you don't look before they leap, you don't think about the burn you'll get twirling near the fire. You and your grandmother get a whiff of excitement and off you go, without considering the consequences." His gaze returned to the river. "But people like Tracy, like my father and me, we have to be careful of every step we make."

Will was referring to something other than

the car accident. He'd been fifteen and Tracy eleven when their mother died at work. Mrs. Jackson had been a frequent Sunday visitor at Emma's house, taking part in Rose's theatricals along with Emma, Tracy and, occasionally, Will. Emma had loved Mrs. Jackson's infectious laugh, her boundless energy, her joie de vivre. She and Granny Rose were like sisters and Emma had wanted to be just like them. And she had, up until the accident.

After his mother's death, Will had seldom left his computer except to haul Tracy back home for supper or away from whatever mischief the two girls had gotten into. He'd never come over for Sunday theatricals unless forced. He'd started treating Emma as if she had a contagious disease.

She hadn't realized. She hadn't known.

This was why Will had shunned her all those years, treating each trip or excursion she and Tracy took as if it was hazardous. This was why Will had kept her away from Tracy, because he thought she'd hurt Tracy worse than she had in the accident. He planned to cocoon his sister the same way he'd cocooned himself, burying himself in work instead of living life to the fullest.

Emma wanted to tell him, *I don't leap with-*

out looking. But he wouldn't believe her. He'd spent nearly fifteen years forming an impression of her as someone he and his sister should avoid. Emma wanted to tell him, *You can't cover yourself in bubble wrap the rest of your life.* Instead she said, "You can't hover over Tracy the rest of her life."

"Why not?" He held himself very still, as if he wanted to be swayed by her logic.

"Because she deserves the right to choose her own road, be it safe or risky."

Will shook his head. "She tried your way, Emma. It's better if she stays on my road from now on."

"Don't do this." Emma touched his shoulder as he turned to go. "You'll lose her."

Will turned back, his gaze anguished. "Can you guarantee I won't lose her if I let her go her own way?"

Emma couldn't. No one could.

CHAPTER SIX

WILL WAS THE first to arrive in the small, one-hundred-year-old church where the town council held its meetings. He'd tried all afternoon to shake off Emma's warning that his form of protection would push Tracy away. He'd attempted to forget the sincerity in Emma's explanation, to ignore how listening to her threatened to erode his sense of purpose. What he felt didn't matter. Keeping Tracy safe did.

Would Tracy forgive her, even if Will couldn't? He feared the answer was yes.

The meeting started in less than an hour. Will forced himself to shut out thoughts of Emma and concentrate on the task at hand. He needed the council to set aside their no-growth policy and rezone their land for commercial use so that Harmony Valley could thrive another one hundred and fifty years.

No sound disturbed the church. The sun elbowed its way through the grimy side windows, past ancient wooden pews, flooding the entry with dust motes and light. The church had been built so the morning sun would illuminate the minister delivering his sermon. The altar was shadowed now and the place smelled musty. No matter. Will planned to set up his laptop and projector so his PowerPoint presentation could be seen on the wall behind the now-gloomy pulpit.

Flynn and Slade came in behind him, their feet echoing on the wooden planked floor.

Slade paused to give each of them a brief once-over. It wasn't every day Flynn and Will wore suits and ties.

"About time you guys showed some class." Slade approved their outfits with a nod.

The three men proceeded up the aisle to set up the presentation.

While they worked, nerves wavered in Will's gut. There was more at stake than a new business venture, but he had to appear confident and put forth their strongest arguments.

Once the laptop was powered up, the projector connected and the PowerPoint presentation showing on the front wall, Will flipped through a few pages, including their architectural renderings of the new buildings. Since the wall behind the pulpit had been plastered over, it wasn't the smoothest of screens or the sharpest of images, but everything was visible.

"Oh. My. God," Tracy said from the back of the church.

"I thought this was a small winery," their dad added, coming in behind her. "And why does it look like a mission? The Franciscans never settled this far north."

"The mission style says California." And Will liked how the arches resembled those at Stanford—orderly, established, impressive.

"Wrong. For H-H-Harmony. Valley. Too big."

"There goes another supporter," Slade muttered.

"It's not too big." Will spared Tracy a glance that he hoped disguised his irritation. He was tired of fighting with her on everything.

"We're not going to build a mom-and-pop operation," Flynn said, as if sensing Will needed backup.

"Too big," Tracy repeated.

The door to the church opened and Emma blew in, as if ushered forward by a strong wind.

"TRACY!" HEART POUNDING apprehensively, Emma nearly bowled Tracy over as she enveloped her in a tight hug.

Tracy's halfhearted reception doused Emma in doubt.

Was Will right? Was Tracy not ready to see her?

Will stood at the altar, as still and silent as if he were a religious relic. Only his eyes gave away his feelings. *Don't hurt her,* they said.

Emma nodded, ever so subtly, to let him know she understood. And then she let Tracy go.

Granny Rose stepped through the doorway. "It's our precious Tracy." She gave Tracy a hug. It was hard to tell who was thinner or frailer.

Emma drew a breath and held on to her carefully honed patience. "I can't tell you how much I've missed you. I felt so bad about the accident." She hesitated. She didn't want to hurt Will, not now that she knew why he'd kept her away, but she had to let Tracy know she hadn't abandoned her. "I've been trying to come visit, but no one would let me in."

"No. One?" Tracy glanced at Will and then her father, her mouth pulling to one side in the start of a scowl.

Will's scowl was already in place.

"But none of that matters now." Emma smiled gently. "You're here and I'm here."

Other residents streamed into the church before Emma could say anything more. They also greeted Tracy, who acknowledged each with a small smile and a nod.

"Do you want to sit together and catch up before the meeting?" Emma asked her as soon as there was a break.

Tracy cast a nervous glance around the church. "No."

Emma had lost her.

She couldn't breathe, couldn't speak. She could only stand and stare at the woman who used to be the one person she shared everything with.

"Not. Here." Tracy turned back to Emma. "My h-house. Tomorrow. Nine."

Emma had researched aphasia when Granny Rose had told her that was what Tracy struggled with. She knew it affected her speech. But listening to her friend was different. Each of Tracy's labored words cut a tiny piece from Emma's heart.

"Thank you. Oh, thank you." Emma hugged Tracy again.

But this time Tracy stood as stiff and un-bending as the old oak tree in the town square.

"MADAME SECRETARY, DO we have any old busi-ness?" Larry Finkelstein, Harmony Valley's mayor, spoke with all the enthusiasm of a clairvoyant foretelling bad news on the cloudy horizon. From the council's table on the altar, the gray-haired former hippie's words rever-berated through the church as the sun dipped behind the mountains bordering the valley.

Emma shifted in the creaky front-row pew, looking at Tracy, who sat on the opposite bench with Will, Flynn and Slade. Her cheeks were pink, but sunken. Her faded jeans and pea-green T-shirt hung off her bony frame, the drab clothing breathing more life than Tracy herself.

After agreeing to meet, Tracy had stayed as far away from Emma as possible. Was she embarrassed by her condition? Or, as Will im-plied, was their friendship irrevocably broken and tomorrow's meeting just a formality?

Emma's fingers twined tightly together.

Unanswered questions lined up like planes waiting to land at the airport. Did Tracy bear any other physical effects from the accident? She hadn't limped. Did her aphasia limit her ability to text or type? Had she thought about returning to work or their shared apartment in the city? Was she confident enough to try?

Emma would have to wait until tomorrow to find out.

She hoped Will would let her in.

Will. He sat ramrod straight, as if he were a general about to rally the troops.

Emma's pulse kicked up in artistic appreciation. Will's profile was worthy of a talented sketch artist. Straight nose, strong chin, every blond hair in place. His charcoal pinstripe suit and soft gray shirt blended together with just the right pop of color from a swirling-patterned burgundy tie. Dressed for business, Will embodied everything cold and calculated about corporate America.

In her scuffed shoes, pink cotton skirt and green blouse, Emma felt positively dowdy. But she and the town didn't have to spruce themselves up to present a good image. Harmony Valley was a last, rare slice of Americana, as untouched by corporate America as Granny Rose.

Still, Emma had to give Will some respect. He hadn't made a scene when she'd talked to Tracy. He'd stood his ground and accepted Tracy's decision, which must have been hard

for him considering what he thought of her
and the lengths he'd gone to all these months
to keep her away.

Will caught Emma looking at him. He
quirked an eyebrow as if to say she shouldn't
get her hopes up.

She smirked at him before glancing over her
shoulder, counting nearly forty people in the
six-pew church. That was more than half the
town. She hoped none of them liked whatever
Will was about to say.

Mildred Parsons, the council's secretary,
cleared her throat. "Mr. Jackson's zoning permits are up for review tonight." Mildred patted
her white, teased curls and gave Will a broad
smile that traced the round lines of her oval
face. "Do you have anything new to present
to us today, Mr. Jackson?"

"Yes." Will's confident voice rang up to the
church rafters.

The crack of Mayor Larry's gavel on the
council table echoed through the church. "Mr.
Jackson has the floor for ten minutes."

Will stood, holding a remote control device
smaller than Emma's car-key fob.

Given Harmony Valley's sleepy character,
Emma expected this to go about as well as a
Democrat presenting at the Republican con-

vention. But then she happened to glance at Mrs. Chambers, who'd been sitting behind Will. The older woman's wrinkled, full-cheeked smile was positively dreamy. And aimed directly at Will. Other gray-haired women in Mrs. Chambers's vicinity looked at Will with the same worshipful expression. What was going on here?

Considering Granny Rose's comments, Emma hadn't expected much support for the winery. Now she wasn't so sure.

Will thanked the council and the town for the opportunity to present to them again. His practiced smile elicited sighs from many of the female members of the audience.

Granny Rose scowled. Mayor Larry tugged at the neck of his blue tie-dyed T-shirt and studied the crowd as if gauging their reaction. Twenty years younger than Rose, he'd always been one to follow popular opinion, hence his eight terms in office.

Emma looked to Tracy to see what she thought of Will winning over a gaggle of grandmas.

Tracy blessed her brother with a sisterly eye roll.

Will noticed. His smile dimmed. "Harmony Valley was established in 1851 by a group of

forty-niners who hadn't had much luck pan-
ning for gold anywhere else." Will brought
up a faded picture of two bearded gold min-
ers and their pack mules.

A series of faded black-and-white photos
depicting the town's history followed in a slow
slideshow on the wall. "Through the years,
Harmony Valley has been a trading post, a
sheep ranch and eventually was subdivided
into smaller family farms, one of which was
an outlaw's hideout."

"That'd be my great-grandfather Nedder-
man." Councilwoman Agnes Villanova was so
short she looked like a child sitting at a table of
adult councilors. She stretched her short frame
pridefully upward until she almost reached
Rose's shoulder. "They called him Big Nose
Ned." She beamed at Will, who proceeded to
talk about several slides that looked like eye
charts with tiny numbers showing years of ne-
glect to infrastructure, declining tax revenue
and negative population growth.

Emma's eyes glazed. She crossed one leg
over the other, bouncing her foot lightly to
keep herself awake. The figures Will showed
were like Greek to Emma, but his verbal sum-
mary was depressing. When had things gotten so bad? She'd known the population had

declined significantly, but she hadn't realized Harmony Valley was on the brink of becoming a ghost town.

Emma shot another glance Tracy's way, but Tracy was studying the charts with a frown.

"Historically, Harmony Valley has changed in response to the times." Will worked the audience with eye contact as he paced the space in front of Emma's pew. For a man who'd made his fortune designing programs for computers, he was surprisingly at ease in front of a crowd. "The stimulus for that change has always been the local economy. When the gold didn't pan out, ranching took over. When ranching played out, the grain mill opened. And then there was an accident at the grain mill." Will paused.

Collectively, the town seemed to honor their dead with a moment of silence.

"Now, ladies and gentleman, it's time for Harmony Valley to make another change—to become an exclusive wine destination." Will stopped in front of Emma, blocking her view of the presentation.

She stopped her foot from bouncing and craned her neck so she could see around him.

With a click of a button, Will brought up an architect's rendering of a huge California-style mission dominating a small vineyard. It was as if extraterrestrial missionaries had landed their mother ship. Gone was the hundred-year-old Henderson farmhouse. Gone was the Hendersons' red barn with its metal corrugated roof. Gone was the quaint, small-town charm of Harmony Valley.

Pews creaked as bodies shifted for a better look. Unintelligible murmurs filled the church like an out-of-sync choir.

Larry rapped the gavel against his palm. "Is that your corporate office or the winery? In either case I don't want it near my house."

"I can't tell what it is." Mildred squinted at the wall, rotating her head as if trying to focus her thick trifocals.

Next to Mildred, Agnes was frowning.

Rose crossed her arms over her skinny chest. "In this case, young man, size does matter."

The crowd's rumblings built, popping like kernels of popcorn.

Emma couldn't contain her grin. Where were Will's supporters now?

If Will had any doubts, he didn't show it. He spoke in an authoritative voice that carried over the crowd and drew their attention back to him. "In addition to the winery, our partnership is willing to invest in town, opening businesses in the town square. A gift shop. A five-star restaurant. And a wine-tasting shop." His renderings showed soulless glass windows, modern interiors and a stark-white tablecloth establishment with a sleek bar. "This will move us to a tourism-based economy that will take Harmony Valley into the current century. Other businesses will return. In five years, we're projecting we can attract contractors to build a new housing tract, perhaps as large as one hundred new homes."

At the town council table, Mayor Larry pounded his gavel harder on the table, Agnes rubbed a hand over her forehead and Granny Rose's mouth gaped open. Mildred still squinted at the wall.

Will was unflappable. "This increase in population and their need to be linked with the outside world will require changes to the town square." A complete view of the new town square flashed on the wall. A chrome-and-steel gazebo with a towering pole replaced the oak tree. The circumference of the square was reduced by more than half in order to make way for extra parking and a stoplight. "Our communications tower in the town square will provide each resident with free wireless internet and make cell-phone service possible in the valley for the first time. And people will attribute this council with the imagination and confidence to launch that change."

Someone behind Emma made a sound of disgust. A voice in the back muttered angrily.

At any moment someone in the pews would stand up and shout a protest. At any moment a council member would move to reject Will's proposal. At any moment...

"What have you done to the town square?" Rose looked puzzled. "Where are we supposed to gather? To hold events like the Spring Festival and the Summer Fair? What you're proposing is a complete change to who we are."

Finally, the voice of reason. Seconded by many voices in the crowd.

But not by Granny Rose's peers on the council table. They still seemed dumbfounded.

"Where's the oak tree in the town square?" Rose demanded.

"We plan to replace it with a hot-spot gazebo." Will kept smiling. It was a smile Emma recognized. The one the boss gave you when he told you he liked the work you'd done and then turned around and rejected it completely. Insert knife in back.

"A hot spot?" Her grandmother's expression pinched with uncompromising wrinkles. "Young man, we don't abide that kind of behavior in this town."

To his credit, Will didn't chuckle at Rose's misunderstanding. "It's a communications tower housed in a chrome-and-steel gazebo with a solar-powered fan. It's called a hot spot because of the signal it sends out."

Rose huffed. "The tree stays. And the lawn. And you can remove the traffic light while you're at it."

There were murmurs of approval.

"Is that the town square? All I see is gray." Mildred squinted. If only she could see, maybe she'd regret asking Will and his friends to start a business in Harmony Valley.

"You're trying to erase our history, not build upon our roots," Mayor Larry said in a voice loud enough to reach those in the back of the church too proud to wear hearing aids. "When you first came to us with this proposal, I assumed you were talking about a small winery that would blend into the landscape, not change everything. What's the square footage on that monstrous building you showed? How many visitors are you projecting each day?"

Emma wasn't sure if Mayor Larry had read the mood of the room or was still offended by the mission-style mother ship being parked across from his house. Either way, Will wasn't likely to receive approval to rezone his land. The council was clearly split. Emma attempted to signal Granny Rose to make a motion. But her grandmother had a faraway look in her eyes.

"We're trying to turn the fortunes of Harmony Valley around," Will insisted with the composure an experienced trial lawyer used with prickly juries. "Position it for future growth and sustainability. Bring back the medical clinic. Reopen our schools and fire station. Build parks and playgrounds for your grandchildren and great-grandchildren. Create a town where families don't have to move away to chase jobs. Where generations of residents live together. Wouldn't you like your family to live down the block?"

"Not like this." Granny Rose snapped back to the present and shook her finger at Will. "Not when the size of your changes threatens the traditions and values of this town. Just because we don't have the world wide web doesn't mean we don't hear about the outside world. This is our home. You've shown us no respect."

Larry nodded in agreement.

Agnes opened her mouth to say something, but hesitated. Mildred still looked lost. Their families had been the most recent to move away from Harmony Valley. According to Granny Rose, Agnes had taken her daughter's leaving particularly hard.

"This is exactly like what happened to Napa! Huge corporations built wineries. Old homes were torn down to make room for golf courses, day spas and luxury mansions." Granny Rose stood, sending her folding chair crashing to the wood floor. She leaned on the table and swung her head around as she looked about the church with wild, feral eyes. "The devil was behind the loss of Napa! And now the devil's sent this Beelzebub to destroy Harmony Valley, as well."

"Granny Rose!" Emma leaped to her feet. She pushed Will aside and charged up the altar stairs, cradling an arm across her grandmother's shoulders.

Everyone stopped talking, even Will, who seemed to have an answer to every issue raised, except when it came to accusations involving the devil.

Granny Rose stared at Emma, slack jawed. Blinked. "What? I…"

"It's all right," Emma said softly.

The look Tracy gave Emma was pitying. The scrutiny from those in the pews was worse.

This was all Will's fault. He'd upset her grandmother with his too-much, too-soon vision of progress and his insensitive suggestion that they chop down the oak tree in the town square. Emma took Granny Rose by the arm and led her down the altar steps.

There was something wrong with her grandmother.

Was this how Rose would finish out her life? Prancing about in long johns and shouting about the devil?

Emma felt sick.

It couldn't be dementia. It just couldn't. There had to be some other explanation. Granny Rose had been clear as crystal today until Will's presentation. Yes, Rose loved the theater and could be overly dramatic. But this was beyond drama.

The one consolation was that Will didn't have enough votes for approval to rezone his land. Mayor Larry clearly hated his architectural plans and Emma was taking Rose home before a motion or a vote could take place.

Emma held Will's gaze. "Now who's looking before they leap? Who didn't think through the repercussions?"

"I'm sorry," Will murmured as they passed him.

Despite seeing the regret in his eyes, Emma couldn't forgive him.

In that moment, she understood Will's bitterness regarding the car accident, the fear of loss, the uncertainty of a loved one's future.

She understood and witnessed firsthand the powerful obstacle those feelings created in the path of forgiveness.

CHAPTER SEVEN

"THAT COULDN'T HAVE gone worse." Will slid his laptop into his brown leather messenger bag, trying not to think about the bewildered look on Rose's face when Emma had come to her rescue. His head pounded and he felt like the worst of bullies, even if what he was fighting for would benefit everyone in town, including Rose.

Right after Emma and her grandmother left, Agnes had moved that they table the issue of rezoning the winery property until a special meeting the following Monday night. Mildred seconded. And Will's hopes for approval today were crushed beneath the mayor's gavel. The church had quickly emptied out.

"Agreed." Slade smoothed his tie beneath his tailored black suit jacket.

"Look at the bright side." Flynn zipped the soft-sided projector case closed. "We didn't get rejected."

"We didn't get approved," Slade pointed out.

"For the love of Mike," Will's father, Ben, said in a loud voice. "Why don't you just say it? You were asked to start a small-town business to inject some life into this place and you turned it into a multimillion-dollar makeover to satisfy your egos. Your plans provoked Rose, who's never been anything but kind to you boys, not to mention unease in the rest of the crowd. That's not something to be proud of."

Flynn and Slade did the "your dad's embarrassing me" shuffle, busying themselves with the already-closed projector case. Tracy stared out the window at the fast-approaching night.

That left Will to defend their proposal. "Dad, you don't understand what we're trying to do."

"Don't patronize me like you do the rest of the town. I may belong to AARP, but I'm not stupid. I'm sure once you complete construction of this monstrosity and open for business it'll make a nice article in one of those business magazines you're so fond of reading. But by then the heart of this town will be destroyed."

Will took a deep breath. "Profits and ego had nothing to do with our plans."

"Loss is more like it," Slade murmured, not at all helpfully.

His father shook his head. "Tracy, let's go home."

Tracy left without looking at Will.

His head pounded harder.

"He'll come around," Slade said.

"And so will Tracy." Flynn settled his baseball cap on his head.

"He's right. Everything was too big. And the mission style? What were we thinking?" Will massaged his temple. Programming impossible code was turning out to be more enjoyable than helping his hometown and providing a future for his sister.

Flynn tugged his tie loose and slipped it into his jacket pocket. "So? What do we do? Scale back our plans?"

"Yes." Will shouldered his laptop bag. "Maybe we go back to the idea of restoring the barn for the main winery and the old farmhouse for the tasting room. We'll need to let our supporters know about the changes and meet with the rest of the residents."

Slade looked grim. "And hope we don't alienate anyone else."

"No sweat." Flynn shrugged. "People love us."

"Most did. Until tonight," Slade muttered.

They talked about the situation all the way back to Flynn's grandfather's house.

Edwin was watching *Family Feud,* but muted the program when he saw them. "Tell me why you have glum faces. I've had a few calls, but I want to hear it from you." He lowered the footrest on his plaid recliner and sat up like the career military man he was, unswerving and ready for action. After they'd recapped the night's events, he said, "No campaign was ever won without overcoming a few challenges."

"A few?" Will had to respect Edwin's strategic acumen, even if he didn't feel as optimistic. The old man attacked a goal much the same way Will approached a programming challenge—research, what-if scenarios and a plan for the steps needed to succeed.

Weeks ago, Edwin had covered the kitchen table with an aerial map of Harmony Valley, highlighting the homes of residents that had committed to them in blue. Undecideds were in yellow. The opposition in orange.

Rose's house was very orange.

"I'm worried about Rose. She was extremely upset." As was Emma. Will bent over to read the skinny yellow sticky notes Edwin had added to the map while they'd been gone. Each one was planted on a house with a scheduled meeting date and time. Based on the number of houses flagged, Edwin wanted them to continue their door-knocking campaign to woo the town.

The old soldier leaned heavily on his cane as he walked to the kitchen table, lowering himself carefully into a wooden captain's chair. "I love this town and these people. But sometimes they get in their own way. Your businesses will be the shot in the arm this place needs. Progress never comes without a price."

Will frowned. "Meaning Rose and her composure?"

"Yes. She and the town council have kept this place a sleepy haven for far too long. Tomorrow morning I'll handle damage control calls to our allies, and you three continue your ambassador visits." Edwin turned back to the map. "Now, pay attention to these yellow flags. Those are residents that aren't for or against us. I'll need you to convince those on the fence that the winery is a good thing. I've created a dossier on each yellow resident." He handed Flynn a lined pad filled with indecipherable scribbles. "Please read them this time."

Will, Flynn and Slade exchanged glances.

Edwin's strategizing sometimes went too far. Will preferred reacting to people face-to-face, not playing to what Edwin considered their vulnerabilities. The men appreciated his help, but Will didn't want to get carried away. Besides, guilt drummed insistently at his temples, flaring into regret every time he thought about the look on Rose's face at the town council meeting. Despite Tracy being priority number one, Will would lose sleep over Rose's reaction. "Is there anything we can do for Rose?"

"Don't chop down the town square's oak tree?" Slade smiled slyly.

"And forget that sexy hot spot you planned?" Flynn grinned.

Will held up his hands in surrender. "Go back to the architectural drawing board?"

"Forget architects, trees and hot spots. And forget Rose." Edwin covered Rose's house on the map with one hand. "Rose is an unbendable force. She's a rock and we're the stream that has to move around her."

The three friends exchanged silent looks

that asked the same question: Was saving Harmony Valley worth upsetting the town's emotional foundation?

Will didn't want to answer that question.

"THAT WAS AGNES." Emma hung up her grandmother's rotary phone.

Agnes had explained to Emma that Rose had suffered several similar episodes at night since the winery project had first come before the town council four weeks ago.

"Traitor." Granny Rose paced the living room. Her gaze was as restless as her feet, bouncing about without a target. "Do you think Will blackmailed Agnes to get her support? How else could she look at his plans and not throw him out?"

Emma didn't want to think about Will. It'd been an hour since they left the meeting and her grandmother was still upset. Emma couldn't blame her. The proposed makeover of Harmony Valley was totally wrong. And her grandmother's uncharacteristic outburst meant all was not right with her health. Emma had to call the doctor in the morning and get Granny Rose evaluated. For the first time since she was a teenager, she regretted that there was no internet here. She'd feel better researching Rose's symptoms on the web.

If only she could discuss her condition with Tracy. So much hung on tomorrow morning—Granny Rose's health, Emma and Tracy's friendship. Emma wished she was as skilled at putting feelings into words as she was at visually expressing herself through art. It made her meeting with Tracy that much more daunting. What if she said something wrong?

"Come sit down with me, Granny."

"I can't sit still. We're under siege." The pacing continued. Granny Rose scrubbed at her face, turned and paced some more. "Devil take me. I should have known something was up. That computer nerd and his friends have been scurrying around town busier than fleas on a stray dog. And they're always over at Edwin Blonkowski's house."

Emma couldn't remember if paranoia was a symptom of dementia. Regardless, in the state Granny Rose was in, she'd never agree to be tested for it. "Granny Rose, Mr. B. is Flynn's grandfather. He raised Flynn. His house has the best porch on the river. Of course they're going to hang out there."

Her grandmother stopped her pacing in front of Emma, her expression fenced in determined lines. "Edwin was military intelligence. Military intelligence, Emma. He's masterminded campaigns and coordinated spies in at least three wars. The last time we packed a town council meeting was the recall election of 1982. He was behind the opposition that put Mayor Larry in office. I agreed with Edwin back then, but now..."

Emma started to argue. Edwin Blonkowski was a big old teddy bear. He'd had an open-door policy with his grandkids and their friends. Emma had sat at his table and eaten cookies after baseball games while he explained old military maps to a group of ten-year-olds. She'd listened to his stories about various wars on his porch. He was... He'd been...brilliant. Maybe her grandmother was right to worry about Edwin.

But that didn't mean she was 100 percent healthy. Emma couldn't overlook Agnes's comments and Granny Rose's behavior from the night before. But maybe things weren't so dire; maybe she could be cautiously hopeful.

Granny Rose resumed her pacing. "We're under siege. Under siege and in danger. You should be careful who you talk to. There could be spies everywhere."

Unease danced on spider legs down Emma's

spine. She was definitely calling the doctor in the morning. And her mother. The long johns with a tutu. The breakdown at the town council meeting. The James Bond movie theme playing in her head.

Her grandmother needed a distraction.

Who was she kidding? Emma needed a distraction.

She flipped through the records in Granny's collection and put a disc on the record player. The orchestral strains of "Let Me Entertain You" from *Gypsy* filled the room. Granny Rose stopped her pacing, tilted her head and closed her eyes. The lines on her forehead smoothed. Her lips curled upward as she drew a breath and sang along.

Emma sank onto the couch, watching as her grandmother reclaimed her equilibrium. A wave of sadness enveloped her in a cold embrace.

Tomorrow loomed with questions and answers Emma dreaded hearing from Granny Rose's doctor.

And she was finally going to discover if she and Tracy were still friends.

CHAPTER EIGHT

"WHAT A BEAUTIFUL day," Granny Rose said cheerfully the next morning, pouring Emma a cup of coffee. She wore white slacks, a crimson button-down cotton shirt and snowy Princess Leia braids over each ear. The agitation and paranoia of the night before were gone. "Our garden club is going to the San Francisco Botanical Garden. Although there might be a shower or two here today, the weather in the city will be spectacular."

"No!" The word burst out of Emma with a heave that sent her stomach pitching in panic. She'd tossed and turned all night waiting until morning came. "I need you here while I make phone calls." To her mother and the doctor. "And what about the winery initiative? Are you giving up the fight?"

"I'm not taking a day off. I'm picking my battles and my battlefield." Granny Rose set Emma's coffee cup on the table and then sat down opposite her, so calm and unlike the restless, suspicious woman from the night before. "Besides, Will's not getting my vote. I made that very clear last night."

"He won't back down."

Granny Rose laughed. "Will can't get anything approved without three votes. It's a stalemate. Larry and me versus Agnes and Mildred."

"What if Larry caves in?"

"He won't."

"What if he does?"

"Mildred is practically blind. She couldn't see how wrong Will's ideas were. She's in charge of the Spring Festival. Where will she hold it if the town square becomes the size of her carport? Besides, Agnes and Mildred are going into the city with me today." Granny Rose came over to hug Emma, bringing the scent of rose water with her. "Who knows? I could sway them back to no growth. It's a long car ride. What are you doing after you visit with Tracy? Something creative I hope." She pulled out a coloring book from beneath a stack of mail on the table and pushed it toward Emma. Her grandmother had scattered the books around the house, believing the simplest creative exercise fed deeper artistic expression.

With a sigh, Emma dutifully flipped through the coloring book, recognizing some of the pages she'd meticulously filled in when she was younger. Much, much younger.

When she held the coloring book, Emma didn't feel the same trepidation she did when she held a paintbrush. A small victory over fear, but a victory nonetheless. Suddenly, she was reluctant to let the book go. She could feel a crayon or pencil inside the newsprint pages and was struck with the urge to color something.

"Don't look like it's the end of the world. That dear girl will forgive you. I know it. Now, I hope you make time for your muse." Granny Rose took one of Emma's hands in hers. "I look forward to seeing what you've done when I get back. It's been too long since the world has experienced an Emma Willoughby work of art."

The world would have to wait a lot longer.

Someone honked in the driveway.

"That'll be Agnes." Granny gathered her purse and camera. "I'll be back in time to make dinner. Toodles!"

After finishing her coffee, Emma took out the bike. But instead of heading for Parish Hill, where she might encounter Will, she rode out East Street and crisscrossed town. She needed some exercise before making her calls. And she hoped the ride would calm her nerves before she went to see Tracy.

Emma pedaled past abandoned homes with knee-high weeds in front, past tidy vineyards and green pastures filled with plump sheep, past charming little houses with flowers blooming around garden gnomes and plaster fairies. The houses in Harmony Valley were a hodgepodge of eras and styles—Victorian, arts-and-crafts bungalows, cottages and the more recent one-story ranch-style home. But none of them looked like a corporate California mission.

If Will had his way, the character of the town would change into something sterile and soulless. If Will had his way, Emma's well of inspiration would be poisoned, and she and Tracy would never rekindle their friendship.

Will would not have his way.

SHORTLY AFTER EIGHT, Emma had talked to Granny Rose's doctor. He'd said it sounded like Sundowner's Syndrome, a form of dementia exacerbated by stress and fatigue with symptoms that manifested themselves mostly at the end of the day. But he couldn't be sure.

He wanted to see Rose and agreed to have his nurse call her tomorrow to make an appointment under the guise of a checkup. In the meantime, Emma was to make sure her grandmother got plenty of rest and avoided stress.

When she hung up the phone, Emma knew what she had to do—stop Will's mission-style mother ship from landing in Harmony Valley so her grandmother wouldn't have to.

Emma next left a voice mail for her mother, updating her on Granny Rose and the doctor's opinion, and asking her to please, please, please call the house.

And then the doubt set in. What if Mr. Blonkowski *was* coordinating the winery campaign? Perhaps he didn't realize how upsetting it was to Rose. Emma had gone to school with Flynn, Mr. B.'s grandson, who'd witnessed Rose's episode. Perhaps she could persuade Flynn to stop being such a radical agent of change.

And so, at eight-thirty, Emma knocked on Edwin Blonkowski's door. She had barely enough time to squeak in a visit with Mr. B. and Flynn before her visit with Tracy at nine.

"Emma." Mr. B. shuffled to his screen door in a pair of stained blue coveralls, leaning heavily on a cane. His hair was salty, his nose more bulbous than ever, but his blue eyes were as sharp as they'd been eight years earlier. "How are you?"

Before she could decide how or what to ask, Mr. B. had a question of his own. "Do you remember the painting you did of Flynn all those years ago?"

"Vaguely." Of all the things she wanted to discuss, painting hadn't made the list. She hid her hands in the drape of her long skirt.

"I still have it in my bedroom. Would you like to see it?"

And torture herself by examining one of her early works? Not really. "About the winery…"

But Mr. B. was already shuffling down the hall, leaving Emma out on the porch. She heard him moving around in the back of the house. And then something clattered to the floor.

"Mr. B.? Are you all right?" Emma opened the screen door, stepping onto the black-and-white linoleum in the foyer. "Is Flynn home?"

"I'm fine," Mr. B. called. "I knocked over some books trying to get the picture down."

To her left, in the living room, a muted rerun of some game show played on the television. To her right, a map covered the kitchen table. Emma drifted closer, her Indian print, ankle-length skirt swishing with each step. She'd loved those yellowed maps as a kid. Mr. B. had marked battles and enemy lines on them and in the process brought history to life.

But this wasn't an old war map. This was a map of Harmony Valley. Houses were high-lighted in blue and orange and yellow. Mrs. Chambers's cottage in blue. Granny Rose's house in orange. Yellow sticky notes on several houses were labeled with dates and times. Those with today's date were on the east side of Harmony Valley. 9:00 a.m. Ten. Eleven. Drinks with Mayor Larry at El Rosal. And so on. Each appointment had a name scribbled beneath it. Flynn. Slade. Will. Sometimes a combination of the three.

Granny Rose was right. Mr. B. was directing the offensive with the precision of General MacArthur. Harmony Valley wasn't prepared for such an onslaught. The combined forces of Will and his friends plus Flynn's grandfather would demolish the charming town and build it into something cold and industrial.

Anger shuddered like cracking ice beneath Emma's skin, freezing her limbs until she stood with rigid indecisiveness over the map. She wanted to rip it into tiny pieces, scattering its shreds into the river. But that wouldn't stop them.

Emma couldn't break her gaze away from the orange highlighting Granny Rose's home. Her grandmother had been marked as the enemy. All those years ago Mr. B. had been adamant about one thing—wars had been lost when generals didn't understand their adversary. He'd used examples from history where guerilla warfare had led to successful coups, because no one could predict the opposition's tactics in advance. No one knew what the opposing army was willing to sacrifice to win.

A declaration of war unfurled its battle flag in Emma's chest, sending resolve spreading like the warming rays of dawn.

Mr. B. knew Granny Rose, but he didn't know Emma, as well. Not the adult Emma anyway. She'd lead the guerilla forces. Well... an immovable force of one.

It was a little after eight-thirty. Emma was due to see Tracy at nine. At one, Will would be out at... Emma leaned over. Felix Libby's house. And then—

Something else tumbled to the floor at the rear of the house.

"Mr. B.? Are you sure you're okay?"

"Fine. I'm fine. I finally got the wire free."

Emma drifted back to the foyer and pretended to watch TV, her mind busy planning her next move.

Mr. B. shuffled down the hall, about as intimidating in appearance as a character on Sesame Street. Emma knew better. She wanted to rail against him for betraying Harmony Valley, but before she could say anything, he handed her a framed, dusty canvas. Apprehension hit the pause button on honorable intentions.

Emma took the painting gingerly, afraid of dropping it, willing her hands not to shake. Her eyes followed the brushstrokes first—too short and heavy. The colors in the painting clashed; the blue of his eyes too rich, Flynn's reddish-brown hair too bright. There was too much background and not enough of her subject. Even then she'd been fascinated with landscapes.

Her heartbeat quickened.

She'd tried to paint Flynn winding up for a pitch. She'd gotten his body proportions wrong—too much butt, not enough torso. Yet, from what she remembered, she'd captured Flynn's determined expression—the tug of his chin to the right, the tense set to his mouth, the young, piercing gaze of a fierce competitor.

Emma wanted to close her eyes and bring back that feeling of joy she'd had when painting; she wanted to hum to herself as she led her brush in a soft caress over the canvas. Her ears felt like they were being stuffed with cotton and her hands trembled. If she didn't collect herself soon, she'd be in no shape to talk to Tracy.

Emma gave the painting back to Mr. B., a bittersweet pang of regret making her fingers numb and cold.

"It's my favorite picture." Mr. B.'s gruff voice filtered through the cotton in her ears.

"I'm glad you enjoy it. About the winery—"

"I'm sorry change upsets your grandmother." The older man's expression was reserved. "But change has to happen if the town is to survive. You want Harmony Valley to survive, don't you?"

"Of course, but—"

"And you realize that every choice has a cost, every path chosen sacrifices something down another road?"

"Yes, but—"

His broad smile challenged his bulbous nose for prominence on his face. "Then the boys can count on your support. Now, you'd best be on your way. You don't want to be late to see Tracy."

"How did you—"

"There are no secrets in Harmony Valley. I can assure you that will never change."

"Some things should change," Emma muttered after she left, turning down the river path that would lead her to Tracy.

"I WANT. YOU. To go." Tracy resisted stomping her feet. That would make her look childish. She resisted tugging her jeans up higher on her rail-thin hips. That would make her look weak. Lacking polished speech, she had to carefully control the visual impressions she made, especially with her brother.

Will leaned against the archway separating the kitchen from the living room. He crossed his arms over his chest. "I'm not leaving you alone with her."

"Dad left." Tracy had told her father she wanted to speak to Emma alone, and he'd gone to pick up fertilizer in Santa Rosa. He wouldn't be back for hours.

Emma was due to arrive any minute and Tracy didn't want Will chaperoning. He'd kept Emma from her for six months. Six months! It felt like a lifetime. A lifetime without the friend who'd kept her secrets and shared her dreams.

The aching loneliness. The gut-clenching worry. The raging anger. No one understood what she was going through. But Emma would. She wouldn't talk to Tracy like she was a child. And because of that, speech would come easier to Tracy. She imagined words tumbling out of her mouth as quickly as laughter.

"Why. Can't—"

"Are you sure you want to see her?"

Tracy made a sound that was half growl, half yowl. She hated how Will always doubted Emma. She hated aphasia and the fact that she couldn't string together a quick argument. She could sing along with rapper Pitbull in her head, but open her mouth and it was as if she couldn't crank her brain's handle fast enough to pump out the words.

Hot tears threatened to spill onto her cheeks. She blinked and turned away from Will, snatching up her notepad and pen, scratching out a message.

Tracy shoved the notepad beneath Will's nose.

I want to talk to Emma alone.

Because she needed Emma to help her escape from Will and Harmony Valley. She'd decided to return to their San Francisco apartment.

With barely a glance at her scribbled command, Will shook his head.

"Leave. Me—"

"I'm not leaving you alone. You're not sure you want to see her. I can tell."

The way Will tried to read her mind and finished her sentences made her feel stupid. In the eyes of her brother, Tracy was handicapped, disabled, incapable of living independently. Tracy felt as insignificant as a plain number two pencil in a mechanical pencil world. "No!"

But the truth was, she didn't know. Tracy had been dozing in the passenger seat. And yesterday—

"Don't forget Emma was dancing yesterday. When was the last time you danced?"

Tracy's breath hitched. To keep from speaking, she ground her teeth. Her brother didn't need to know what had happened the night before the accident. They'd been in Las Vegas, after all.

Someone knocked at the door.

Tracy glared at him. One last command for him to leave.

Will didn't budge, of course.

She'd have to find another time to talk to Emma about moving back to the apartment. The settlements from Emma's insurance and the trucking company that owned the big rig involved in the collision would pay Tracy's share of the rent until she was able to return to work. Whatever work someone with her challenges could get. She'd do anything to regain her independence.

Still, her hand hesitated on the doorknob. Her plan was contingent upon her liking whatever Emma had to say. What if Will was right? She'd seemed remorseful last night, but there could be more to Emma's story. Details Tracy couldn't forgive her for.

What if Emma heard her speak and didn't want to be friends anymore?

Emma knocked again.

"If you're not sure…" Will's voice skated with cutting blades over her nerves. "Don't let her in."

Tracy clenched her teeth and turned the tarnished brass knob.

"TRACY, I'VE MISSED you so much." Emma sank into the couch beneath the dusty trout mounted on the wall. She set the shoebox on the cushion next to her.

Tracy looked young and rebellious. There was a set to her mouth, a slant to her sharp blue eyes and the bright orange T-shirt that used to fit her listed slightly toward one shoulder. Will stood guard a few feet away, his arms crossed over his chest, staring at Emma. He'd struck the exact same pose before her and Tracy's prom, driving home from college just so he could try to put the fear of God into their dates. She'd felt his eyes upon her that night, too, and she'd burned with the feeling of feminine power. She would have burned with embarrassment to know what he'd really thought of her back then—reckless, irresponsible, a threat to the safety of his sister.

Today his gaze on Emma was so intense it threatened to ignite a fire in her veins. She was certain he didn't intend to convey interest in her. It had to be her artistic, misdirected passion. She lifted her chin as if to tell him he couldn't intimidate her and angled her body directly toward Tracy. "Do you remember the accident?"

Tracy's apprehension swept through the room like a chill winter draft. She hunched on her dad's brown leather recliner, the cor-

'ners of her mouth drooping as she murmured, "Some."

"I won't recount the crash," Emma was quick to reassure her.

Tracy's shoulders went from rigid to merely tense.

"You have to know...I am so sorry." Just saying the words nearly unbraided the ribbons of fear, worry and guilt that had bound Emma's heart to her toes for six months. "We'd been on the road for a couple of hours. You were sleeping because..."

Tracy had met someone in Las Vegas and they'd gone to a late-night, private party. Emma was practically positive Tracy hadn't told her brother about that.

Emma slid a glance in Will's direction, but forced herself not to look at his face, afraid he'd realize she wasn't about to tell the entire truth. Instead, she stared at his expensive running shoes. "Because I had kept you out late the night before."

Her gaze slipped back to Tracy, whose cheeks were tinged pink.

"We'd driven through the Tehachapi mountains earlier and I started visualizing a grouping of snowy peaks I'd seen." The striations of gray. The shimmer of marbled granite beneath the delicate snowflake-like blanket of snow. Just thinking about the landscape caused Emma's hands to tremble. She laced her fingers together, not wanting Tracy to know she bore hidden scars from the accident. Her artistic block was nothing compared to the challenges Tracy faced. "You know how some landscapes call to me."

Tracy gave a small, almost imperceptible nod.

Over by the kitchen, Will sniffed, as if trying to catch the scent of what Emma wasn't saying.

Emma knotted her fingers tighter. "I didn't fall asleep. I remember a billboard we passed. I remember the song playing on the radio. I remember seeing the mountains like a picture ahead of me on the road. But all of a sudden the truck was there and—"

Tracy swallowed thickly. The blood had drained from her face.

"And then it happened." Emma's fingers convulsed as they'd done on the wheel that day. "They flew you to one hospital and drove me to another. The worst of my injuries wouldn't show up for days." She hadn't meant to mention that.

Out of the corner of her eye, Emma saw Will cock his head.

"Your. Injuries?"

Silently cursing her blabbing mouth, Emma chose her words carefully. "My injuries are nothing compared to yours." So she'd lost her talent. That was inconsequential compared to Tracy losing her ability to speak fluently. Emma was desperate to make amends. Someday she'd tell Tracy what she'd lost. But not today. "By the time I was released and arrived at your hospital, I couldn't get in, but I tried to see you." Emma fought to keep the desperation out of her voice, afraid she was failing. "And I raised money for your medical bills."

"We used your funds to establish a charitable foundation in Tracy's name for those with aphasia who can't afford speech therapy." Will stared at his shoes, as if he was reluctant to admit that Emma had done something good.

"That's nice." With a millionaire for a brother, Tracy had no need for financial aid, but Emma had wanted to do something. She handed the shoebox to Tracy. "And I kept coming back every week, even when they transferred you to Greenhaven."

Tracy placed the cardboard box on the coffee table and lifted the lid. "Oh." She gave a small smile, picking up one of the tiny dolls. Farmer Carina. Her hair was the same straw blond as Tracy's.

Emma's smile had never felt so big. "I brought a different one to the hospital every Sunday."

Tracy turned accusing eyes on Will. "Why. Keep. This. From—"

"The doctors didn't want you upset."

"You. Should. Have—"

Will tossed a hand in Emma's direction as easily as he'd tossed aside Tracy's wishes. "If I'd asked you, I'd risk upsetting you."

"Say. Sorry."

Listening to Tracy's struggle to speak, comparing her halting cadence to how she used to speak, magnified Emma's guilt.

Maybe Will was right. Maybe Tracy did need more therapy before she tried to resume her life in the city. People could be impatient and cruel. They'd judge Tracy's intelligence by her speech pattern. Tracy would hate it. And Will knew it.

The air in the room thickened with regrets and what-might-have-beens. This was why Will had brought Tracy back to Harmony Valley. Not only to protect her from Emma, but to protect her fragile ego from the rest of the world. The pace here was slower. The people more understanding than those ladder-climbing, backstabbing executives at the ad agency. Emma felt like hugging Will for putting Tracy's needs above his own.

And then he had to ruin it. "If I say I'm sorry, Emma will know I don't mean it. I did what I thought was right. And I'd do it again."

That coldhearted, pigheaded—

"I can't. Wait. To—"

"To get out of here. Yeah, I know." There was an undercurrent of sadness in Will's voice that made it hard to remember he was cold-hearted and pigheaded. "Can we have this discussion after your next round of therapy?"

"Will!" Tracy dropped the doll back into the box and bunched her fingers into a fist.

Emma remembered Tracy brimming with emotion and talking a mile a minute. Blurting out joyful observations on life. Blasting her brother when he tried to boss her around. Her speech may have become more deliberate, but the way Tracy poured emotion into her staccato sentences was exactly the same.

Emma reached across the coffee table to cover Tracy's skeletal fist with her palm. "You can do anything you want. That hasn't

changed. And neither has Will's overprotec-
tiveness."

Tracy's smile was so powerful it punc-
tured the thick layer of guilt Emma had been
wrapped in for months. She could feel it de-
flate, draining out of her until her limbs felt
featherlight and her heartbeat calmed.

"What do you want to do?" Tracy wasn't
ready to face the fast-paced world yet. Emma
softened her tone, gentled her voice and tried
to lessen the blow for Tracy. "We can go back
to the city. But Will is right about one thing.
We should wait until you finish more therapy."

"No!" Tracy and Will protested in unison.
They exchanged frustrated scowls.

Tracy yanked her hand from beneath Emma's.

"But…" Emma looked from Will to Tracy,
trying to interpret their moods. And failing.
"Will said you had more therapy to complete."

Will loomed over Emma. "She's not going
back to the city. Not with you. Not ever."

"No. Therapy." Tracy's face scrunched in
horror. "No." She ran to the back of the house,
slamming the door to her bedroom so hard it
rattled the walls, rattling Emma's hopes for
reconciliation, leaving her in a numb, ear-
ringing state of paralysis.

Things had been going so well. Why had they fallen apart?

Emma stared at her hands, replaying the conversation in her head.

"Do you see what you've done?" Will held the door open. She hadn't noticed him move.

"What I've done?" Emma's lungs labored in quick, ragged spurts, fueling her outrage. "I see what you've done. Tracy doesn't have to say a word when you're around. You complete every sentence for her. You said she needed more therapy. Oh, I fell right into that one, didn't I? What therapy is going to help when you're acting as her crutch?"

"Leave. Now."

Emma stood with a swish of her long skirt and walked toward the doorway. "This isn't over."

She barely made it out before he slammed the door at her back. "None of it is over."

CHAPTER NINE

WILL WAS DROWNING in cats.

A big orange tomcat with scarred ears curled on his lap. A delicate gray tabby perched on his shoulder. A spindly, purring Siamese with one eye rubbed against his arm. A black cat leaped onto his knees. Kittens of all sizes and colors tumbled around his ankles.

After kicking Emma out of the house, Will had tried to talk to Tracy, but she'd locked her bedroom door and wouldn't come out or speak to him. Hadn't he warned her letting Emma in was a bad idea? He couldn't let it matter that Emma's sincerity and mysterious injuries had touched him and also nudged his curiosity. But Emma didn't have to deal with the fallout of her actions. He did.

If only Tracy could hear the Morse code message pounding at his temples: *Emma was trouble. Emma was trouble.* And he was afraid they hadn't seen the last of her. Emma was too stubborn to go away.

A fluffy white kitten bit into Will's shoe-lace, tumbled onto its back and kicked at the lace with ferocious pink-padded hind feet.

Will chuckled.

There looked to be at least twenty cats in the living room, sleeping, scuffling and stalking. It was simultaneously heartwarming and claustrophobic.

The bundle of fluff that had captured his shoelace pulled with such determination his shoe came untied.

Will chuckled again.

"I can't live in a big city." Felix stared at Will through platter-thick glasses. He was a retired fire chief from Healdsburg, formerly the chief of Harmony Valley's volunteer fire department. Now the big, burly man with a heart of gold rescued cats. "Big cities won't let you have more than a couple cats. This winery of yours won't hurt my rescues, will it?"

"No." At least Will hoped not. If it came to that, he'd fight for Felix's right to rescue as many cats as he could.

As if sensing Will had fudged an answer, the Siamese nipped Will's biceps. It was only a love bite, but Will picked the cat up to prevent more chomping.

The Siamese snuggled against his chest,

ivory fur as soft as mink. It purred as loud as a small motorboat.

"I try to find homes for my rescues, but that's not always possible." With hands the size of footballs, Felix picked up the ball of fur at Will's feet, disengaged its claws from Will's shoelace and cuddled it in the crook of his thick neck.

"I'd love to see you at the next town council meeting." Will checked his watch. It was after one-thirty. He started divesting himself of cats, revealing a coat of cat hair on his jeans and polo shirt. "Bringing the city back to life will mean more services. Maybe even a vet, seeing as how Dr. Wentworth wants to retire." He tied his shoe before traversing the feline labyrinth to the door, the Siamese close at his heels.

"A new vet would be a dream come true." Felix followed him out, shutting the Siamese in. "Oh, there's Emma. She used to play with my granddaughter, Frances, in the summer. Hullo, Emma! Can I interest you in a kitten?"

Will turned to see Emma walking up the driveway, flashing a smooth smile that kicked his heart into a new gear and promised trouble. The body-hugging dark blue T-shirt and ankle-length, blue Indian-print skirt she wore swayed in tandem with her long, dark hair. There was something about Emma that demanded his attention and he couldn't figure out what it was, no matter how long he looked at her.

Emma greeted Felix with a hug, careful not to dislodge the old man's kitten. "No pets allowed in my building. So no type of animal, be it dog or cat or *louse*—" she narrowed her eyes at Will "—would be a good fit for me."

A less perceptive man wouldn't notice the hungry glint of payback in her eyes. A man with more common sense might have worried about the coincidence of her appearance. Will just wanted to move on to his next appointment.

"I was hoping you'd finally changed your mind and decided to settle down in Harmony Valley with Rose," Felix said.

"Nope. I'm still living in the city."

The Siamese cat yowled behind Felix's screen door, as if wanting in on whatever Emma had planned.

"Good news, Emma." Felix glowed. "Will says there's a chance we'll get a new vet if the town council rezones the Henderson property."

"Have you heard the details of Will's plans?"

Emma smirked at Will. Then her gaze slid casually to Felix's immaculately kept white arts-and-craft house with a wraparound porch. "They're tearing down the Henderson house and barn. Oh, and they presented plans for a subdivision. One hundred houses, right, Will?"

Will clamped his mouth closed. He'd forgotten Felix was involved in the Preservation Society. Edwin had mentioned it in his dossier.

"Really?" Felix's expression hardened. "A cat chewed my phone cable. I'll have to get a new one so I can stay up to date on the news."

Will attempted a smile. "Thanks to Rose, we've realized we need to preserve and revitalize existing structures. But the important things are the return of services, not necessarily how we get them."

"Bring your architectural plans by and let me be the judge," Felix said coolly.

In less than a minute Emma had undermined Will's efforts. He wanted to strangle her. Instead, he extended his hand toward Felix. "Hope to see you at the meeting on Monday."

As Felix returned to his cats, Emma walked with Will down the driveway. Not surprisingly, clouds gathered overhead. Emma most likely brought rain clouds wherever she went.

"Weren't you going to visit Felix?" he asked with forceful cheer.

"I did. Now I'm going to visit someone else." Emma purred as innocently as the one-eyed Siamese had, right before it bit him.

The suspicion he'd ignored when she'd first shown up resurfaced. Her appearance at Felix's house wasn't a coincidence. Will brushed cat hair off his clothing, creating a whirlwind of flying fur. "You're not coming with me."

"I'm not *with* you. But I'm going to go…this way." She turned left, heading south on Madison Avenue. "Have you talked to Mr. Mionetti lately?"

"No." It was his next destination. *How had she known?*

"I'd love to catch up with Mr. Mionetti." Emma's chin was in the air, her gaze fixed firmly ahead. The bandage on her forehead peeked beneath her bangs, as if proclaiming she needed looking after just as much as Tracy did.

He was reminded of the time Emma had talked Tracy into floating down the Harmony River the spring after his mother died. It had been too early in the season, and the river had been running too fast. They'd hit a patch of rapids and Tracy had broken her ankle on a jutting rock. His dad had driven Tracy to the hospital. Will had been tasked with walking Emma home. He'd told her exactly what he thought of her irresponsible influence on his sister. Emma hadn't even defended herself. She'd simply walked with her nose in the air.

And here was Emma causing trouble again. She'd undermined him with Felix and she clearly planned to do the same with Mr. Mionetti.

Will didn't believe in pussyfooting around. "You can forget whatever scheme you've cooked up and head on home."

Her chin inched higher and she opened her mouth to speak, but Will wasn't finished.

"I'd like to apologize to Rose. I hadn't realized how much our plans would upset her."

Emma blew out a puff of air. "Conspicuously absent in your little speech was an apology to me for banning me from Tracy's bedside."

"I'm not going to apologize for that. You proved this morning that I was justified in keeping you away. You upset Tracy."

"You were as much to blame for upsetting her as I was." She pinned him with a direct gaze that wouldn't let him deny it. "For years, you've been trying to control Tracy's life and, for now, you've succeeded. Which is probably why you've moved on to controlling Harmony Valley. You think you can change things here any way you like, regardless of the wishes of our friends and neighbors. Is that what becoming a millionaire does to people like you? Does money give you the right to be in control of everything?"

"My fortune has nothing to do with this. I'm trying to improve the standard of living here and save a dying town." With effort, he kept his cool. He could reason with Emma all day, until she fell silent, until she fell prey to his logic or to his kiss. A kiss would be quicker.

Where had that crazy thought come from?

Will stumbled. Just because he was losing his mind didn't mean he had to lose command of his limbs or his lips.

Emma marched on, oblivious to his torment. "Like cementing over the town's heritage is so honorable we should all bow down before you. I think not."

For one moment, Will considered bypassing Mr. Mionetti's house and heading back to town. He'd always known Emma and Tracy had a special bond, but he'd only seen the unpredictable, unreliable Emma, the one who made him feel justified in keeping her away.

But this Emma, this grown-up Emma, made him see her as a beautiful, compassionate woman—whose stubbornness wore at his patience.

They turned at the street's only weeping willow, walking down a long, straight lane bound by rusty barbed wire, gnarled, tilted fence posts and olive trees. The lane bordered a pasture and ended at a beige ranch home surrounded by a white picket fence. The sheep in the pasture retreated, bleating nervously as he and Emma passed.

"I can take it from here," Will said. "It's Tuesday. Shouldn't you be working?"

"I cleared off my calendar so I could help you today."

"Help me?" He'd sooner accept help from a rattlesnake. At least they gave warning before a strike. "How do you propose to help me?"

"You'll see." She grinned.

A shaggy sheepdog behind the picket fence began barking at their approach. His deep, warning bark was strained, perhaps by his collar, which was connected to a taut chain.

Will slowed. He had a deep respect for the territoriality of farm dogs, having been treed by a German shepherd in his youth.

Emma didn't seem at all worried. She

opened the gate and walked in, crossing the lawn to the dog.

Will followed, closing the gate behind them.

"Hey, Shep." Emma knelt near the beast, who still halfheartedly barked in Will's direction. There was a metallic click. Then Emma stood, holding the free end of Shep's chain. "Oops."

Shep shook himself off, taking two drunken steps sideways. Will knew in one heart-stuttering moment when the large dog realized he was free. Shep's eyes locked on to Will like he was hungry and Will was a meaty soup bone. With a bellowing bark, Shep leaped forward.

Will opened the gate, stepped through and closed it again.

Shep loped along in slow motion, plopping to the ground in an exhausted heap on the other side of the gate. His eyes were rheumy and his muzzle a peppery gray. He panted as if he'd run uphill for miles, not twenty feet of flat ground.

"Good boy, Shep." Emma had trailed after the dog and bent to scratch him behind his ears. "Lucky you. Shep doesn't move like he used to."

Will desperately wanted to wipe that superior expression off Emma's face. He was torn between the best way to do so—wrap his hands around her slender neck or claim domination of her mouth with his.

His hands fisted. His lips pressed together.

"What's all this racket?" Mr. Mionetti walked out. The old man was beanpole-thin and looked as if a strong wind could blow him over. "Who's there? And why is Shep loose?"

The sheepdog shuffled over to his reedy master.

"I'm sorry, Mr. Mionetti. It's me, Emma Willoughby, Rose Cascia's granddaughter." Emma slid a sly glance Will's way. "Do you remember Will Jackson? Ben Jackson's son? He has an appointment with you today. He wants to build a winery on the Henderson property."

The urge to strangle became more urgent.

"Heard about that. Don't like wineries." Mr. Mionetti's lips rippled into a thin, wrinkly frown. "Every year or so another winery comes around here wanting to plant their vines on my land. As if I don't make a good living with my sheep. Some people are just plain dumb."

Like Will, who hadn't paid as much attention as Emma had to Harmony Valley residents when he lived here. He'd been too busy honing his computer skills.

Emma's grin stretched to annoying proportions.

"Don't need to speak to another winery flunky." Mr. Mionetti barked his dismissal louder than Shep.

Leaving Will to wonder how badly his winery chances with Mr. Mionetti could possibly be hurt if he duct taped Emma to the weeping willow at the end of the lane.

"I LIKE THE color yellow," Emma said as she and Will walked up Mr. Mionetti's lane past sheep and olive trees under an increasingly cloudy sky. Even a rain cloud couldn't dim the thrill of thwarting Will at two houses. Victory put a bounce in her step. Taunting him about those yellow Post-it flags she'd seen back at Mr. B.'s house was sweet icing on her delicious lemon cake. "Some people think yellow is indecisive and middle ground. But I think yellow is a sunny, decisive color that's averse to change."

"Did you break into Edwin's house? Or did he let you in?" Will's anger filled every syllable. His hand darted toward Emma's arm.

She danced out of reach. "I'll never tell, and

the great thing about Harmony Valley is your cell phone doesn't work here. So you can't call Mr. B. or your friends until you find a landline. You're going to Snarky Sam's next, right?" She laughed. For the first time in a long time, her laughter reached deep into the recesses of her guilt-ridden soul.

And then fat raindrops started to fall, as if even Mother Nature was against her.

They ran for the broad weeping willow at the end of the drive.

"I'd forgotten how fickle the weather is here." Will parted the curtain of branches beneath the willow just as it started to pour, holding them open for Emma, then turning away once she was inside. He crossed his arms over his chest in the male version of a pout.

"It'll pass in a few minutes." She hoped that was true. It was a long walk home without an umbrella.

"I can wait. I've got a few minutes before going to Sam's and time after that before I have drinks with Mayor Larry."

"While you're having cocktails maybe I'll swing by and check on Tracy."

He surprised her by remaining silent.

A frisson of apprehension skittered over her skin. She stared out across the wet landscape, trying to recall the details of Mr. B.'s map, letting the patter of rain fill the silence.

Gradually, she noticed the breathtaking 360-degree perspective from beneath the weeping willow. Sheep dotted the green grass of Mr. Mionetti's farm. Plump, green grapevines grew across the road, advancing up the hillside. The valanced branches of the willow shifted with sinuous grace. And the rain softened every view, deepened the multiple shades of green with a gemlike polish.

She'd start the painting with the sky, brushing in layers of gray. Then she'd paint the rich umber of the earth and the iron gray of the puddles. She'd paint the grapevines next. Neatly. A regimented order with tendrils reaching like a mother's hand to sweep up a wandering child into a loving embrace. Then she'd paint the willow's branches, some of which dragged on the ground like fashionable drapes. And far off in the distance a sliver of—

"What? You're not talking to me now?" Will's voice carried more than a hint of annoyance.

The rest of what he said or didn't say was drowned out by the memory of protesting brakes and the whine of a large, powerful engine. The landscape she'd been composing faded away as her vision fogged over.

Emma reached out. Her hand connected with the willow's tree trunk. Cool, rough bark. She wiped at her damp forehead with her other hand, fighting the clammy, dank feeling of fear and failure.

"You look awful." Will stepped into Emma's line of tunneled vision. "Sit," he commanded, tugging her down, kneeling next to her. "Put your head between your knees."

"Has anyone ever told you you're too bossy?"

"Only Tracy and you. And you don't count."

Emma pushed at Will's hands with her own, but his were steadier, stronger in purpose. Under his guidance, her knees became earmuffs. She closed her eyes when her brain started registering the soil's various brown shades contrasted against the blues of her skirt. She breathed in the scent of fabric softener, of rich, musty earth, cleansing rain and Will's woodsy aftershave.

Thunder rumbled in the distance, its grumbling slower than her heart rate.

Emma tried to sit up, but Will kept her head firmly between her legs. It became harder to fill her lungs with air. "Please…"

"Tell me what's wrong. I can help." Will Jackson at his most annoying.

"Let me breathe!" She pushed up hard enough to break free of his hold. The back of her head bounced off the tree trunk. "Ow."

He draped his arm across her shoulders as if to keep her from falling over. "What is it with you and head wounds?"

Emma gritted her teeth. "You don't have to hold on to me. I'm not going to pass out."

"You could have fooled me a minute ago." His arm stayed. Steady. Reassuring.

"Seen a lot of people faint, have you?" The pain chased away the last of the fog around the edges of her vision, but not the woodsy scent of Will.

"You'd be surprised at how often women faint at the sight of me."

"You wish."

Thunder rumbled above the hills to the east, over the vineyards.

Emma refused to look. She focused on the ground at her feet.

A fat raindrop splashed onto the nape of her neck. It rolled down her spine in a haphazard way that made her shiver.

Will rubbed her shoulder.

She risked a glance at him.

His blue eyes were gentled with concern. How could such an overbearing, infuriating man have such expressive, beautiful eyes? They brimmed with the promise of a gentleman, of doors held open, chairs pulled out, of concern for others.

Yeah, right.

He cupped her chin and examined her face so intently, she blushed.

"I'm fine."

"Tell me what happened." An order. No surprise there.

"Nothing happened."

"Panic attack," he surmised. "You were somewhere else for a while. Battling demons."

Emma clamped her lips shut. She didn't want to say anything. Her fears were her own. She hadn't told anyone—not even Granny Rose—about the debilitating dread she felt when she tried to paint or sketch. For a moment, Emma gave her own fears priority instead of Tracy's condition. What would she do if she couldn't reclaim her art? Who would she become?

She wanted to curl in on herself. But she knew that however adrift she felt, Tracy felt much worse. If Tracy could bear it, so could she.

The rain eased. Just a few more minutes and

she'd be able to walk away. What she wouldn't give to be able to retreat to Granny Rose's house and crawl into bed.

"I had a fear once," Will said softly.

This was a media moment. Perfect specimens like Will never admitted weakness. "Only one?"

"I was afraid of spiders."

"Really?" Emma didn't believe him for a minute.

"Big ones. Little ones. Hairy ones. It didn't matter. If they had eight legs, they freaked me out." There was something in his husky voice, an earnestness that drew her gaze to his and wouldn't let go. She could spend hours trying to capture the layers of hurt in his eyes with her sketch pencil or brush.

Time slowed as they stared at each other, as she realized that behind his pain was something softer. Warmer. Something she had to be imagining. Something that answered the longing that she knew must be in her own eyes.

Holy raging wildfire.

Emma tugged her gaze free. She needed to defuse the moment, to return to their combative state. Now she knew why she'd categorized Will as public enemy number one. He was attractive. To her. And she…

"This fear of spiders... Did it start when you were four?" she whispered, half-jokingly.

"I was fifteen."

Whatever comeback she felt forming dissipated in a whoosh of air. She knew what had happened to him at fifteen.

"My mother had just died and I didn't like the idea of her in a coffin." His eyes softened to a deeper blue and his gaze met Emma's, but she suspected he was seeing a memory, not her. Will never looked at her that way. "I saw a spider outside my window the morning she died. And another the day we buried her. I thought it was a sign. An omen of death."

"That's silly." But Emma had to force the words past a throat tight with compassion. Many times she'd wished Will's mother had been her own. Emma's mom always put the needs of others ahead of her daughter's. Will's mom never had. She baked cookies, talked about boys and gave the best hugs, next to Granny Rose, of course. When she'd died in that explosion, Emma had grieved almost as much as Will and Tracy.

"Every fear is silly when you say it out loud." Will stood and held out his hand to her.

Emma accepted his help. His hand was larger than hers—strong, warm, the hand of a man you could rely on. His touch was as intimate as a caress, a promise of more caresses to come. Tempting. So tempting, this need to be held and let someone else shoulder her fears.

Emma knew she should pull away, knew she should step back.

Instead, her gaze drifted up his arm, an arm waiting to draw her closer. Drifted farther to his mouth, to his lips, slightly parted, waiting to meet her own. Drifted higher to his intense blue eyes, and a gaze waiting for her to forget that they were at cross purposes.

Will seemed to hold back, as if looking for any indication that she would accept the promise of this something, so nebulous, that swirled intangibly between them, yet at the same time so strong she could almost feel it—*feel him*—warm and solid and real.

Air became trapped in her lungs, sending heat flaming through her veins.

If she leaned forward, the wait would be over, the promise of more accepted.

From the next valley over, thunder murmured.

And still Will held her hand. Still, they gazed at each other. Still, neither of them moved to submit to the need swirling between them.

The need to touch, to feel, to kiss.

"No!" She couldn't kiss Will. She couldn't want to kiss Will. He hadn't forgiven her for the accident. And probably never would.

Emma snatched her hand free and stepped out of reach, flexing her fingers as if she could banish his warmth. But she couldn't banish what he'd awoken in her, this unwanted awareness. She could only deny it.

Will's expression didn't change. He didn't smile. He didn't smirk. He didn't laugh off what had almost happened. Was the idea of a kiss all in her head? His nonreaction almost made her rush forward and kiss his indifference away.

Foolish idea, that. Emma drew a deep breath and licked her lips.

Will, Mr. Control, dropped his gaze to Emma's mouth. Heat flickered in his eyes. His gaze locked on hers once more.

Emma held her breath. He was going to kiss her now.

Dread scuffled with anticipation in her belly as she waited for Will to decide.

But nothing happened. Will didn't move.

The rain tapered off to an intermittent mist. A blue jay swooped past with a squawk of indignation.

Emma swallowed and stepped back. She

was knee-quakingly grateful that neither of them had succumbed to temptation. She'd almost made a colossal mistake on multiple levels. It was as if the willow tree they'd stepped beneath was neutral territory. She edged closer to the border of branches. "I know what you think of me. In your eyes, I'm the loose cannon. The one people get hurt around." They needed to get that issue up front, not talk about kisses. "But your opinion doesn't matter to me. Tracy's does. I'm not going to give up on our friendship. And I don't think Tracy is, either."

Will's brow furrowed.

"And I'm against change here, just like Granny Rose. I'm trying to stop your winery." Emma drew a deep breath, remembering too late her grandmother's warning about Will and his ability to charm her. "I won't let you have your way without a fight." Not with Tracy, not with the town and certainly not with her own feelings.

"There's more at stake here for me than a dying town," he said, his voice a husky threat.

The rain stopped. The sun winked at the edges of the willow.

She'd almost kissed Will. If it had been anyone else she'd almost kissed, she'd be rushing to tell Tracy.

Instead, she tossed out a challenge. "Snarky Sam's. Last one there can't talk for five minutes." Emma slipped through the damp willow branches and took off at a run, picking up her skirt, sandals slapping against the wet pavement as she reached Madison Avenue.

Will overtook her in twenty yards and quickly put an ever-lengthening distance between them.

Emma had been counting on that. She needed breathing room.

And Sam didn't take kindly to interruptions.

CHAPTER TEN

SNARKY SAM'S WAS part antiques store, part pawn shop, located at the entrance to town on Main Street, where the sidewalks started. It was a mile away from the weeping willow where Emma had had her panic attack and Will had come close to kissing her.

Thankfully, Will hadn't given in to that system-shaking chemistry. A kiss was something even Edwin couldn't strategize around.

There would be no kisses.

Not with the woman who'd almost killed his sister.

Under the willow, Will had watched Emma shrink from an energetic, confident beauty to a withdrawn, fragile woman. It was like watching a spring flower wither on the vine. He'd meant to soothe her, to chase away her fears and bring that annoying grin back to her face.

Backfired. Big time.

He didn't know where this attraction had come from, but he needed to get rid of it. Fast.

The rain had moved on and the sun was breaking through what remained of the clouds.

In a way, Will would have been better off if he'd kissed Emma. Then he wouldn't be obsessing about how her lips would feel on his, how her body would feel pressed against him. This was Emma, for crying out loud. He'd bandaged her skinned knees, pulled her pigtails and dunked her in the river, same as he'd done to his sister. But if she was like a sister to him, he wouldn't be feeling this attraction.

Will needed to focus on Sam Smith. Sam's business was barely hanging on, and Will was ready to offer him an opportunity. Emma was three blocks back. Will had more than enough time to break the ice with Sam and make his point before his five minutes were up.

The sidewalk in front of the shop was littered with antiques and what Will would call junk, all dripping with raindrops. A wooden baby cradle, a washboard, an old bicycle, a wood chipper.

He opened the wood-framed glass door, setting off a bell. The air in the shop was stale and musty; the merchandise dusty and dated.

Hanging on didn't begin to describe Sam's business.

"You pawning or buying?" A gnarled sprite of a man in a blue-checked flannel shirt put his comic book down to eye Will. He sat behind a display counter loaded with old jewelry, but his suffer-no-fools attitude was front and center.

Will felt about as welcome as a fat tick on a show dog. "Neither."

"No soliciting. Says so on the door. You get me?" Sam raised his comic book again. Spider-Man swung across the cover. The edges of the page were as yellow and age-worn as Sam.

Edwin's notes had indicated Sam would be open to more sales, but sales of what? It was hard to get a handle on the man when the store seemed to sell everything from knick-knacks to small appliances to jewelry to really bad taxidermy. A skunk wearing a Sherlock Holmes outfit stood on a table to his right, while a raccoon wearing a bikini strutted to his left.

The eight-week marathon of activity to obtain approvals for the winery finally kicked in. Will's body felt heavy, his motivation sagged. But he was here, so he ignored both and assembled his smile. "I'm not buying or selling."

Sam lowered the comic book, revealing a deeply set scowl. "If you ain't pawning and you ain't selling, you're in the wrong establishment. I'm a man of business. Don't have time to waste." Spider-Man swung back into place.

Will's smile remained locked on target. "I'm Will Jackson. My business partners and I are building a winery on the old Henderson property."

Sam dropped the comic book on the glass counter, a puff of dust rising in protest. "I call bull. The town council hasn't approved a nail you plan to hammer."

"That's true. The town council is holding hearings."

"They're stalling. Supposed you'd be smart enough to know that. Although if you ain't, you might as well give up now."

Will considered his options.

"Looks like one of Felix's cats got your tongue."

Will forced a self-conscious chuckle and brushed off a few more cat hairs from his polo. "You boxed me into a corner. If I agree that the council is stalling, I'll look critical of the council. If I disagree, I'll look naive."

"Very smart, but Edwin should have told

you, I don't take sides. I won't hang signs for you or tolerate protestors on my sidewalk."

Will switched topics, indicating the collection of coffee tables, ceramic statues and lamps with a wave of his hand. "What's your bestselling item?"

"Nobody buys anything from me anymore," Sam snapped. "I lend money. Ninety-day terms. Come about day seventy-five I put their item out on the sidewalk as a reminder that I'll need my money or I'm going to own whatever they've pawned. Folks here need short-term loans to make ends meet." Sam thumbed his fist toward the back of the store. "I've got ten blenders back there, seven bread machines, three treadmills and one rusted-out wheelbarrow. I don't plan to sell any of it." His gaze landed on a locked set of glass shelves to his left filled with colorful glass plates, cups and bowls. Some of the snark blew out of him. He almost smiled. "My wife used to sell antiques, back when there were people working in this town. She loved Depression glass." The scowl returned. "But folks in Harmony Valley have more than enough things. You get me?"

Sam had tipped his hand and exposed the heart of his concerns. "How would you like to sell Depression glass again?"

"I'm an old man. I don't think I want to work that hard." Sam tapped the Spider-Man comic on the counter with one gnarled finger. "This is starting to sound like a solicitation. I think it's time for you to move along. You get me?"

The bell rang behind Will. He didn't turn. The very air in the room shifted and his body tensed as if readying to pounce. He knew who'd come in. Emma.

Anger rooted him to the scuffed linoleum. Anger at Emma. Anger at the corner he'd backed himself into. She'd wanted him to get to the shop first or she wouldn't have challenged him to that race, giving him five uninterrupted minutes with Sam. Which he'd blown.

"Well if it ain't Emma Willoughby." Sam snorted. "I can see this is shaping up to be another civil war. No, no. Don't deny it. I can see it by the way you're looking at this young man there ain't no love lost between you. I'm not much interested in wine or art. And since I'm very busy, and neither of you have commerce with me, I'll have to ask you both to leave."

"If you'd let me explain," Will began.

"You two are disrupting my workday. I'd

call the sheriff, but he'd take thirty minutes to get here from Cloverdale."

"I'm going, Sam. And I'll take this bit of rubbish out with me." Emma opened the door, waiting until Will was outside to grin.

It was hard to believe that sometime in the past hour he'd wanted to kiss those lips. "You knew! You knew Sam wouldn't take sides when you challenged me to that race."

"Did you ever pay attention to anything besides the farm and your computers when you lived here?" She laughed, but the sound died off when her gaze landed on Sam's window.

She was looking toward the corner of the display, at something half-hidden behind the wood chipper. Will shifted so he could see what had caught her attention. It was an oil painting of Harmony Valley as seen from the top of Parish Hill.

The amused, upward crinkle to Emma's eyes fell. Her smile flattened. Her body stilled. The teasing air of superiority from seconds ago vanished, revealing the vulnerable woman he'd discovered beneath the willow. The woman he yearned to hold again.

Residual anger grappled with the need to comfort and protect.

Protect?

For a moment, Will was perplexed. And then he realized his was a natural reaction. He'd protected Emma most of the early years of her life. After his mother died, his focus had turned primarily to Tracy and by extension Emma. It was only logical his old habits would reassert themselves when he saw Emma's distress.

"Did you paint that?" His voice jarred her, although he hadn't spoken much louder than a whisper.

She drew a breath and looked away. "I captured the heart of this place, don't you think?" She turned and walked briskly toward the town square, as if she couldn't get away from the painting fast enough.

Will wasn't an artist. He couldn't distinguish passion in a painting, this one or otherwise. What he did see was the burned silo frame, the empty parking spaces along Main Street, the lack of life. Now that she'd put some distance between them, his brain kicked back into gear.

He hurried to catch up to her. "How prophetic that you painted the town without people, since that's where it's headed if the town council doesn't rezone the Henderson property."

"You see everything too literally." There was strength in her voice again, although her eyes still had a worried slant.

"It's why I'm good with computers."

"And why you stumble with people."

"Do you know why everyone under the age of sixty left Harmony Valley?" Will managed to speak in a measured voice, as if he were an outsider with nothing at stake. "They had mouths to feed, college bills, mortgages. The town council forced them out with a no-growth policy that was shortsighted. It's why everyone left."

Emma frowned.

Sensing he was near scoring a point, Will pressed on. "You heard what Sam said. It takes emergency services thirty minutes to get here. Heaven help someone if there's a fire. Or worse." With the advanced age of Harmony Valley's older residents, it was only a matter of time until tragedy arrived.

His father drove by, his white pickup truck headed toward the center of town. He saw Will and waved.

"Harmony Valley has a volunteer fire department." Emma's information was maddeningly out-of-date.

"Had. They shut it down when Felix failed

the fitness exam. Property-insurance rates increased when they lost that service. That's what finally broke Agnes's daughter. She couldn't afford to live here anymore."

Emma stopped at the corner of what had been the town's grocery store. Its brick wall was faded and crumbled at the base. El Rosal had picked up the grocery slack, selling staples out of their restaurant lobby. She cocked her head as she considered him. "Are you telling me you're only building this humongous winery and investing in town so they can restore emergency services? There's nothing in it for you?"

Will didn't refute her quickly enough.

"Come on. Spill it." She laughed.

A few minutes ago her laughter had danced across the bounds of his anger. Now he recognized it as something more—her armor against the world. Against him.

She smirked. "I can wait all day. Cleared my calendar, remember?"

He didn't want to tell her about his hopes for Tracy. He knew what her response would be—worse than Slade's. But he didn't see that he had a choice. "You're going to take this wrong."

"Try me." Her grin lit a fire in his gut, challenged him to defend his intentions.

They were good intentions. And good intentions deserved a good defense. Always. "I want Tracy to work here. At the winery. Or somewhere in town."

"There you go again." Emma's hands bobbed and floated and accused. "Wrapping Tracy up, boxing her in, shipping her off. Taking charge when you know Tracy wouldn't want this."

"I know what I'm doing. You may consider it overbearing—"

"Consider?" She huffed. "Do you have a plan for everyone in town? Including me?"

If she hadn't read him so well, he might have denied it or changed the subject.

But Emma was too perceptive. "You do! I should have known." She gestured for him to continue, quickly.

"All right. Since you want to know. I have no concrete plans, only preferences." Not all of which would see the light of day, like kissing Emma. He definitely wasn't making plans for that, but some niggling part of him refused to let go of the idea.

"Give. What are you thinking?" That grin again. Soon to disappear. "I can't wait to hear your preferences about me."

She wouldn't appreciate hearing what he had to say, but she'd asked and it was better to lay it out in front of her now. Her reaction might squelch his attraction to her. "I'd like some council members to retire so we can accelerate progress in town. I'd like to tear down some buildings that aren't up to earthquake code. This is California. You never know when or where the next big one will strike." He pointed to the crumbling brick at the bottom of the old grocery-store wall. And then came the personal stuff. "I'd like Tracy to give up her half of your apartment and move in with Dad. I'd like you to go paint somewhere far away from Tracy." And him. "I'd like you to—"

"That's enough." Emma's chin was up, along with her hackles. "I get your point, especially when it comes to me. You don't care about this place or anybody but yourself."

It was exactly the opposite. He cared more than he wanted to admit. He should leave and let her think poorly of him. Instead, he tried to reason with her. "Careful, Emma. You're letting emotion get in the way of logic. I care more than you know."

"Then you have a funny way of showing it. I have emotions. I express them. And I respect free will." Her hands fisted her skirt. "It's Tracy's future. The same for the town. And my life. They're our choices, not yours."

Her verbal jabs landed, striking a nerve. Will's shoulders pinched. She was acting as if he didn't care when he often felt he cared too much. It was why he pushed so hard for change.

But she wasn't finished. "I agree the town council should try to restore emergency services, but don't fault people like my grandmother and Mayor Larry for trying to protect the town's heritage and way of life just because you can't recognize how important that is."

Another blow landed. He was supposed to form a negative opinion of her, not the other way around.

"Protect their lifestyle?" Will closed the distance between them until he could smell the flowery scent of her hair. He lowered his voice until she had to angle her head toward him to capture every word. "They grew pot up on Parish Hill. Did you know that? I left that out of my little history lesson last night at the council meeting, but apparently it was once a vital part of the economy here."

Emma choked on a lungful of air, so close

he could reach out and kiss her. "That's not true."

His mouth worked over potential arguments, but his body kept urging him to use his lips in a completely different way.

Clamping his mouth firmly shut, Will took a step back. Then another.

"Ask Rose." He crossed the street, heading toward Slade's house, away from the accusations he resented, away from the grin that burned up his insides, away from the attraction that had him wanting something he could never have with Emma.

Her in his arms.

EMMA MARCHED HOME under a cloud-spotted sky. The things Will had accused her grandmother and town council of. *Slap-slap, slap-slap*. The way he'd implied Emma took everything he said personally. *Slap-slap-slap*. The way the logic of his argument about emergency services made sense. *Slap-slap*. The way her heart didn't want to listen. *Slap*.

A lone dandelion at the side of the road beckoned. Emma marched determinedly past it.

Will thought dandelion wishes were a waste of time. Will thought dandelion wishes spread weeds into the world. Will thought—

Emma spun around and plucked the dandelion free. She didn't care what Will thought. She and Tracy had been making dandelion wishes since they were kids.

She turned toward home, stopping in the middle of the bridge over Harmony River. She tried to catch her breath. She tried to be as calm as the water flowing beneath her.

It wasn't possible. Not even with a dandelion wish at the ready.

What would she wish for?

She could wish that Will would give up on his winery and go away. She could wish that Will would realize that her friendship with Tracy transcended accidents, mental challenges and artistic blocks. Or wish away the pull of Will's appeal on both an artistic and a physical level. Or wish to erase that near kiss. And the suspicion that Will had wanted to kiss her again as they'd argued on Main Street.

Emma huffed. All her wishes involved Will.

Because Will needed to go away.

She blew the dandelion fluff out over the water.

The seeds twirled and pirouetted in a cluster that dispersed in the air before drifting slowly down to the water. Harmony Valley might change, but dandelion wishes would not.

Emma's pulse calmed. Her frustration ebbed.

After the last fluff had disappeared down-river, Emma headed home. She let herself in the back door and poured a glass of lemonade, drinking it on the rear porch steps. In her self-appointed role as Harmony Valley's unofficial protector, she should shadow Will the rest of the afternoon. But that near kiss felt like a dodged bullet, and Emma wasn't ready to risk another showdown.

She stared at the landscape, wondering what Tracy was doing, wondering if she could go find her and try apologizing again. It was probably too soon. Her attention turned to her surroundings. The lawn sloped gently toward the bending river, framed on one side by the eucalyptus grove and wild blackberries, and on the other by Granny's vegetable garden. It was the perfect place to paint.

If she had the courage to paint.

Emma sagged against the porch railing. Moping solved nothing. A few minutes later, she'd wrestled the wooden easel downstairs to the lawn. A few minutes more and a canvas sat on the easel. Trying to paint was better than trying to avoid thinking about it.

At least in theory.

Left hand clutching her sketching pencil

over the canvas, Emma squinted at the landscape and fought the shakes, fought to quiet
the cacophony of the accident.

A cloud drifted across the sun, shading the
landscape, sucking the warmth out of the air.
Emma's arms prickled with goose bumps. Her
determination wavered.

Maybe she could control her fears if she
skipped a step—no sketching, just painting.
She squirted oil paint on her wooden painter's palette, her hands steady as set concrete.
She started with big gobs of blue, yellow, red
and white, then mixed colors with a brush
to get different shades of brown, green, blue
and gray. She didn't usually work with more
than one color at a time, but it had been so
long since she'd mixed any paint that creating
the shades brought a long-lost feeling of joy.
But it was a silent joy. There was no musical
soundtrack playing in her head. She'd take the
silence as long as her talent returned.

It wasn't until she carefully loaded the tip of
a brush with murky green that her hand succumbed to that familiar tremble. With stilted,
determined strokes, Emma tried to outline the
edge of the river. But it was as if she'd gone
back in time. The shrill complaint of braking
rubber on pavement. The warning rumble of

a big rig engine. She no longer saw the river. Images from the accident flashed before her. Heart stopping. Breath stealing.

Gasping, she stumbled back, blinked away the harrowing memories. All she'd succeeded in doing was to paint a green line that might have passed for a caterpillar if she was in kindergarten. Her shoulders slumped in defeat.

She dropped her palette and paintbrush onto the grass, and ran into the house, intending to go up to her room. But at the end of the hall was a picture she'd painted of Yosemite's Half Dome. The realization hit her that she'd never paint like that again.

Emma walked out the front door, collapsing on the porch swing, listening to red-winged blackbirds chatter to each other in the eucalyptus grove. The only birds she heard in the city were seagulls. And that was a backdrop to angry commuter car horns, chants from irate protesters and the constant chatter of people on cell phones.

Harmony Valley was special just the way it was. And yet, it wasn't perfect. Emma didn't want to acknowledge the truth in Will's arguments. But how could she not? There were too many elderly people living here to have emergency services so far away. What if Granny

Rose fell? What if Mr. B. had another heart attack?

And eventually, without any new businesses and no one younger than sixty, the town would die out. Emma didn't want that, either. But that didn't mean Harmony Valley had to be torn down and rebuilt with cookie-cutter subdivisions. If the oak tree in the town square came down and the landscape in the valley changed, its character would change.

Maybe Emma would be more open to the town being developed if other things in her life were certain. Granny Rose's mental health. Tracy's friendship and forgiveness. Her own ability to follow through on her passion.

Every fear is silly when you say it out loud.

Will's words. He'd meant that some fears weren't based in fact. But Emma had seen the world through an artist's perspective all her life. She'd been so lost behind an artist's lens that she'd crashed. She was lucky she hadn't killed Tracy. Who knew that being an artist was such a dangerous profession?

Her glance landed on the coloring book on the patio table. Emma picked it up and opened it to a fresh page, marked by a forest-green crayon.

Emma traced the heavy black lines with the nubby green crayon.

Lightning didn't strike, but her heart was pounding so fiercely she couldn't hear the birds anymore.

All Emma had was green. Her hand barely trembled as she started shading the drawings with long, even strokes. Her mind shifted into neutral as she patiently colored within the lines. When she was done her hands were steady, her heart calm.

Emma stared once more at Parish Hill and murmured, "Someday."

But when she returned her attention to the coloring book, it wasn't a landscape she sketched in the margin, but her grandmother's beloved face.

WHAT WAS WRONG with Emma?

From behind blackberry bushes near the river, Tracy had tried to psych herself into talking to Emma. She'd watched her start to paint and then throw down her paintbrush in disgust. Emma never gave up on a painting after a few short minutes. And when she'd stomped out to the front porch, Tracy couldn't squelch her curiosity. She'd stayed hidden in the eucalyptus grove as she rounded the house.

Emma wasn't getting any additional paint supplies. She was sitting in the porch swing, coloring.

Tracy worked her way back around to the blackberry bushes bordering the backyard, but the canvas was facing the house so she couldn't see what Emma had painted.

When Emma told Tracy that she should wait to move back to the city until she'd had more therapy, Tracy had wanted to run away. She'd wanted Emma to say she'd do whatever Tracy needed, whatever she wanted to make her happy, not treat her like an invalid.

Tracy would die of embarrassment if Emma caught her spying, but she had to find out what was on that canvas. Emma had mentioned some injury and Tracy was curious. Had she broken her fingers or wrist? Was her vision wonky?

Tracy darted out from the cover of the blackberry bushes. It took her ten seconds to get to the easel. Her breath came in labored gasps and her leg muscles shook as if they'd give out at any moment.

And there was Emma's latest masterpiece. A green worm.

No wonder Emma was upset. It looked like

a finger painting. Tracy had made better pictures than that in therapy.

She picked up the brush—it still had green on it—and painted antennae on the worm. And then wings. Lifting the palette, she dabbed white polka dots on the creature. She filled in the blue sky, plastered the bottom of the canvas with black. Finally there was no blank bit of canvas left.

Power surged through her veins. She'd done something without permission and now felt like she could take on the world. And all because she'd painted a picture on a canvas. Wait until Emma found out.

Tracy grinned, admiring her work once more. And then terror struck.

Oh, dear God. Emma was going to come out here and discover what she'd done. She could be watching her right now.

Tracy spun around, her nervous gaze darting to the windows and doors, but no one came out.

How would she explain this? Will would think she needed to see a psychiatrist, or at the least that she missed the rudimentary arts and crafts at Evergreen. He meant well, but he thought a mosquito bite meant she'd contract the West Nile virus.

What was she going to do? She didn't want anyone to know. Not Will or Emma. She didn't want to be sent back to the hospital.

She dropped the palette and brush on the grass, grabbed the canvas and ran.

CHAPTER ELEVEN

"WHAT'S UP, WILL?" Slade stepped out of his kitchen onto the back porch, looking like he'd been in earnest negotiations and had lost. Black hair bunched to one side as if fisted in frustration; tie knot loose, the ends flapping in the breeze. "You don't even like basketball."

In the middle of trying to make a layup into the rusted hoop bolted above Slade's detached garage, Will didn't bother answering. Emma was his problem, not Slade's.

The ball bounced off the rim and into the grass separating Slade's driveway from Old Man Takata's. When Slade hadn't answered the door, Will had needed something to wear down the sharp edge of frustration.

"I heard you knock," Slade continued. "But I was on the landline with my divorce lawyer. This lack of cell service is starting to get old. I may have to purchase my own communications tower and put it in the backyard."

Will picked up the ball and gestured toward

the house. "I was beginning to think you had a woman in there."

Slade came down the steps and held out his hands, asking for the ball. "A woman? No woman is coming inside this house ever again. Do you know what the bridge club calls this place?"

"No." Will passed the basketball to him.

"The Death and Divorce house. No family has lived here untouched. The idea of a woman in there makes me cringe." Slade dribbled twice on the cracking pavement and then put up a beautiful, arcing shot that went through the orange metal hoop without touching it. And Slade did it in khakis, dress shirt and a tie, with a grin that dismissed his earlier annoyance with his ex-wife's legal maneuvering. "Correction. The idea of *anyone* in that house makes me cringe."

Will rebounded the shot, refusing to be envious of Slade's skill. "If it bothers you that much, you can sleep on the top bunk at my house. My dad wants to keep the bunk bed for his grandchildren." Not that he had any grandchildren on the horizon.

"I'll survive."

And that was the problem with Slade. He was all about survival. It would have creeped

Will out to sleep down the hall from the room where his father committed suicide. Not that he would have chosen the bunk bed, either. A man had to have some pride. Will dribbled toward the basket, intending to try for another layup.

Slade intercepted him, blocking his path, forcing Will to transition to a pull-up jump shot that Slade easily swatted away.

"Denied!" Slade ran down the ball. "If you would've spent more time when you lived here shooting hoops than on your computer—"

"We wouldn't be rich."

"I hate it when you're right." Slade put up another fifteen footer, which would have swished if the hoop had a net.

Will bit back a curse. He'd always been the last kid picked on a team—he loved sports, but he sucked at them. He let the ball bounce to the grass on the side of the driveway. "Come on. We need to meet up with Flynn at El Rosal. Wouldn't want to miss drinks with Mayor Larry."

When they reached the town square, Flynn paced beneath the oak tree, settling and resetting his Giants cap on his head.

"I don't know how your visits went, but I was accused of being a little upstart, a disgrace to Harmony Valley and an unprincipled child." Flynn ticked off his negative attributes on his fingers. "I feel like I should be twisting my villainous mustache."

Slade patted Flynn on the back. "I'm no better than Donald Trump."

"I don't respect the free will of others and I can't see the heart in this town," Will added. "People think I'm a control freak."

"Sorry, dude." Slade couldn't quite contain a grin. "That last one I can't argue with."

"Me, either." Flynn's grin didn't sting like Emma's had. "But let me tell you. When I'm old, I'm coming up with more colorful putdowns." He opened the door to El Rosal. "Oh, I nearly forgot. Grandpa Ed talked a television reporter into coming by this week to interview you." Flynn pointed at Will.

"Me? Why not you or Slade?"

"He said you're the most photogenic. Pretty boy." Flynn grinned.

They entered El Rosal. The small Mexican restaurant was the only sit-down option in town, the only takeout option in town and the only bar in town. The chairs and tables were painted bright primary colors. Mexican pop poured out of the speakers, while baseball played on a television screen over the bar.

About fifteen residents had come in for dinner, a drink or company.

Larry sat at the corner of the bar, where he could see and talk to anyone in the restaurant—the tie-dye king lording over his subjects. In his sixties, Larry was among the younger residents of Harmony Valley, tall with a lanky body kept toned by his vegetarianism and love of yoga. But the lack of body fat gave away every emotion in his bony face.

Flynn paused on the threshold. "Ten bucks says Mayor Larry started a tab for us."

Slade ran a hand through his hair. "You're beginning to sound like me."

"I'll take that bet," Will said.

Mayor Larry was well-off, having married into wealth the second time around. He could afford to pay for a round of drinks.

Larry caught sight of them and waved. "Well, hullo, boys! Juan, get these boys a beer." The mayor slapped Flynn on the back when he took the stool next to him. "I started a tab for you. Hope you don't mind."

Flynn held out his hand toward Will.

Who dug in his wallet for a ten.

Will's dad sat at a table in the corner alone. His faded blue-flannel shirt made his thin blond hair look nearly gray. "Can I talk to you for a minute?" he called to Will.

"Can it wait? We have a meeting."

"It can't wait. Sit." Ben pulled out the royal blue chair next to him. He was nursing a bottle of beer and working his way through a basket of tortilla chips. "I saw you with Emma today. It looked like you were arguing."

It could have been worse. He could have been caught kissing Emma. If that were the case, he imagined his father would be prepping an entirely different conversation.

"For Tracy's sake, you've got to work things out with Emma." His dad tapped the table with a forefinger. "Accidents happen, usually because of a combination of coincidence and bad luck, topped with a dose of poor judgment. The important thing to remember is that the crash was an accident. If you don't move on from it, it can control your life."

"Do you know how hard it is to stay strong for Tracy? Blaming Emma…" Will looked away, toward the ball game. "Blaming Emma gives me strength." What would happen to that strength if he forgave Emma? If he kissed her? If he—

"Your sister is home now. She's doing well. Let this thing with Emma go."

How could he forgive Emma? "Did you forgive Harmony Valley Grain after Mom's death? Would you have been able to sell them your corn if they hadn't closed down?"

"Thankfully, I didn't have to make that decision," Ben said, staring out the window toward the old grain silo. "Forgiveness takes more energy than anger ever could. Someday the anger's going to go away and you'll be left with nothing. And then you'll be wondering where the time went. I hope you realize that before it's too late." And then he stood up and left.

Will sat very still. The clank of dishes, the jumbled chorus of voices, the roar of the televised crowd at the baseball game after a hit all closed in around him, shrouding him in an uneasy bitterness he didn't want to let go of.

Will felt small and petty, like a boy holding on to a grudge for a school-yard slight. Causing his sister injuries that could last a lifetime wasn't inconsequential. Emma was to blame. She'd admitted it.

Why did he have to forgive her?

How could he ever forgive her?

EMMA WAS STILL doodling in the coloring book when Agnes's faded green Buick pulled into the drive.

The three councilwomen got out of the car with the slow deliberation of the elderly. Emma could remember a time when they had practically danced out of the vehicle and up the stairs, ribbing each other good-naturedly and singing snatches of show tunes.

"How was the botanical garden?" Emma hurried down to help Mildred.

Granny Rose popped her head up from the backseat. "We saw the most beautiful *Rhododendron occidentale*. It was pink with darker pink striations that you would have loved. So delicate. So vibrant. I wish you'd stretch yourself and paint flowers."

At this point, Emma would be happy to complete a paint-by-number project.

"Took us forever to see everything. What's that old saying?" Mildred's usual round, warm smile was noticeably absent. She looked worn-out as she hefted her briefcase-size purse onto her shoulder. "You're only as fast as your slowest team member? I'm always holding up the show."

"You're not." Agnes, who stood five feet tall on a good day, wrestled Mildred's candy-apple-red walker out of the trunk, snapped it out and wheeled it over to her friend.

"We brought home a bucket of chicken,

mashed potatoes and biscuits. None of us felt like cooking." Granny Rose walked by, arms full of food containers. "I had the most marvelous nap in the car. I never nap, but I do feel gloriously refreshed." She paused at the front door, taking in the porch swing and the coloring book on the cushion. She turned to Emma with a look that questioned.

Emma shrugged, too self-conscious and unsure of what her crayon doodles of her grandmother's face meant to say anything.

Granny Rose grinned and went inside.

"I miss driving," Mildred said. "Sometimes I feel like I should ride in the trunk with my walker."

"You're not baggage," Agnes scolded, and then for Emma's benefit added, "She's been feeling sorry for herself since her daughter and grandkids moved down to Healdsburg. She can't drive anymore and they can't come see her every weekend."

"I can too drive." Mildred lumbered over to the steps. She set the walker aside and gripped the handrail.

"You can't see the road. For the safety of others, you've chosen not to drive." Agnes gestured for Emma to carry the walker up while she climbed behind Mildred, her hand at her back to steady her if needed.

"Well, I can choose to drive again, can't I? I still have my license."

"It expires in three months. That's one less thing you need to tote around in that luggage-size purse of yours. You've got everything but the kitchen sink in there."

"I like to be prepared," Mildred grumbled.

"Oh, you are. I went searching in her bag for breath mints today," Agnes told Emma. "Do you know what I found?"

Emma shook her head.

Mildred stopped climbing. "Not this again."

"A wrench!" Agnes crowed.

Mildred's round cheeks brightened with color. "You never know when you'll need to tighten a loose bolt."

"That's for sure." Agnes winked at Emma.

Once they'd helped Mildred up the steps, she wheeled herself into the dining room with all the agility of the race-car driver she'd once been.

Emma went to the kitchen to help Granny Rose, sparing a moment between gathering napkins and utensils to look out the back window. She stopped digging in the silverware drawer for forks. "Granny, did you bring in the canvas I was working on?" She'd die of embarrassment if she had.

"No, dear. I thought it was odd that you'd left your easel and paints out there. But sometimes you get distracted and scatter your things around."

"I'm not thirteen. And a twenty-by-twenty-four-inch canvas is missing. It's too heavy to have been blown away in the wind."

"You can look for it after dinner. Come sit down."

"Yes, let's eat." Mildred had taken a seat at the table. "I've got bingo tonight with Will. He's been driving me ever since he came back to town. Poor boy has no luck."

"Really?" Canvas forgotten, Emma set the table with knives, forks and napkins. "Do you think he'll bring Tracy?"

"I don't know," Mildred said. "Do you want me to call and ask?"

"No, thanks." Emma tried to keep the excitement out of her voice. "I'll call later."

Granny Rose met Emma's questioning glance with a nod of agreement. It looked like they were going to play bingo tonight.

After they'd all dished out plates and started to eat, Emma asked, "When was Harmony Valley's economy based on marijuana?"

The grandfather clock ticked several long seconds in the silence.

The elderly trio passed around indecipherable glances that had Emma's heart sinking. They put their chicken back on their plates and meticulously wiped their fingers.

"Emma," Agnes began, ever the group's spokesperson. "It's not what you think."

"How do you know what I think?"

"Because we can see the condemnation in your eyes," Granny Rose said gently.

"I'll reserve judgment if you tell me the truth." Uncertainty fluttered restlessly in her stomach. How would Emma know if they told her the truth? She only knew what she wanted to hear—that Will was wrong.

"It happened in 1970," Mildred said softly. "Long before you were born."

"We were protesting the war." Agnes took up the story. "People of all ages came from various states to join the student protests in San Francisco. When it was over, a lot of people didn't have the means to return home."

"And a couple were on the lam," Mildred cut in.

Rose and Agnes shushed her.

Agnes cleared her throat. "Civil disobedience is a trivial charge. Anyway, we brought some people home with us. After all, Harmony Valley has always been a place that gives shelter to the world-weary. And our weary camped out on Parish Hill."

The fluttering in Emma's stomach eased. Their story sounded plausible. "Larry was with them?" Mayor Larry was the town's most ardent love child.

"Yes. The town loved Larry and his friends. They brought a young, refreshing culture." Granny Rose's face glowed with pride, as if she was responsible for expanding the valley's cultural base. "Larry and Delilah knit sweaters and tie-dyed T-shirts. Others sang and played music in the town square."

"They baked the most delicious brownies," Mildred added sweetly.

Agnes and Rose exchanged glances.

If Emma hadn't been horrified, she might have laughed.

"How were we to know a few of them were growing marijuana up there?" Granny Rose poked her mashed potatoes with her fork. "They didn't cause any trouble. I don't think anyone here would have found out about their side business except someone—who is no longer a resident here—tried to sell several pounds of their crop to an undercover police-man in Santa Rosa."

"But what about Larry? How did he get elected if he broke the law?"

Agnes spun her wineglass slowly on the table. "Larry denied any involvement and we believed him. After all, he and Delilah were busy making a lot of sweaters."

"But—"

"Emma, it was the seventies," Granny Rose argued gently. "And you know what Larry's like. He's so interested in inner peace he can't remember to water his lawn. How could he grow anything?"

Will had implied something entirely different than the story her grandmother and friends recounted. Emma sighed, grateful he'd had it wrong. "So you three weren't growing mari-juana? Or smoking doobies?"

Indignant protests erupted like the fits and starts of Yellowstone's Old Faithful.

When the trio was done claiming they'd never so much as inhaled, Emma sank back into her chair. "And it was only that one year?"

They all fervently assured her that it had been.

"Who told you this? It's not a part of our history we're proud of." Granny Rose leaned forward, a frown wrinkling her delicate brow. "I don't need to ask. It was Will, wasn't it?"

Mildred and Agnes exchanged glances that indicated this wasn't the first time today Rose had spoken Will's name in the same way she'd curse invading gophers in her vegetable garden.

"Is that who you want to put your faith in?" Granny Rose demanded of her friends. "A man who's willing to besmirch our town's good name? A man who would imply to my granddaughter that we grew cannabis?"

"But what about the good things Will and his friends want to do?" Mildred put forth timidly. "They want to reopen the medical clinic and the volunteer fire station."

"That man has filled everyone's head with nonsense." Granny picked up a chicken leg and shook it at them collectively. "Do you know how many small towns in America thrive even though they're located more than twenty minutes from the nearest emergency services?"

Emma took in the two other women's blank faces and answered for them all. "No."

"Me, either. But it's a lot, trust me. I'm sure there are towns in a similar situation as Harmony Valley." Rose moved the chicken leg closer as if readying to take a bite, and then lowered it again. "It's a choice we make. If you choose a home off the beaten path, you won't have all the services you would in the city."

Agnes frowned, her petite features moving uncharacteristically downward. "We're getting to an age, Rose, where we need those services."

Granny Rose shook her head. "We're getting to an age, Agnes, when we'll die. I'd rather turn up my toes here at home. But if you prefer, follow your daughter to the city."

"If this winery initiative doesn't pass, I will," Agnes retorted.

Emma wanted to side with her grandmother, but for the good of the residents she held dear, it was increasingly clear that elements of Will's proposal made sense.

Which was a shame, since nothing else she felt about him did.

CHAPTER TWELVE

"I FEEL LUCKY," Mildred said to Will and Tracy as she wheeled her walker into the church's multipurpose room in Cloverdale. Mildred scoped out a table and settled her short, plump frame into a folding chair, releasing her walker to one side. "Let's boogie."

"Let's boogie," Tracy repeated. Then she laughed.

The smile on Will's face probably looked goofy. He didn't care. He couldn't believe the change in Tracy after only two days in Harmony Valley. She'd chattered with Mildred the entire ride. Her smile hadn't faded since she'd climbed into his truck. Not once. She had to stay and work at the winery.

Sure, she wasn't stringing together complex sentences, but her speech was smoother and she was laughing more. It was a gift. One Will wasn't going to question after the day he'd had. The frustrations of getting the winery off the ground, Emma's meddling, his father's unsolicited advice—none of it mattered if Tracy's condition improved. He needed to broach the topic of working for him again before Emma spoke to her.

Tracy helped Mildred scoot her chair closer to the table. "Next time. I'll drive. To bingo."

Will's smile dimmed, but only a little. "When the doctor clears you."

His comment earned him a scowl from Tracy.

"I used to drive here," Mildred said. "I could bring us next week. I have my license."

Will gave Mildred's thick glasses a double take. "I thought you weren't supposed to drive." Emma had a better chance of obtaining his permission to transport Tracy to bingo than Mildred did. And Emma's chance currently stood at zero.

"Agnes told you that, didn't she? She thinks I can't see the road. My vision is fine. Let me tell you, I used to time myself driving the loop on Parish Hill. I know that road like the back of my hand. My best time was under five minutes."

"A record that will have to stand." He drew Tracy aside. "I want to ask you something."

She beamed expectantly at him, the way she

used to when they were kids, as if he was her hero and could do no wrong.

And he knew. He knew as soon as the words *I want you to stay here and work for the winery* left his mouth, that smile of hers would disappear. He could hear Emma telling him, "I told you so." And she was right. Tracy didn't want to stay in Harmony Valley and if he tried to force her to... Well, the words Tracy would use to describe him wouldn't be pretty.

"What?"

He couldn't ask her. At least not yet. He'd suggest a job to her when the winery was approved. By then she may have realized that she was blossoming in Harmony Valley. "I'm a tyrannical idiot."

She laughed. "Yes. You are." She claimed a folding chair next to Mildred and fanned her cheeks with a bingo card.

Will stood like a dolt, unable to take his eyes off his happy sister. He didn't think he could stand not knowing what the future held for her.

"Luck needs a boost. First, you've got to blow off all the bad juju, like this." Mildred demonstrated by blowing across the face of one of her cards as if it was a birthday cake loaded with candles. "Then you place it front and center on the table."

For Mildred, bingo was all about the ritual. In the six weeks he'd been taking her to bingo, she wore the same lucky shirt—a faded black Justin Bieber T-shirt one of her granddaughters had given her with the wise Canadian philosopher's advice: *Never Say Never.* She always made Will take the back road into town so she could hold her breath as they drove over the old Russian River bridge. She'd buy an evening's worth of cards with two tens—never a twenty. And she always sat in the middle of a table on the right-hand side of the room.

With another laugh that lifted Will's spirits, Tracy did as Mildred instructed. "Now what?"

"Now we use all our lucky charms." Mildred waved over one of the hostesses and gave her a white plastic travel mug with her husband's picture on it, requesting a coffee. Then she withdrew a plastic container from her backpack-size purse. From it she took out her good luck charms—a hot pink rabbit's foot, a three-inch-high wooden tiki, a black polished marble-size stone and a five-dollar poker chip from the old Sands hotel in Las Vegas.

"I need. Lucky charms." Tracy grinned.

"You collect them as you age, dear, like

sunspots and ex-husbands." Mildred picked up the pink rabbit's foot. "Until then, you can borrow this."

Grinning again, Will took a seat on the other side of Mildred, leaving a chair open between them. That seat was usually occupied by a retired school bus driver named Earl, who had a thing for peanut-butter cookies and Mildred, although his COPD sometimes kept him at home. He checked his cell phone for text and email messages.

The noise in the church hall became more raucous as seats filled up at the folding tables. But one voice rose above the others. A voice belonging to someone with dark hair, an Indian-print blue skirt and the ability to increase his blood pressure.

"Tracy, can I sit next to you?" Emma's smile was bright and hopeful.

Will stood, prepared to escort Emma out the door, or at least to another table. All his sister had to do was say the word.

Tracy glanced up at Emma. Will couldn't see his sister's face, but he could see Emma's clearly, watched as her smile lost its grip.

"No, no." Tracy's tone was firm with just a hint of standoffishness. Then she patted the chair next to her at the end of the table. "Rose."

"Of course I'll sit with you, Tracy." Rose appeared behind Emma in a dark skirt and muff-like braids over each ear. "And Emma will sit on the other side of Mildred." Rose paused, a hand on the back of her chair. She took one look at Will before advising Emma, "Scoot as far away from the computer nerd as you can and tell me if he tries anything."

Emma's cheeks bloomed a soft rose that matched the color of her lips.

Add lechery to the list of sins Rose had assigned him.

"Granny, please stop." Emma reached for the chair on the other side of Mildred.

At the last moment, Will remembered he didn't want Emma at their table and gripped a section of the chair back. His fingers brushed against Emma's cold ones. He quelled the impulse to shift his hand over hers, to warm her fingers beneath his own.

Emma snatched her hand away, cradling it against her stomach as if his touch burned.

"I'm saving this seat for Mildred's friend Earl." His voice sounded too gruff, too intimate. The tone of a lover.

Unwisely, Will waited for their eyes to

meet, waited to see again the longing in her gaze and know it was him she wanted. Him.

Emma didn't look at Will. Instead, she glanced around, a slightly desperate tremble to her lips, as if her vague smile was her last and only defense against the tension between them.

Most people had already taken their seats, but there were one or two chairs available at the tables in the back. It was better for Will's sanity if Emma sat as far away from him as possible.

"It's okay." Mildred glanced up at Will. "I don't think Earl is coming tonight. He would have arrived on the senior-center bus, and those people came in five minutes ago."

Emma's gaze caught on Will's hand, still on her chair, before she accepted Mildred's invitation. "Thanks. I'll move if Earl shows up." She took the metal chair and pulled it out until Will's hand dropped away.

Will sat at the end of the table next to Emma. Why couldn't he just ignore her and let the attraction he felt for her fade?

Because Emma wasn't easy to ignore. She was bright and colorful and wounded, hurt by the loss of Tracy's friendship and burdened with panic attacks, the source of which he had yet to uncover. A result of the car accident?

And yet, as much as he knew Emma was hurting, and that he was the cause of some of that pain, he couldn't let his guard down. He could feel compassion, but he couldn't let himself forgive. The fear of losing Tracy—and the memory of his grief when his mother died—was too debilitating.

"It's nice of Tracy to sit and visit with Rose tonight. I'll have plenty of time to visit with Tracy later." Emma spoke hopefully, somehow managing to put a semiconfident smile on her face despite the death-grip clasp of her hands in her lap.

Will leaned back so he could see Tracy. She was demonstrating Mildred's lucky card-blowing technique to Rose.

"So much. Luck," she said. "Big winners. All of us."

"Even Emma?" Rose asked with wide, innocent eyes.

A few days ago, Will would have applauded when Tracy didn't answer.

Tonight, he was aware of how much Tracy's silence hurt Emma.

Everyone wanted him to give Emma a second chance. The more he listened to her side, the more he put himself in her strappy shoes, the more he realized there were two sides to every story, two sides to every hurt, two sides to forgiveness.

Maybe his father was right. Maybe Will was only making the situation between the two friends worse. Maybe he should try harder to forgive.

For Tracy.

"FIRST GAME OF the night, ladies and gentlemen. Let's get things rolling." The emcee of the event was a soft-spoken minister who morphed into a corny cross between a comedian and a game-show host when he picked up a microphone. "*B* twelve. *B* twelve. That's *B* as in *butterfly,* twelve. Butterflies may look harmless, but they have been known to swarm like bees, which would send any pacemaker into overdrive."

Emma didn't have *B* twelve. She felt like she didn't have a lot of things—hope for a damaged friendship, confidence in her talent, common sense enough to know that pursuing these unexpected feelings toward Will would be disastrous. She arranged her bingo chips in neat little stacks.

Will put his arm across the back of her chair

and leaned in close. He did that a lot, as if he wanted to close the distance between them so only she heard what he said. He probably had no idea of the effect he had on her—how the woodsy hint of his aftershave drew her closer, how the varying intensity of his eyes, from electric to soft baby blue, enthralled her. "Are you okay? I'd offer to drive Rose home so you could leave, but I doubt she'd accept a ride from me."

"I'm here to play bingo." Emma tried to feel happy just being in the same room as Tracy, but with Will in her space it was hard to think of anything but him.

"Do you hear Tracy talking? Her speech has been better this evening than it's been in weeks." His fingers touched the thin cotton over her shoulder blade.

Emma held herself very still. "Maybe my visit this morning helped her."

Will surprised her by not arguing the point. "Tracy's passed another milestone. We should all be celebrating." He sounded upbeat, but his words had the opposite effect on Emma. Despite wishing Tracy well, she wanted to share those milestones with her friend.

"She looks wonderful," Emma said. "And so happy." Maybe Will was right. Maybe Tracy was better off without her. "You haven't talked to her about working for you, have you?"

He removed his arm from the back of her chair.

"*G* fifty-eight. *G* fifty-eight. That's *G* as in George, fifty-eight. We've got three Georges here tonight and one has a birthday." The minister led the room in song.

When the singing ended, Emma turned, scooting her bottom to the farthest edge of her seat, giving her breathing room. "Well?"

His eyes were a flat, cold blue as he shrugged. "I've floated the idea past her. She rejected it, but she could get used to it. No sense forcing the issue until we get our property rezoned."

"I've been thinking about you—" *Don't say that!* She rushed on. "Your winery and Harmony Valley. You're right. The town needs emergency services."

The stare he gave her was probing, assessing, skeptical.

She tamped down her annoyance. "I might be able to make things easier for you. With Granny Rose."

His expression didn't change.

"And in return, you could...perhaps..."

Emma plunged on "…not make a fuss when I ask Tracy to go shopping with me."

"Only if I drive." Will blinked, as if surprised at his own answer.

Hope burst inside Emma, expanding her chest with the air she hadn't realized she'd been denying herself. "Really? You don't mind?"

"I don't mind if you ask because she's going to say no," he grumbled.

"Thank you!" Before Emma realized what she was doing, she leaned in and kissed Will's cheek. It was warm and lightly stubbled. She fell back in her chair, heat spreading in places it had no right to.

He rubbed his cheek. "Emma…" The way he said her name—slowly and with wonder—caused a flutter in her stomach.

A flutter that died when he turned away from her without another word.

"*G* fifty-three. *G* fifty-three. That's *G* rhymes with *C* for *cat,* fifty-three. Did you know that cats have a sixty-note vocal range? But they probably still couldn't sing 'Happy Birthday' in tune."

The patter of polite laughter filled the room, but Emma barely heard.

There were fools, and there were people who did foolish things.

At that moment, she couldn't decide which she was.

CHAPTER THIRTEEN

EMMA DROVE BACK to Cloverdale the next afternoon to use the wireless connection at Starbucks. She'd finished a print ad for one client and needed to upload it to their password-protected website for review.

While she enjoyed a skinny latte and checked her email, she accepted two more print-ad assignments from the advertising agency Tracy used to work for. She'd wanted to take out her sketchbook and pencil while she enjoyed her coffee, but her fingers got clammy at the thought.

Miracle of miracles, her mother had sent her an email and left her a voice mail. Both mentioned her murder case wasn't due to be handed over to jury for deliberations until early next week. As soon as a verdict came in, she'd come down from Sacramento for a visit. Yes, Emma should call the doctor. No, she didn't want the character of Harmony Valley to change, either. Love, etc., Mom.

Will had invited Emma to the Harmony Valley Lions Club meeting later that afternoon. She'd promised to try to broach the topic of the winery with her grandmother if he promised to respect the character of Harmony Valley, something Will admitted he and his partners were already trying to do. Unfortunately, Emma hadn't found the right moment to discuss the winery with Granny Rose.

"What did I miss?" Emma asked her grandmother when she slid into the church pew just after four o'clock, craning her neck to see if Tracy was there.

She wasn't.

"You missed nothing. Will is saying the same old, same old," Granny Rose whispered, sparing a breath to blow a lock of white hair off her forehead.

"They didn't mention anything about scaling back their designs or respecting the character of the town?" She'd expected that much, at least.

"They said they've decided to restore the existing buildings, but I don't believe them. Look at that. It's that hoochy hot spot again. Looks like the perfect place for someone like Will to be an exhibitionist. He hasn't made a play for you, has he?"

Given the small size of the church and the urgency of her grandmother's question, everyone heard her, including Will. He was up on the altar, as he'd been the night of the council meeting, looking handsome in khakis and a burgundy polo. He stopped talking and pinned Emma with a dark look that demanded she rein in her grandmother.

Dark, demanding looks from Will were something Emma absolutely did not need.

She'd spent a fair amount of time lecturing herself on the perils of infatuation. As lectures went, she'd thought the message had sunk into her brain.

Obviously not. She could almost smell Will's aftershave from four rows back.

Cheeks heating, Emma waited for the meeting to resume before whispering, "Did the doctor call?"

"Your doctor didn't call," Granny Rose whispered back, her gaze locked on Will. "I don't know who your doctor is."

Emma swallowed her exasperation. "Did *your* doctor call?"

"Yes. How did you know?" Granny Rose spared Emma a quick glance.

Sam, who was sitting in front of them, frowned over his shoulder.

"They called the other day," Emma lied, wishing her grandmother could read lips. "While you were working on *The Music Man*. What did they want?"

"They wanted me to come in for a checkup, but I'm much too busy."

Emma blew out a frustrated breath.

Granny Rose tilted her face toward Emma, still keeping Will in her sights. "You should call your doctor if you're not feeling well. At my age, I expect I'll feel good until the moment I keel over. But that's just the way I am. At your age, even the most minor problem could turn into something that could kill you. Like the Big C. Cancer isn't something you postpone. If it's cancer you're worried about, head right home and call your doctor."

"I feel fine. I don't have cancer." Knock on wood.

"I'm just saying. I've seen enough people in this town ignore those little warning signs and then *bam*—" Granny Rose snapped her fingers "—you check into the Eternal Rest Motel. Why, just this spring, Nadine Tarkley dropped dead of heart failure hefting a bag of kitty litter out of the back of her Caddy." She paused, looking at Will skeptically. "I wonder if that computer nerd lifts a lot of kitty litter."

That strange feeling—the one that Emma had when she'd first come back to town and found Granny Rose in her long johns—did the jitterbug in Emma's gut. "We should go." Before Granny worked herself into one of her off-kilter fits. Before Will accused her of not holding up her end of the bargain they'd made last night about her trying to make Granny see the value in change.

Emma gripped Granny Rose's arm and scooted down the pew, trying to bring her grandmother with her.

Granny brushed off Emma's grip. "Not yet. They're coming to the finale. I didn't get to see it Monday night, since we had to leave the council meeting early."

Emma checked the projected image on the wall. It was the same one they'd walked out on Monday night. The oak tree was gone, replaced by the modern-looking hot spot. The square footage of the town square's lawn had been reduced to the size of a large bedroom to make room for more parking.

And next to the rendering stood Will. "Although our partnership is only proposing a few businesses, we hope that their success sometime next year will attract other entrepreneurs to the area. We see opportunities for a sandwich shop, a bakery, an ice cream—"

"Or gelato parlor," Flynn interrupted from the front pew.

Slade elbowed him.

Will continued as if they hadn't spoken. "An office supply store where you can make copies and ship items, a beauty salon, an auto-mechanic shop. The opportunities are endless."

"I used to own a bridal shop," Mae Gardner piped up. She was tall with unnaturally red hair, a love of heavy makeup and gossip. "Someone could open a bridal shop."

"Bridal shops require a pool of local brides, Mae," Sam pointed out.

"Well, then, someone should open a beauty shop. We haven't had one since Nadine died," Mae said, looking inconvenienced.

"Ladies come to my barbershop for hair-cuts." Phil Lambridge turned in his chair to look at Mae.

"Not this lady," Mae huffed.

And who could blame her? Phil's hands shook as they rested on the pew railing. It was a wonder anyone trusted him with sharp scissors near their ears.

Bald Mario Rodriguez piped up from the second row. "I'd like to see a coffee shop. It would be great to have a cup of coffee away from the missus."

Laughter sprinkled through the room like a light and welcome rain shower. This was the Harmony Valley Emma loved, full of character and spunk.

Will ignored the outbursts and aimed his control fob at the screen.

Her grandmother angled forward.

Emma held her breath. Waiting to see what Granny Rose did next was like sitting in the front car of a roller coaster at the top of the first big hill, anticipating a stomach-dropping ride.

"All good suggestions." Will pressed a button. "In closing, we'd like to thank our supporters, including Agnes Villanova, Mildred Parsons and Edwin Blonkowski."

Granny Rose stood. "What assurance do we have that you won't sell us downriver? How do we know you aren't going to take our approvals and government bottling permits and sell for a profit to some big corporation?" Her grandmother spoke in a businesslike voice, the one that had won her the town's respect and a seat on the town council. She directed her words to the crowd. "If a corporation buys them out, they'll bulldoze our houses, our histories, our memories, precisely as they did in Napa and Healdsburg and a dozen other small towns. Do you remember how they bulldozed a hillside in Healdsburg, changing the entire landscape? Have you driven by the cavernous warehouses?" Granny Rose pointed at the twelve Lions in the audience. "That big corporation they sell to will knock on your door and buy you out. They'll buy out everyone until there's nothing left of Harmony Valley. Nothing."

Her proverbial roller coaster had dropped over the edge and everyone in the church seemed to be recovering from the ride. Emma hoped it was over.

Will exchanged a quick, frustrated glance with Emma. "That's not our plan."

"How about a contract?" Sam asked, a snarky challenge in his tone.

Slade shook his head ever so slightly at Will.

"That's what I thought." Granny Rose turned to Emma, as calm as if they'd finished watching an enjoyable musical. "Now I'm ready to go."

Emma was happy to oblige.

"We're committed to Harmony Valley," Will called after them.

Her grandmother ignored him.

Out on the sidewalk, Emma was beside herself. "Can they really do that?" Was this why Will had looked at her funny last night at bingo when she'd offered a truce?

"Yes. I called a friend of mine that used to live in Napa. She told me exactly what happened. Oh, she told me, all right." Granny pounded one delicate fist into her palm. "Some global winery will swoop down on us like Sherman did with Atlanta. Do you know how valuable Sonoma County wines have become? We may be in the middle of nowhere, but half our acreage is vineyards. And another big chunk is idle, ripe for the planting."

"Wow."

"Wow is right. I can't stand by and watch this happen, Emma. You know that, don't you?" Granny Rose stopped to look at the town square and the oak tree where her husband had proposed. "Hot spot, my fanny. The oak tree stays."

"We need to calm down and think about this rationally." The last thing Emma wanted was Granny stressed out and sinking into an episode like she'd experienced at the council meeting Monday night. Her grandmother was already half wound up.

"Rose!" Will's long strides ate up the distance between them.

"Here comes Beelzebub," said Granny Rose, a tempestuous set to her features.

"Calm down," Emma whispered as she caught Will's eye. "And listen to what he has to say."

Her grandmother harrumphed.

"Rose, why do you think we'd go to all the trouble, not to mention the expense, of seeking winery approvals only to sell them off?"

"It would be different if you were going to settle here, young man, but your heart lies out there." Granny Rose gestured to the one road out of town. "A business here could only be a burden to you. And your partner with the tie looks like he'd jump at the chance for a deal."

"We plan to leave a representative here," Will said. "Someone who'll watch out for our interests, as well as the town's."

"An employee is not a guarantee that you're setting down roots." Granny put one hand on her slim hip.

"We're also taking your suggestions into account—reducing the size of our facility, preserving the oak tree. We're exploring the possibility of using the existing farm buildings."

"Words. I don't trust words." Granny Rose slid a glance toward the oak tree. "I'm going to make everyone see the danger of putting our future in your hands."

Will gave Emma a look that said "help me out here."

"I'm sure Will can come up with some kind of guarantee." Like the fact that he wanted his sister to run the place. She gave him a look that said "come clean."

Will remained suspiciously mute.

Her grandmother fairly vibrated with unexploded tension. It was time to get her home.

"When you figure it out, Will, you can let us know." Emma took her grandmother firmly by the arm and headed for home. "After dinner, I'm dropping you off with Agnes to watch baseball. Mayor Larry invited me to bowl. I want you to promise you won't make trouble while I'm gone."

"Emma—"

"Promise me. No trouble while I'm gone."

"I promise." Granny Rose's angelic expression was almost too good to be believed.

"I KNOW WE challenged you to a game during league." Mayor Larry parked his bag on the floor, dug inside and tried to shake the wrinkles out of his purple-and-green tie-dyed bowling shirt. "But Takata had a colonoscopy this morning and couldn't drag his butt out of bed. We had to scramble for a replacement player this morning." Larry buttoned his bowling shirt over a black Grateful Dead T-shirt.

"Some people need to seriously examine their priorities." Sam collapsed in the scorer's chair, winded after his walk from the parking lot.

"We welcome the challenge." Will deposited Sam's bowling bag at his feet. After this afternoon's blowup with Rose, he was nostalgic for their cramped apartment and near-empty bank account. At least then he'd been the master of his own destiny. Maybe if he had an idea for an app, he'd be more resilient to these winery setbacks.

Felix was changing his shoes in a lane seat next to Larry. The big man's bowling shirt was sprinkled with cat hair. "I won't be needing to see your architectural plans, Will, since I'm not going to support any sellout."

Will was still reeling from Rose's accusation that they were only applying for permits to sell out the entire town. More unsettling was Slade's claim that he'd support a lucrative offer. He couldn't reassure people they wouldn't sell if both his partners didn't agree.

Flynn claimed a chair on the opposite side of the double bowling lane, raising his voice to be heard over balls crashing into pins. "We aren't going to all this trouble just to sell out."

Felix grumbled something Will couldn't hear. How were they supposed to save Harmony Valley when no one trusted them?

Tracy's carefree laughter carried from the shoe counter. She and Slade were paying for four pairs of shoes. Miraculously, Tracy had been in a good mood for days. Granted, she locked herself in her room most of the time, but when she came out, she was smiling. Her happiness was the only thing keeping Will from giving up on the winery.

"Hey, guys."

The sound of Emma's voice was like a hard reboot to Will's heart—a quick, unexpected *stop,* followed by a not-so-gentle *go.*

Emma blessed Will with that challenging grin. The one that said "make me stop smiling." "I'm here to bowl."

"With whom?" Will asked, at the same moment Larry said, "Right on time, teammate."

"I don't think this is a good idea," Will said

to Emma, gesturing toward Tracy, who was shopping the ball aisle.

"It doesn't bother me." Emma waved at Tracy, who quickly looked away. Emma's smile wavered. "It doesn't bother me," she repeated, but softly and almost to herself. "Would you rather I ask her to go shopping?"

"No."

"We start in five minutes and Emma still doesn't have shoes," Sam pointed out, pausing after having entered *E* on the fourth line of the electronic scoreboard posted above them.

"I'm on it." Emma picked up her purse and left.

Slade took a practice ball. Although he'd rolled up his sleeves, his gray shirt looked freshly pressed, even though it was the end of the day.

From the row of seats on the other side of the score table, Flynn checked something on his cell phone. They were all phone addicts any time they reentered civilization.

"What's. She doing. Here?" Tracy held a green ball against her stomach.

Will's gaze strayed to Emma at the shoe counter. "Larry invited her to bowl."

"No one. Told me," Tracy said petulantly, depositing her ball in the ball rack.

"Likewise." Will shrugged. "You've been friends a long time. You should talk to her."

At his words, Flynn's head came up from his phone. He scrutinized Will, who shrugged again. Much as he didn't want to admit it, Tracy and Emma missed each other.

"I will. Soon." Tracy glanced toward the shoe counter.

Emma returned before he could question Tracy further. His sister claimed a seat on the other side of the lane from both Will and Emma.

While he put on his bowling shoes, Emma multitasked, slipping off her sandals as she held up her end of the bargain they'd made at bingo. "Larry, are you going to vote for Will's winery next Monday, because I've been thinking—"

"This is league, Emma." Larry waggled his finger at her. "We don't talk shop here. Bowling is existential."

"If I'd known you were coming, I would have warned you about Larry's rules." Will tried not to stare at Emma's orange toenails, the graceful arch of her foot. "But thanks for trying. At least no one can say you're a quitter."

"Not about that, at least," Emma said cryptically, producing a pair of black socks from her purse. "I'm operating on faith. I need more than your word that you won't sell the town out."

Felix stared at Will, waiting for reassurance he couldn't give until Slade backed off from the dollar signs.

"I told you I don't want to sell." Will rubbed his palms on his thighs and changed the subject. "A bit of advice. Don't suck. Larry likes to win."

Emma slid her feet into the faded red-and-white leather shoes. "Regardless of which team wins, I bet I bowl better than you tonight."

He'd forgotten how competitive Emma was. "Bring it. Loser pays for lunch at El Rosal." It was a friendly bet, something that might shake her composure and make her lose that grin. His own composure was rock solid. His heart wasn't thudding in his chest because of her. That was just precompetition adrenaline.

She double knotted her laces.

Will rubbed his forehead. There was no way Emma's feet could look good in scuffed bowling shoes.

Emma watched a bowler in the next lane. She rolled her shoulders back and forth. Pinwheeled her arms in big circles. Stretched them behind her back.

Doubt tweaked the edge of Will's confidence, as if he'd accepted a golf game with a big money bet and discovered he was playing against Tiger Woods.

Emma turned to the mayor. "Hey, Larry, can I take a practice ball?"

"No time for that." The mayor stepped up to the ball rack.

"Give me a minute." Moving past him, Emma tested the approach to the line, walking through her motion and follow-through. She grabbed the brush hanging from the scoring table and sat next to Will, brushing the bottoms of her shoes.

"Were you, perhaps, a bowling pro at some point and no one told me?" Will fought the unlikely suspicion that someone had painted a big *S* on his chest. *S* standing for *Sucker,* not *Superman*.

"Emma had. Bowling. For P.E. In school." Tracy's death-ray vision was trained on Will. It was the you're-making-a-fool-of-yourself-stop-it younger-sister stare that was the bane of older brothers everywhere. He'd have thought he'd be used to it by now, especially since she'd used it more these past few months than the past few years combined.

"What happened to basketball and soccer?" Slade was frowning at his orange-and-black bowling shoes, as if an investor might suddenly walk into the bowling alley to meet him, take one look at his tacky footwear and walk out.

"Budget cuts. Our P.E. teacher lost his job, so the school improvised." Flynn wiped his bowling ball. "Larry volunteered to teach bowling and yoga. Felix volunteered to teach golf. Volunteers kept Harmony Valley schools open for years."

"I took. Yoga," Tracy said.

"And I took golf," Flynn said. "How about we golf tomorrow?"

"Can't. Got a pacemaker check in the morning." Mayor Larry led off for his team. He bowled like Fred Flintstone, too high on his toes. Two swings of the ball and he had a spare.

Slade led off for Will's team and got a spare.

Sam bowled next. The spritely old man staggered through his approach as if his chartreuse ball was too heavy for him. But he picked up a spare, as did Flynn and Felix. Tracy knocked down six pins. Her arms were so weak that her ball lacked momentum.

Then it was Will's turn. He just missed picking up a spare. He might have been a tad distracted by a woman with dark hair and delectable toes.

Will returned to the seat next to Emma. Might as well get into her head. "Pretty tough going last, isn't it?"

"Spoken like the person who just went last for his team." Emma stepped confidently to the ball rack, her left hand hovering briefly over the fan.

"Gutter ball," Will murmured, for luck.

"We're all good sports here." Felix frowned at him.

Will shrugged. What could he say? His competitive side was yin to his control freak's yang.

Emma stood at the ready, head bowed over the ball as if she was gazing into it to see her fortune. She lined herself up, swung the ball back and let it fly with the fine-tuned precision of a professional athlete. Strike.

Mayor Larry hooted and high-fived Felix.

Emma could barely keep a bike upright and she bowled like that? Will was in trouble.

"I'm going for a water." Emma breezed by him. "Does anyone want anything?"

After she'd taken orders and left, Tracy came over to sit next to Will. "Quit. Flirting. With Emma."

Mayor Larry stepped up to bowl.

"I'm not flirting," Will protested. "She annoys me. Always has."

Tracy rolled her eyes. "You suck. At dating."

Flynn and Slade tried to camouflage their chuckles.

"What are you talking about? I have no trouble getting dates." Or at least he hadn't until they'd come to Harmony Valley. Not that there was a dating pool in the small town.

She shook her head. "You suck. At keep... keeping. Girl. Friends."

"You're worried about me breaking Emma's heart?" Will would never understand his sister. "You won't talk to her and yet you're trying to protect her?"

She nodded. "Have you. Forgiven her?"

"No."

"Then. She's. Off-limits."

She had a point. Will held up his hands in surrender. Tracy returned to her seat. Flynn said something that made her laugh.

On her next turn, Emma bowled another strike. She plopped into the seat next to him, dropping a challenge. "You better bowl the game of your life, because I'm going to wipe the floor with you."

Without thinking, Will countered with a challenge of his own. "Easier here than on Parish Hill."

"Really?" Emma raised an eyebrow. "You want to go there? Your running shoes against my bike?"

"I'll make it easy on you. It's not a race to the top, just to see who can go the farthest before quitting."

Tracy's scowl promised Will the kind of retribution only a sister could deliver, making him hesitate only a moment before specifying a time for their race.

After all, competition wasn't dating.

CHAPTER FOURTEEN

"GRANNY ROSE, I'M home." Emma came through the back door into the mudroom.

Although Mayor Larry refused to discuss the winery project with her, he'd told her several times she was welcome to bowl on his team anytime. That was what came of beating Will two out of three times. She'd have to think about how to use that to her advantage in turning Larry into a supporter of change. One who'd lock out any corporate deal Will might make behind the town's back.

"I'm in here, reading," Granny Rose called from her bedroom.

Emma poked her head in the door, relieved that Granny Rose was sitting in a chair next to the bed, looking sweet and grandmotherly.

She bid Granny good-night and went upstairs, thinking about Will and his challenge. She'd been foolish to accept a race up Parish Hill, even if he did make her feel alive again. For half a year she'd felt guilty for living.

And that guilt had kept her from painting.

Emma stood in front of the easel she'd hauled back up to her room and frowned at the blank canvas. She'd never found the one with the ugly green caterpillar. Fairies? Thieves? Pranksters? Nothing was going as it should. Not with Tracy, not with her art or the town. And her truce with Will? It had gotten her nowhere. Emma could no longer afford to be patient, sitting around and waiting. She had to be the agent of change.

She rifled through her paint-supply box until she found a pencil with a sharpened tip. This week, she'd colored and sketched her grandmother's face in crayon. Surely, she could sketch a landscape with pencil.

Emma tried a pine tree first, but as soon as she started, the truck's diesel engine roared to life, making her hands tremble. She might as well have drawn a triangle with a trunk. The so-called tree had no life. No energy.

Emma sighed. She picked up a crayon in her supply box. Burnt umber.

Her grandmother's face came to mind. Indignant. Sly. Gleeful.

Emma started to sketch with crayon. She filled the canvas with different versions of her grandmother's expressive face, capturing her myriad emotions.

"Granny Rose!" Emma cried out when she realized what she'd done. Here was something new, something fresh. Delight sprinted through her veins. "Granny Rose, come see!"

Her grandmother didn't answer.

A wave of uncertainty had Emma running downstairs.

Maybe she was asleep. Maybe she was in the bathroom. Maybe—

Her calls to her grandmother grew softer as she hurried down the first-floor hallway. She peeked into Granny Rose's bedroom. The book she'd been reading rested on the chair. The antique four-poster bed was neatly made. Granny Rose's work boots weren't lined up by the closet.

Emma spun around and headed for the kitchen.

"Granny Rose?" Her words echoed in the empty kitchen, fell into silence in the living room, were carried off by the wind when Emma stepped out on the porch.

Emma called Agnes and told her Granny Rose was missing. "Was she calm when you left her after the ball game?" She'd been peaceful when Emma came home.

"For Rose, lately, she was calm…. Almost too calm."

I can't stand by and let this happen.

Emma recalled the way her grandmother had looked at the oak tree after the Lions Club meeting. "She promised not to make trouble while I was bowling." And she hadn't. She'd waited until Emma was home and lost in the creative process.

Guilt stabbed at her, so sharp she wanted to double over. "This is my fault—"

"Now, Emma, don't—"

"I've got to find her." Worst-case scenarios flipped through her head—heart attack, broken hip, drowning. She would not imagine Granny as a vigilante, going for a direct assault at Will and his friends.

"I'll call around and see if anyone else has seen her," Agnes offered. "Don't worry. Rose is passionate, but she's not foolish."

Emma hoped her grandmother's friend was right.

HAVING STOPPED FOR pizza after bowling, Will and Tracy were just walking through the door as their dad was heading out.

"Rose is missing," Ben said.

Will didn't hesitate. "I'll help." If Rose was

upset, it was most likely his fault. He turned around and followed Ben out into the darkness. They could complete a preliminary search through town quicker than the time it would take for the sheriff to arrive. "Where was she last seen?"

"Emma talked to her when she came home. When she checked on Rose later, she was gone. Something's been off with Rose lately." There was no mistaking the disappointment in Ben's gaze when it connected with Will's. "Don't have to tell you that. Heard you want to sell out the town."

Ouch. His own father doubted him. "Not now, Dad. We'll talk after we find Rose."

"I'm coming. Too." Tracy shut the door behind her and ran to Will's truck.

"Granny Rose!" Emma called, crossing the bridge into town. She wrapped the ends of her thin sweater tighter around her and tried to ignore the vise of worry clamped around her chest that made it hard to breathe.

The sun had long since gone down. Although they were miles from the ocean, a cool breeze rode through the valley, chilling the air. And it would only get colder as the night progressed.

This was all her fault. She shouldn't have tried sketching. This was why she could no longer be an artist. Car accidents. Missing grandmothers. No one was safe in Emma's care.

Her throat closed.

Wanting a child, a family. Those were dreams she had no right to.

Emma hurried across the bridge, hesitating at the crossroads on the other side. She could continue along Washington Street toward Edwin's house or head for the town square.

I can't stand by and let this happen.

The oak tree. Granny Rose had to be at the oak tree. Emma ran toward the square and was rewarded by the sound of a thin, warbly voice improvising a song.

"Granny Rose!" Emma ran around the corner of El Rosal and into the square.

Her grandmother sat on the wrought-iron bench beneath the oak tree, wearing a light blue windbreaker. She stopped singing when she saw Emma approach.

"What are you doing?" Emma called to her again just as a truck pulled into the opposite side of the square and parked.

Her grandmother looked confused. "I'm protesting."

"But it's the middle of the night."

"But someone's here." Her voice sounded thin, yet hopeful. "Maybe it's a camera crew."

"Please, it's time to go home." Emma knelt at her grandmother's feet and took her hand.

"I can't." Granny stared expectantly at the figures approaching. "Oh, it's *him*." She slumped back on the bench.

Will and Tracy emerged from the shadows on the far side of the square.

All Emma's hopes of saving her grandmother's reputation evaporated.

"It's okay," Emma called to them, trying to sound calm. "We're heading home."

"We'll drive you." Will's deep, kind voice shouldn't have made Emma want to sob with relief.

"Thank you. No need. We can walk home from here." Emma stood.

"Get rid of them," Granny Rose whispered. "I can't go home yet."

"What do you mean?" Emma whispered back, gently tugging on Granny's hand. "Protest over. Come on."

Her grandmother sighed. "I handcuffed myself to this bench and threw the key over there." She shook her right wrist. Something metal rattled. "Or did I throw it behind me?"

The air rushed out of Emma's lungs and she sank to her knees again.

Will and Tracy had been close enough to hear Granny Rose's predicament. "Tracy, run down the block to Slade's house," Will said. "Tell him we need a couple flashlights and a hacksaw or some bolt cutters." He could have been instructing his sister to run next door to borrow a cup of sugar. Tracy ran off, her footsteps a soft, steady pad on the grass.

"Young man, I will stay here until the populace of Harmony Valley realizes your winery is all part of a bigger plot to increase your bank account." Granny Rose's tone belied her predicament.

"You're more likely to find villains in one of your musicals than you are among me and my friends," Will said. "You can suspect me of schemes and treachery, Rose, but I assure you, this winery is important to me in the long-term. I won't sell."

Granny Rose huffed in scorn.

"If he says he won't sell, he'll do everything in his power not to sell," Emma said. Will had always been true to his word, whether he was promising Tracy's dad he'd watch over them or committing to work with them at a soup kitchen.

"I see how this is." Granny Rose sniffed. "You've convinced Emma to support your plan instead of me."

Will gave a long-suffering sigh.

"Granny Rose, I love you. But even you have to admit the town needs emergency services. What would happen to Mr. B. if he had another heart attack? What if Mildred fell? I don't care if it's a winery that brings those things back or a new grain mill. I want everyone here to be safe."

Granny Rose snorted.

The cold from the ground was seeping through Emma's jeans. She perched on the metal bench next to her grandmother. The longer they sat in silence, the more Emma thought about the danger her grandmother had put herself in. "I could have gone to bed," she said, anger percolating in her veins. "You would have been out here all night. Freezing."

"It's not that cold," Granny Rose said stubbornly.

"It's cold enough," Emma said. "Where did you get those handcuffs?"

Granny lifted her nose in the air. "Every woman should own a pair of handcuffs."

Will laughed, his gaze seeking Emma's, sending heat creeping into her cheeks. "I'm glad I've had this chance to get to know you better, Rose."

"You mean before I die and you bulldoze Harmony Valley?"

"No, because you've given new meaning to the phrase hot spot. If we do build one here, I'm going to have them weld your handcuffs above the door, just like they do with horseshoes. For luck."

Granny turned away from them. "Now you're trying to embarrass me."

Emma was the one who was embarrassed. "With good cause. You can't handcuff yourself around town, even if you are trying to save an old tree."

"My Rupert proposed to me right here. He dropped to one knee." Granny Rose's voice drifted dreamily. "He was so handsome and we were so in love. How could anybody chop down our tree?"

Emma reached out for Will's hand and spoke softly. "Don't get rid of her tree. Please."

He didn't answer, but when Emma would have released Will's hand, he held on to hers.

She tried to remind herself that Will was an indulgence she couldn't afford. Still, she drew his hand closer and rested her forehead on the back of it. She just needed to borrow his strength.

After a moment, Will said, "Rose, did you ever race anyone up Parish Hill? Rupert, perhaps?"

Her grandmother didn't turn. "Why ever would I do that?"

"Pity." Will squeezed Emma's hand lightly. "You probably would have won by force of will alone."

Emma laughed, grateful that Will had been the one who'd found them. She reclaimed her hand when Tracy's light footsteps announced her return.

"He's. Coming." Tracy hunched over, hands on her knees as she tried to catch her breath.

"Thanks," Emma said.

"Any. Time."

"Let's hope I'm never in this situation again." Emma glanced up at Will and then looked at Tracy. "It's probably not the best time to ask, but I'm going to anyway. Would you like to go shopping tomorrow?"

"May-be," Tracy struggled with the word.

Maybe was better than *no*.

THE ONLY GOOD thing about Tracy's doctor not allowing her to drive was that she could get out of cars quicker and be in her bedroom before Will or her dad came through the front door.

She hopped out of Will's truck as soon as he stopped in the driveway. Once inside her room, she locked the door behind her.

Black walls greeted her. Tracy had found several gallons of paint in the barn. Black primer. White. Beige. She'd used up all the black on the walls and ceiling of her small room. Her bed was an island in the midst of her own version of art therapy.

Painting helped her sort things out. She may only be finding zen through painting walls, but still, she could finally see why Emma loved working with paints so much. And right now, things needed sorting.

What had happened to Will hating Emma? He was such a hypocrite. He'd kept Tracy away from her friend all this time and now he was being nice to her? He couldn't have forgiven Emma for the accident. He would have told Tracy.

And Emma? Rose had clearly tipped her rocker too far backward. The dear woman's out-of-character behavior had to be tough on Emma. Tracy wished she could talk to her about it but, of course, she couldn't hold a decent conversation with anyone.

She bunched up her pink chenille bathrobe and shoved it along the crack at the bottom of the door to prevent paint fumes from drifting into the hallway. Heaven forbid Will found out what she was doing. He'd think she'd lost her mind.

"Good night, Tracy." Will's footsteps sounded farther down the hall.

Tracy opened her window, letting in a brisk breeze that did nothing to cool the heated frustration that built inside her. The more time she spent with people who talked easily, the higher her frustration level. She needed an outlet.

And then she began to paint, white over black. White clouds. A white sun. A white picket fence. Nothing as detailed and true to life as Emma would have done. But it didn't matter. Tracy worked at a pace that had her breathing heavily and sweating. She painted until long after midnight, long after she heard anyone moving about the house. She painted until her arm ached and there wasn't any more white paint left in the can.

She stood in the midst of chaos and anger. But it was chaos and anger of her making. A feeling of joy spread through her chest.

She wasn't in control outside her bedroom. But here, she was queen and master of all things. No one completed her sentences in her room. No one treated her like an invalid. Here she felt like she had before the accident—in charge of her own destiny.

She didn't want to think about how small her world had become.

She'd take things one day at a time.

Tomorrow, she'd have to get more paint.

Fire-engine red would do nicely.

Paint smudged, exhausted and smiling, Tracy crawled into bed.

CHAPTER FIFTEEN

WILL WAS WAITING for her.

The realization made Emma pedal faster.

He was stretching, getting ready for their race up Parish Hill. But he spotted Emma the moment she crossed the bridge into view. He'd tossed out a challenge last night at the bowling alley and again when they'd rescued Granny Rose. She hadn't planned on showing up, preferring to stay with her grandmother. But Agnes had appeared early to have coffee with Granny, who was lucid once more and planning her daily rehearsal of *The Music Man*.

And somehow, this prickly friendship she and Will had developed was helping to soothe the hurt between her and Tracy. Emma wasn't going to examine her feelings more closely because this was as far as their friendship went—bowling challenges and races up Parish Hill.

Ahead, the fog hovered low above him, like a canopy, and clung to the ground in wispy tendrils at his ankles. Beads of water dotted his blond hair like a crown. The morning was gray. And still he managed to look bright, shiny, glowing.

When she got closer, Will grinned and spun around, heading toward Parish Hill.

Emma pumped the pedals. Soon she was inching past him up the first switchback.

"Careful of those gears." His voice was deep, but on the verge of breathlessness.

She didn't waste words. She didn't dwell on those places inside her that sparked when he spoke. She concentrated all her being into pedaling, all her focus into staying on the bike. There would be no changing gears today. She'd stay in the same one all the way.

Second hill. Third. Emma pulled away. Her lungs strained. Her legs threatened to drop off. This ranked among one of the stupidest things she'd ever done. She'd made a tactical error. He'd outmaneuvered her. Emma was out in front and he was a full switchback below her. If she collapsed or quit first, all Will had to do was take a few steps farther and he'd win.

She needed a distraction. The bright orange of a poppy petal. The rich brown of the earth. The glint of sunshine off a blue jay's wing.

The growl of a motor filled her ears. Tires squealed.

Gripping her handlebars, Emma flashed back to the accident, but the sounds were different, higher pitched, farther away. This wasn't a memory induced by her mentally composing a painting.

Emma yelled a warning.

More rubber protested on pavement.

A car was coming fast. Too fast.

And then a vintage blue Volkswagen Beetle exploded around the corner above her, swinging wide, right at Emma.

Ice filled her limbs, her lungs, her veins.

Time slowed.

The car drifted. Tires screeched on a trajectory of death.

Emma's.

She jerked the handlebars and pumped the pedals. Her front tire bounced off the pavement at the same time the car's rear fender clipped the bike's sprockets, whipping her off the road.

Airborne, she felt the wind rush over her, muting the sound of the rampaging car.

Emma plummeted through the air toward the steep slope and tumbled to earth with a breath-stealing thud. She rolled and tumbled. The world spun in a kaleidoscope of color. She ate dirt. Banged against rocks and branches and all sorts of hard things that hurt and promised to hurt worse later. She'd never stop rolling. She'd never—

If she didn't stop, she'd slide across the next switchback and into the path of the car.

Panic gave her jellied limbs strength. Emma flung her arms and legs into a big X and flopped onto her back, hoping she'd stretch wide enough to snag something.

Her foot hooked on a tree root with a jolt of pain and she spun to an ankle-twisting halt. Realized she was screaming. Stopped. Gasped for air. Registered the sound and smell of burning rubber. Remembered Will was somewhere on the road below.

She tried to warn him, but her breath came in shallow, rib-racking gasps too weak to form words, much less shout.

The Beetle took the corner, arcing toward Will, who wasn't getting out of the way. He was shouting and waving his arms in the middle of the road, like some B-movie hero who didn't have a stunt double.

"Will," Emma managed to rasp, her mind already flattening him beneath the small car, her heart already mourning him despite him being such a pain.

At the last moment, Will jumped aside, leaped onto the driver's running board and clung to the open window.

With one last earsplitting squeal of tires, the engine died and the car jolted to a stop.

"I'll kill him." Emma wasn't sure if she meant the driver or Will. Probably whoever she reached first.

Groaning, she picked herself up and made her way to the road on shaky legs that threatened to buckle and an ankle that protested every step. Her body felt sluggish and numb, but her brain was reaching for strong words she planned to use very soon.

The entire car, including the windshield, was caked with dust. Emma couldn't see who was driving. Cobwebs covered the headlights, hung like garlands from the hubcaps.

Emma leaned in the open passenger window opposite Will, ready to chew the driver out. And then she realized who it was. "Mildred?"

Mildred's lower lip trembled. Her fingers kneaded the steering wheel. "I just wanted... I just wanted... I just wanted to prove I could still drive." And then she started to cry.

Emma's anger deflated on a gush of air. Mildred had taught Emma to drive when she was fifteen, risking whiplash and Granny Rose's wrath. It was Mildred who'd loaned her a vintage Mercedes-Benz coupe one weekend when Emma was a dateless bridesmaid. It was Mildred who'd traded in her car keys—well, almost all her car keys—for a candy-apple-red walker.

Will's gaze found Emma's. "You okay?"

She nodded. Now that the anger was gone, feeling had started returning to her body. Her battered, scraped up, blood-oozing body. Emma leaned more heavily on the car door. Dirt from her arms sprinkled onto the seat. She could feel debris in her shoes, down her sports bra and up the back of her shorts.

Mildred wiped at a tear. "I'm worthless. I can't see. I can't walk. I can't do anything anymore."

"That's not true." Emma's heart went out to her. "You've been taking care of yourself for years. That's not easy for someone with a walker."

Will gave Emma an approving look.

"Don't try to make me feel better. I've made up my mind. I'm worthless." Mildred's hands dropped to her lap. "Drive me down to the morgue. I've outlived my reason for being."

"No more talk like that. You're on the town council, aren't you? You picked the wrong road, is all. You should stick to straightaways." Will shot Emma a significant look that seemed to say "go with me here."

The problem was a tiny voice in Emma's head wanted to go with Will anywhere, at odds with her artistic dreams, which demanded she go it alone.

"Curves are tough," Emma agreed. Especially curves with fifty-foot drop-offs, bike riders, joggers and unsuspecting squirrels. Mildred was lucky she hadn't killed herself on one of the other switchbacks above them.

"You won't tell Agnes and Rose, will you?" she sniffed. "I'll put the car back in the carport, I promise."

"It'll be our little secret if you let us drive you home," Will assured her, using his forearm to wipe at the caked dirt on the windshield.

Emma very carefully promised nothing. She hoped Will had his fingers crossed behind his back.

"I knew I could trust you." Mildred brightened. "I don't want to interrupt your run.

I should be fine driving home from here. I know the way like the back of my hand."

Will reached in and took the keys from the ignition. "We insist. I'll help you get in the passenger seat, since I don't see your walker in the back."

"I left it in the driveway." Mildred had the grace to blush.

"Hop in the back, Emma." Will was in command mode.

Emma was in no mood to be bossed around. "I can ride my bike home." She turned to look uphill. She didn't see her bike at first. And then she looked higher. The frame had been speared by an oak branch about ten feet below the road where she'd been hit. The slope she'd fallen down was a steep obstacle course of trees, thick fallen branches and rocks the size of Saint Bernards. She could have been killed.

Emma's legs gave out and she crumpled to the pavement.

WILL HAD TO practically lift Emma into the backseat of the old Beetle. She hadn't passed out, but her face was a clammy green color that worried him. She didn't say a word on the drive to Mildred's house. Very un-Emma-like.

They settled Mildred into her favorite recliner. From there, she could see her big-screen television and—if she wasn't legally blind—she could have seen her racing pictures on the wall. Given what he'd heard over the years about her career, Will was curious.

One black-and-white photo showed a vintage race car wrapped around a tree. "Did you crash this car in a race?"

"You could say that. I was forced off the track during my victory lap by some very resentful men." There was regret in her normally sweet-tempered voice. "I got over it. Took a long time, but I got over it."

Despite being banged up pretty bad, Emma made Mildred a cup of tea. She didn't complain or lay blame. But Will wasn't sure her steady state would last much longer.

"I'm borrowing your car to take Emma home," he told Mildred.

"When you bring it back, make sure you hang the keys on the hook by the kitchen door so I can find them when I need them." Mildred started to smile and then seemed to think better of it.

Will helped Emma up from the couch. She had to be hurting, otherwise she'd be telling him not to boss her around. "We'll talk more about driving privileges when I get back."

"Oh. Okay." Mildred sighed.

It only took a few silent minutes to drive to Rose's house. Will was really worried now.

"Thanks for the ride." Emma opened the creaky car door slowly, swinging one foot out at a time.

She moved so carefully Will was able to shut off the car and come around to the passenger side before Emma stood up.

"I can take it from here." She limped forward.

Will took her gently by the arm. "The only reason I didn't drive straight to the hospital is because your pupils aren't dilated and you aren't screaming in pain. I don't think you've had a concussion."

She walked in measured steps toward the porch. "Thanks for the astute diagnosis." She groaned as she lifted her foot onto the first step. "I can go it alone from here."

"Doubtful." Will swept Emma into his arms. She gave a little mewling cry of protest, like one of Felix's kittens, but didn't say another word as he carried her up to the front door. He fumbled with the screen to get in. No one locked their doors in Harmony Valley. "Rose? Are you home?"

"She's working on *The Music Man* with

those kids in Cloverdale this morning. Agnes drove her."

Emma was cradled against his chest as if she belonged there, her arm looped around his neck. They crossed the threshold as if they were a newly married couple, except they weren't married. They weren't in once-in-a-lifetime finery. He reeked of sweat and she smelled like someone had tried to bury her alive.

It was a miracle she hadn't broken her neck on that hill or hit her head. That was twice now that she'd walked away from disaster—once with Tracy and once with him. "You need to buy a lottery ticket."

Emma squirmed. "You can put me down now."

He didn't want to. In his arms, she was safe. "You need a bath." Will turned to the stairs. By the time he got to the second-floor landing he was almost as sweaty and winded as he'd been during their race. He deposited her carefully in the bathroom and started the bathwater.

"I think you've fulfilled your Boy Scout pledge for the day." Emma waved him toward the bathroom door, but even that effort lacked her usual spunk.

Will stepped closer and picked a twig out of her dark hair. It would be so easy to slip his palm into the crook in her neck, draw her close and kiss her, if only to reassure himself that she was okay. He'd watched helplessly as Emma was flung from her bike. The slow-motion horror of it returned to him in a rush. His hands wanted to shake. His breath wanted to catch. His mind wanted to erase the memory.

She could have hit her head and ended up like Tracy. A few days ago he'd wished Tracy's fate on Emma. How ironic that today he felt differently.

"I'm fine. I'll live to bowl another day." Emma's voice was barely above a whisper, as if she, too, was sensing her mortality.

Will looked her up and down one more time to make sure she was indeed fine and still standing before him instead of lying in broken pieces on Parish Hill, with Mildred and her Beetle a mangled mess somewhere nearby. He wouldn't have been able to call for help if anything serious had happened up there. He would've had to run to the top of the hill for cell service or down into town for a landline. But he couldn't have left them if they needed CPR or a tourniquet or a hand to hold as they lay dying.

Will's body did shake then. With rage. The entire town, including Emma, wore blinders. They needed what had become basic necessities, like cell-phone service and a volunteer fire department. "This can't go on."

"I agree," she said on a bone-tired sigh. "I'm not going to race you to the top of Parish Hill anymore. In fact, as soon as I get Granny Rose to the doctor, I'm leaving."

"I mean, the town has to stop fighting us on these changes." His words snapped with anger, no hint of the fear and caring that had spawned them. "What's it going to take? Someone dying? You dying?"

With a growl of possession, Will wrapped both hands around Emma's neck, tugged her close and planted a kiss on her mouth that was far from gentle. Just as quickly, he released her and spun away.

"I… You… Don't…" she sputtered.

He was already on the landing. "I'll be back to check on you in an hour. Answer the door or I'll assume you've passed out and need CPR."

She let loose a primitive yell and then slammed the bathroom door.

Will laughed. It was a maniacal sort of laugh. The kind where you knew you were in deep trouble, but didn't have a clue how to get out.

CHAPTER SIXTEEN

EMMA WASN'T GOING to let Will in after that drive-by kiss of his.

It shouldn't have left her body on fire. It shouldn't have targeted and disabled her speech center with arrow-like accuracy. It shouldn't have lingered in her thoughts.

She'd meant what she'd told him. She was leaving as soon as she knew Granny Rose was going to be okay.

But—

Emma cut off the thought. She locked the doors downstairs and watched for him through her second-story open bedroom window, perched on the sill. She rotated the ice pack she'd made downstairs from one bruise to another—her cheek, her elbow, her thigh. Thank heavens her ankle wasn't sprained. It ached, but it wasn't swollen.

Will emerged from the trees by the river right on time, his expression as grim as the black T-shirt that hugged his chest.

"Hey," she called down to him. "I'm good. Thanks for checking. Go on about your business." She waved him off.

Will shaded his eyes as he looked up at her. "You are my business for the rest of the day."

His declaration sent the same speech-muting arrow to her brain that had disarmed her in the bathroom. By the time she'd regained her senses, he stood in her bedroom doorway.

"How'd you get up here? I locked the doors."

He brushed back a lock of wet hair, the normally bright gold color muted to a somber almost brown. "Everyone in Harmony Valley keeps a spare key above the back door," Will said as he stepped inside.

The room seemed to shrink, along with Emma's ability to breathe.

She shifted the ice pack to her cheek. Maybe she did have a concussion, because she could almost imagine him closing the distance between them and kissing her again. Deeply this time, with more opportunity for her hands to explore the hard planes and contours of his body.

Will paced the room, taking in the empty canvas, empty walls, twin bed and her open, messy suitcases. "Nice light in here. I can see why you chose it. But why aren't any of your pictures on the walls?" He touched the canvas perched on the easel. "And why is this blank? Everyone always talks about you painting nonstop when you're here."

If he hadn't kissed her… If he hadn't barged into her bedroom… If she hadn't wanted him to kiss her again…. That was a lot of "ifs." But without them, Emma might have deflected his question. As it was, she was caught totally off guard. "I haven't been in a creative mood."

The cameos she'd sketched in crayon of her grandmother and hidden in the back of the closet didn't count.

He studied her face, his scrutiny causing her to blush beneath the ice pack, because she knew he knew that deep down she wanted a real kiss.

It was a relief when Will released her from his gaze, once more taking in the blank walls and canvas. "Blocked, huh?"

Emma shifted the ice pack to her elbow and didn't answer.

"Does the empty canvas taunt you until you want to throw it in the trash?"

His insight surprised her. "You have no idea."

"I hear people get over blocks if they take

a break from their work." His blue eyes held understanding, not sympathy. "Try something new."

"Thanks for the advice." She *had* been trying something new—working with crayons. Not much market for Crayola art, but it might keep her sane in her old age.

"Well…you know…" He ran his finger down the side of the canvas. She imagined him running that finger down her neck, along her collarbone. "I'm going through something like that myself."

Emma laughed. "When does a computer programmer get blocked?"

He gripped the corner of canvas so tight she thought he might stretch it out of shape. "Who do you think comes up with the idea for a game or an application?"

Shrew, thy name was Emma. "I'm sorry. I don't know much about technology." Which was why—when added to her passion to create and her inability to protect those around her—whatever was going on between them would never amount to anything. They were worlds apart. She loved her iPhone for its beauty and simplicity. He probably loved his for the amazing things it could do.

Will retreated to the opposite side of the

room, putting his hands behind his back and leaning up against the wall, speaking as if he read her mind. "I may not know much about painting, and you may not know much about computer programming, but we're more alike than you think."

"Being alike doesn't matter. Without forgiveness, whatever this is between us—" and hopefully she wasn't making a fool of herself by admitting she thought there was something "—it can't go anywhere."

Somewhere along the line, this computer nerd had perfected the dark and dangerous look.

Emma needed to remember that as much as Will's attention excited her, if he never forgave her for the accident....

"Do you blame Mildred for what happened to me today?"

His eyes stroked over her, leaving a heat trail even the ice pack couldn't extinguish. "Mildred caused the accident. Of course she's to blame." His words were spoken almost absentmindedly, as if his thoughts weren't totally on the conversation.

Regret clenched its cold fingers around Emma's throat, making it hard to speak. "You don't say that in the same tone of voice you use when you talk about Tracy's accident. Or about me causing it."

Will's gaze hardened.

He didn't forgive her. And chances were he never would. She had to swallow more than once to get the words out, to lay down boundaries that they'd both breached. "Your lack of forgiveness combined with my goals means you have to stop looking at me like that."

"I've tried to stop, but I don't think I can." His voice was soft and hard at the same time, but his eyes had that lost look, like they'd had the other day when he'd talked about being afraid of spiders. "Tell me about your goals, Emma."

This was where she made a stand for what was important to her. This was where he'd realize how poor a choice she was for a relationship— with him or Tracy.

"Whatever was going on in my head the day of the car accident, it was all about those mountains instead of the road and our safety. And now I can't even mentally compose a painting without the fear of that day overtaking me." She couldn't meet his gaze. "I can't look around me without seeing the complex layers and color. I've never been able to look at a forest and not see the trees. To have lost the ability to express the beauty I see around me is like cutting away a piece of who I am. Do you know what that's like? It's more than a block, it's an emptiness where I used to be." She drew a shuddering breath. "But that doesn't matter. Now that I'm sure Tracy will be okay… And after I'm sure Granny Rose is fine, I'm going away. I need to be alone for a long time." Understatement. She was going to be alone forever if that was what it took to reclaim her art.

"So you want to be alone? You need time to get yourself together? I can give you that."

"I'm not asking you to wait for me." Emma gripped the ice pack. "I'm choosing my career over family. And…and…close relationships. That's why I can't kiss you."

To his credit, he considered her words before responding. "You're going through a rough time. But you've been painting for years and no one ever got hurt around you. Your art and your personal relationships can coexist."

She refrained from rolling her eyes. Barely. "This from the person who won't let me drive Tracy shopping. How different would you feel if Tracy had died? Or if Granny Rose was hospitalized after being chained to a park bench all night? I know you believe I should never be trusted with someone else's welfare ever again."

"I thought I heard voices up here." Granny Rose stepped into the room, saving Emma from saying or doing anything more. "Emma, are you talking to yourself again?"

"She's not alone." Will's gruff voice startled Emma's grandmother.

"You!" Granny glanced at the bed, which Emma had made first thing in the morning—thank goodness—before turning her gaze to Will. "What are you doing in here?"

"Checking up on Emma. She crashed her bike on Parish Hill."

Granny Rose rushed over to Emma, lifting her bruised and scraped arms and examining her similarly abused face. "You're sure he didn't hit you?"

"Granny, Will may be many things, but he wouldn't hit a woman," Emma scolded. "I ran off the road and wiped out pretty good. I was lucky Will was there." Not that she could bring herself to look at him while she reassured her grandmother she was fine a dozen more times.

In her concern for Emma, Granny forgot about Will, who was still standing against the wall. But Emma could feel his eyes upon her, feel the heat he refused to quell in his gaze. Was he that determined to get in the last word when Emma had so clearly summed up what was best for the both of them?

Finally, her grandmother stopped fussing and went downstairs to make her famous triple-chocolate cure-all—chocolate-chip cookies, brownies and hot chocolate. It would have been safer to follow her, but Emma had never played it safe. It was true what Will had told her days before by the river. She was willing to twirl near the fire.

"Now that she's home, I should be going." He pushed himself upright. "But think about this, Emma. You didn't drive your grandmother to the town square and handcuff her there. You didn't hand Mildred her car keys. Give the old girls credit for their own actions. This idea you have about sacrificing your relationships to be some kind of lonely, eccentric Picasso is giving power to a silly fear."

Emma shook her head.

"The Emma I grew up with wouldn't let fear get the upper hand. She'd dig in her heels and battle back." He moved into the doorway. "That's the Emma I'll kiss again, despite my better judgment. Despite Rose and Tracy and the trade-off you think you have to make to get your art back. She's there. Inside you. And I will kiss her again. And next time…" His eyes captured hers, an intense clear blue that laid claim. "I'll take my time."

His words plundered her principles and robbed her murmured denial of anything resembling conviction.

"WHAT DO YOU mean you don't want to dance?" Granny Rose demanded later that afternoon. She opened the screen door and gestured for Emma to follow her out.

"I took a tumble on Parish Hill. I could barely make it down the stairs." Who'd have thought Emma would miss Will transporting her from one floor to the other? Emma sat on the bottom step trying to convince her battered body it could make it back to her bedroom, where she'd continue to reject Will's words about fears and kisses. Dancing? Out of the question. "I'm walking like an old lady."

"I'm offended by that remark. Now, come out on the porch. You had a cup of hot chocolate, two brownies and three chocolate-chip cookies. You need to work them off." Granny patted her tush. "So you took a tumble? Let's work out the kinks and move on."

How could Emma move on when she kept

remembering the intensity of Will's gaze? The thrilling threat of a kiss? The annoyance she felt that he didn't believe she had to be alone forever to pursue her art.

"Well, look who's here. It's Tracy." Granny let the screen door bang behind her. "I hope you're ready to dance. Emma's in a feel-sorry-for-me funk. She has nothing to be funky over. It's not like she held a protest and no one came. Would you like to dance with me?"

"Yes." Tracy's voice was rich with silent laughter.

Emma dragged her sorry sack of bones out on the porch.

The big-band sound of Glenn Miller's orchestra spun out of the phonograph, spilled out the open front window.

Emma waved at Tracy, who was grinning as she let Granny Rose lead.

Tracy was out of breath after the first song. "Cut in." She gestured to Emma before collapsing on the porch swing, her legs chicken skinny beneath her blue denim shorts.

"Go easy on me." Emma shuffled forward.

"Why?" Her grandmother held out her hand. "You should always dance like it's your last day on earth."

Soon Emma's muscles had warmed to the

point where she didn't whimper with each step. After two dances, she begged for a halt, and Granny Rose went to the kitchen for water and cookies.

"Will. Told me. Are you. Okay?" Tracy pointed to Emma's bruised face when Emma sank onto the swing.

"I was dancing like it was my last day on earth." It almost had been.

"You fell. Race…racing Will?"

Emma nodded. "I'm not very good at keeping people safe, even myself."

"That's. Not true." Tracy scowled and pounded a fist on her thigh. "Don't. Believe what. Will says."

"It's true."

Tracy made a frustrated sound. "He bosses. Me. He orders. Me. He makes. Me mad." Tracy panted with the effort to get the words out. "You. Too."

"Sometimes," Emma allowed. He could have ordered her into his arms this morning or the other day beneath the willow tree and she might not have minded. "But there's truth to his words. I can't explain what happened in the car that day, but my mind wandered and you got hurt. And now I'm struggling to paint and you're struggling to talk. And you have so much to say."

"Will wants. Me to. Have. Shock. Therapy." Tracy touched her forefingers together and made a zapping noise. "Bye-bye. Brain."

Emma grabbed Tracy's hand. "You tell him you won't do it unless he does it first."

That made Tracy laugh.

"There's got to be other methods. Maybe you just need practice. I'll videotape you reading speeches. You can get up on stage with Granny's production of *The Music Man*."

"Ha! Seventy-ty-six. Trom-bones," Tracy tried to sing, and then shook her head. But she was smiling.

"Now, that's what I like to see." Granny Rose carried a tray with three glasses of water and a plate of cookies. "Two girls sharing confidences on the porch. It's like old times." She set the tray on the table. "What were you talking about? Boys, I bet. You used to stay up all night talking about boys and wedding dresses. Those sleepovers made you the best of friends."

"Granny, we're not thirteen."

"That's it." Granny Rose snapped her fingers. "You girls need a sleepover."

Tracy and Emma exchanged glances and chuckled.

Her grandmother handed out glasses. "You've grown a bit since your last sleepover. You won't both fit in that twin bed upstairs. Tracy, don't you have a bigger bed in your room?"

Tracy rocketed to her feet. "I've got. To go."

"But you just got here," Granny Rose protested as Tracy ran down the steps. She turned to Emma. "What did I say?"

"I have no idea."

CHAPTER SEVENTEEN

"YOU MADE ENOUGH cookies to feed an army," Emma said to Granny Rose as they walked over to the town square on Saturday morning for the Grand Marshal Selection Ceremony. They each carried a big tub of homemade chocolate-chip cookies.

"My cast members make up a small army." Granny Rose chuckled. "I'll get nominated for sure. Don't know if I'll win. It's an honor to be recognized."

"That's what they all say," Emma murmured.

Two weeks before the Spring Festival, the town gathered to recognize the artistic or community contributions of its members. But only one resident was chosen to be the Grand Marshal and preside over the Spring Festival.

This year, Granny Rose had invited her elementary-school production from Cloverdale to sing something from *The Music Man*. Snarky Sam would undoubtedly bring one of his taxidermy projects. Mayor Larry would demonstrate the latest yoga poses. Mrs. Mionetti would bring her latest wool-knitting project. And so on. Residents were a diverse and talented lot.

"Emma, do you have a rock in your shoe? You're limping."

"I'm still working out the kinks from that fall off the bike." Emma's body felt like she'd been run over by a truck. Twice. Will was right. Progress needed to be made before someone died waiting for help. But about the kissing… Will was wrong. Kissing her was a bad idea. If it came to a choice between a kiss and recovering her talent, she'd have to choose paintbrushes and canvas.

Granny Rose laughed. "How sad that there won't be a painting from Emma Willoughby this year."

"I'm no longer a resident, so I can't enter."

There was a chill to the spring morning that seemed to rise from the dewy, fresh-cut grass, making Emma glad she'd chosen to wear black yoga pants and a plum-colored hoodie, which also hid most of her scrapes and bruises. Or maybe it was the chill of anticipation Emma felt. She suspected she'd see Will today. Would he try to kiss her? Or chide her about her silly fears?

They stepped onto the Harmony River bridge. In the distance, Emma could see people buzzing around the perimeter of the town square, setting up tables and chairs.

"Why is it that only Harmony Valley residents show up to this?"

"We like to be true to ourselves. Two weeks from now we'll show off the best of our talents in the Spring Festival, celebrate our town's diversity with floats and open the year's first Farmer's Market."

"Maybe next year there'll be wine poured at the festival."

"I told you not to listen to that computer nerd." Granny Rose frowned.

"I want you to have a safety net here in town. Will's plan isn't perfect, but it's the only plan out there."

"I warned you about Will. He fascinated you even as a child." Granny Rose stopped long enough to shake her finger at Emma. "But he never saw you as more than a nuisance. Nothing has changed. You chase after him and he ignores you."

"That's not true." The words slid slowly

from Emma's lips as she realized the truth beneath the alibis she'd been telling for years.

I have a crush on Will.

Granny Rose huffed and continued walking, leaving Emma alone with her thoughts on the bridge where town lovers traditionally shared a good-night kiss.

I have a crush on Will.

When had that happened?

Emma flipped through memories—rafting, fishing, hiking—going back further and further—Easter-egg hunts, Fourth of July sparklers—until one memory stuck.

This one.

She'd been too small and weak to make a basket on the hoop above Will and Tracy's garage. She'd been trying for what seemed like forever, so long that her best friend had gotten bored and run over to the swing set. But Emma, stubborn even back then, had kept at it in the hot sun. Sweaty, her hands smelling like dirty rubber, she'd dribbled and leaped and wished the ball into the hoop. To no avail.

And then Will had rounded the corner of the house from the barn, looking as hot and dirty as she felt in his scuffed work boots and dusty blue jeans. A few years older, a few feet taller, with a lot more responsibility on his plate.

"You'll never sink that," he'd said.

She'd wanted to toss the ball to the moon, along with every other basketball on the planet.

And then, without warning, Will had lifted her up, basketball and all. Her laughter had filled the air as she'd stretched her arms toward the hoop, barely putting the ball through the orange metal rim. Her feet had come back to earth safely. He'd released her.

She'd scurried after the ball. "Let's do that again."

He'd lifted her over and over, laughing along with her, until his father had called him into the field.

She'd known he had chores. She'd known she'd be in the way. She'd followed him anyway.

A few days ago she'd followed him around Harmony Valley.

Could I have more than a crush on Will?

Heavens, she hoped not.

She was fascinated by the deliberate, yet confident way he moved, the meticulous approach he had toward life, as if unwanted what-if scenarios were weighed, measured and avoided at all costs. She found his protection of Tracy both exasperating and endearing. She enjoyed the way his bossy nature needled her rebel instincts.

But love? She wasn't sure she knew what that meant, how that felt.

And she was determined not to know.

Thankfully, the object of her soon-to-be nonexistent affection was nowhere in sight when Emma collected herself and ventured into the town square. Would it be too much to ask that he and his friends had taken the day off from schmoozing Harmony Valley residents?

Of course he'd be here. Everyone in Harmony Valley came to the ceremony. Which meant Tracy would be here, as well.

Emma deposited her tub of cookies on a table near her grandmother, who was busy welcoming her young performers and their parents. Slipping on her sunglasses, breathing in the smell of fresh-cut grass, she wandered around the square to check out what the residents had done this year.

Snarky Sam had set up a five-foot-tall sawhorse next to his lawn chair. Hanging from it was a deer head with a broad spread of antlers. Sam had somehow given the deer humanlike shoulders and dressed him in a white shirt and black vest, a sloppy gray toupee and a hoop earring.

A group of elementary schoolchildren from Granny Rose's school in blue jeans and T-shirts painted like blue band jackets swarmed around Sam and his work as if he was a rock star.

"Nice," Emma praised the pawn-shop owner over the children's heads.

"It's better than the skunk, don't you think?" Sam's Sherlock Holmes skunk had won him the Grand Marshal title one year. "Worth your vote?"

"Worth somebody's. I can't vote anymore." Wishing him luck, Emma moved on.

Hiro Takata sat at the next table.

"How did the colonoscopy go?" Emma asked politely, hoping the pictures on his table weren't of his insides.

"I'm smooth as a baby's bottom in there." Old Man Takata, as he liked most people younger than him to call him, patted the back of his hip. He used to be an undertaker and still did special requests. He had two framed pictures on his table, both extreme close-ups of Nadine Tarkley's face. "Can you tell which is before and which is after?"

Emma's stomach threatened to sour, but she gamely took a closer look. "I'm going to guess the one with the white silk background is the after." The one where Mrs. Tarkley's dead eyes were closed.

"Correct!" He clapped his hands. "I hear you took my place at bowling. I'll be back week after next."

"I'll hold your spot." Emma moved on.

She was admiring Mrs. Mionetti's knit wool lampshades when Will appeared next to her. He handed her a travel mug. "Thought you might need an extra cup of coffee this morning."

I have a crush on Will.

Emma held the coffee between them like a much-needed barrier. "Where's Tracy?"

"She and my dad went to the hardware store first thing. They should be back soon. Flynn and Slade went into town to catch a movie." He stepped into her space, examining the bruise on her cheek, which Emma thought was barely visible beneath a layer of makeup. "You look good. How do you feel?"

"Okay." *Please don't ask me about my fears.* Emma walked away with a nervous gait she hadn't experienced since high school. She stopped in front of Felix's table.

The big retired fireman had pet crates of adorable kittens. One was occupied by a rather large, one-eyed Siamese. Upon seeing Will, the Siamese started yowling and rubbing against the cage. Will reached in a finger to scratch the cat behind one ear. The Siamese purred.

"Ping's bonded with you," Felix said stiffly to Will. "I'd ask if you'd adopt him, but I want him to have a stable home with a person who cares about others."

Will retracted his finger. "I keep telling you and everyone else—I'm building the winery and running the winery. It's not for sale."

"He's selling." Felix reached into a crate to take out a small white kitten, passing it to one of Granny Rose's musical cast.

Will clenched his jaw. "No, I'm not."

Emma laid a hand on Will's arm. "People would be more likely to believe you if you gave them a reason. An honest reason for starting a winery and retaining ownership." And then she waited for him to admit he was doing it for his dad and Tracy.

Will's lips remained sealed.

Why was he stopping short of reassuring the town of his commitment?

"He's selling," Felix surmised.

"I'm not."

"He's selling," Felix repeated gloomily.

TRACY STOOD NEXT to her dad at the Grand Marshal Selection Ceremony. The sun and light breeze had chased away all traces of fog, leaving the late morning squintably bright. She'd rather be home painting in her dark room, but her father had driven straight from the hardware store in Cloverdale to attend the festivities. Heaven forbid he miss out on a town event.

Tracy's paint cans were in the back of his truck. Thankfully, her dad hadn't asked her why she needed five gallons of paint in five different, loud colors. She would have left, but there were too many cans for her to carry home by herself. Even if she left with one or two, Will would notice and ask questions she didn't want to answer.

"The votes are in," Mayor Larry announced, from the stage set up in front of El Rosal. "And we have a tie between Rose Cascia's *The Music Man*—"

The kids jumped up and down, cheering.

Their parents hovered in the background with benevolent smiles.

"And Sam Smith's Corporate Deer."

Tracy remembered the last time she'd qualified to cast a vote. She'd cast a ballot for Snarky Sam's bikini raccoon. The roadkill taxidermist was always her favorite candidate for Grand Marshal.

"In case of a tie, the town council may appoint an independent board to break it. In this case, we've chosen judges who've left Harmony Valley and made us proud—Will Jackson, Emma Willoughby and Tracy Jackson."

Tracy looked up with a start. "Me?"

Her father hugged her. "You."

"Folks, in case you don't know or don't remember, these are three former Harmony Valley residents, among them a self-made millionaire, an up-and-coming artist and a survivor of a serious accident. Let's bring them up here with a big round of applause."

Tracy gritted her teeth. *Survivor of a serious accident.* Was that her claim to fame? No flippin' way.

"She's the artist," one little boy said, pointing at Tracy's paint-stained fingers.

Tracy tucked her hands in her jeans pockets as she followed Will over to the podium.

She felt the pitying eyes of the townspeople on her and could hear their whispers, "She's the one who can't talk." She couldn't take their judgment, their scrutiny. She edged back, but someone grabbed her arm.

It was Emma.

"Smile," Emma said before Tracy could succumb to panic and shrug her off. "Smile like this is the best day of your life and they'll smile right back at you."

It was either break free of Emma's grip and make a fool of herself as she ran away, or smile. If she ran, the town would qualify her nickname—something like "reclusive serious accident survivor."

So Tracy smiled. She smiled at the kiddies in front of the podium, waving at them as if she was Miss America—there was a laugh. She pointed out people she knew and smiled when they waved back. She worked that smile until her cheeks hurt and she realized Will was talking into the microphone.

"So although I like Sam's Corporate Deer, I have a fondness for *The Music Man*. My vote goes to Rose."

Tracy rolled her eyes.

"If he thinks his vote will get my vote, he can vote again," Rose grumbled from the grass below the podium. She was swaying back and forth as if readying herself for a leap onto the stage. Trouble was coming.

Emma was already halfway down the stairs to calm her grandmother.

Will drew Tracy toward the microphone. There was no question who she was voting for. "Sam."

Her underage *The Music Man* homies in the front row groaned and applauded politely.

"Don't you want to tell us why?" Mayor Larry asked.

No, she didn't. But Emma was still down talking to Rose and Larry was giving Tracy the "go on" hand signal, so Tracy expanded on her answer. "I. Liked it."

The kids applauded. Tracy went back to smiling at anyone who made eye contact with her, wishing she could disappear.

Mayor Larry claimed the microphone and waved Emma back up to the podium. "It comes down to you, Emma."

With one last finger shake at Rose, Emma approached the stage. Her gaze fell on Tracy, frowning in speculation.

Tracy recognized that look. It meant Emma was making a right turn when her GPS and everyone else recommended she turn left.

Pointing at Tracy, Emma grinned, an unspoken *Are you in?*

Tracy shook her head.

"Tough." Emma put her foot on the bottom step. "It's your year."

She couldn't mean... She wouldn't...

Tracy opened her mouth to say no but nothing came out. Rose took advantage of their near-silent exchange, darting past her granddaughter up the stairs. She snatched the microphone from Larry. "This man—" she pointed at Will "—wants to change things here."

Mayor Larry made a grab for the microphone, but at the last minute, Tracy caught hold of his arm. She didn't like Rose picking on Will, but he could take it. She wasn't sure Rose in her current state could stand up to Larry.

Rose cast Tracy a quick smile before trashing Will some more. "I don't know about you, but I want Harmony Valley to survive. We need some new improvements here in town, but we have to choose our allies carefully."

"Granny Rose!" Emma and Rose played tug-of-war with the microphone.

Mayor Larry dropped a string of colorful curses in between platitudes about meddling

members of society upsetting the status quo.
Tracy held on to his arm.

"He won't tell us why he wants to build the
winery," Felix shouted over them all.

"Don't trust the computer nerd!" Rose gave
up the mic and left the podium.

The gathered crowd dissolved into a raucous mess. Neighbor shouting at neighbor.
Fists shaking. Hats tossed to the ground.

"Please!" Emma yelled into the microphone.
"Let me finish casting my vote."

"Too late," Mayor Larry said, shaking Tracy
off. "Besides, you're going to vote for Rose."

"No, I'm not."

"Woo-hoo! Another win!" Sam shouted.

"I'm sorry, Sam, I'm not voting for you
either." Emma's voice carried through the
speakers and seemed to echo down empty
Main Street. "The Grand Marshal is supposed
to represent the best we have to offer. And this
town is a survivor."

Survivor? Tracy cringed at the word. She
started shaking her head. Words. She needed
to find the right words. But the words wouldn't
come.

"And I think this year, the person who best
represents survival—"

No, no, no, no, no.

"—is my dear friend Tracy Jackson. So my vote for Grand Marshal goes to her." Emma was smiling, as if she was giving Tracy the gift at the top of her wish list.

Didn't Emma realize the Grand Marshal had to preside as the master of ceremonies over the Spring Festival events? Had to stand up on stage and speak into a microphone? Tracy's stomach roiled.

After a moment of silence, a few people started to applaud. And then a few more. And then everyone in the town square was applauding, while Tracy struggled not to be sick.

Mayor Larry took the microphone from Emma with a slightly distant look that seemed to be calculating popular opinion against established procedure. He was Tracy's last hope.

"I know we have rules and we counted votes, but I think in this case, we can make an exception." He drew himself up and waved an arm in Tracy's direction. "Our Grand Marshal for this year's Spring Festival is Tracy Jackson!"

Tracy ran to the alley behind El Rosal and vomited.

"AND YOU THINK I'm overbearing?" Will confronted Emma beneath the oak tree.

Mayor Larry was having a powwow with the ladies on the town council over by the stage. Rose was looking abashed, clutching a cookie tin to her chest. The rest of the crowd had dispersed, walking slowly home or climbing into cars.

"Did you see how upset Tracy was?" Will was so close to Emma she could smell coffee on his breath.

"Yes, and I'm sorry for that." Emma lifted her chin. "Yesterday I was joking with Tracy about her getting onstage with Granny Rose's elementary-school kids instead of going to shock therapy. You do know she doesn't want electrodes on her brain?"

He glared at her. "There's been a lot of success with transcranial direct-current stimulation."

"And what kind of success will she have if she's petrified of the therapy?"

He waved her concern aside. "The best and brightest doctors are behind the trials. I was lucky to have gotten her in. You had no right—"

"You keep forgetting she's an adult." Or that she and Tracy had been best friends for more than two decades. "I warned her."

"When?"

"Right before Granny Rose stole the microphone. Tracy could have stopped me." Emma had been half hoping she'd see the old spark in her friend. The you-can't-put-one-over-on-me grin as Tracy leaped forward to prevent her from taking the microphone. But this might be even better. Grand Marshal. It was a perfect challenge for Tracy.

Will scrubbed a hand over his face. He looked tired.

Emma resisted the urge to stroke her palm over his cheek. "She's stopped me before. You don't know how many times—"

"I don't want to know." He half turned away from her, hands on his hips.

"I half expected her to do the same thing this time." Emma felt the beginnings of a grin.

Will shook his head. "This is a perfect example of why I kept you away from Tracy for months. You draw her in and then upset her."

All levity faded. "Really? You think life is always a bowl of cherries jubilee? You upset my grandmother just by breathing. You don't see me on your case about it."

"That's different." His eyes were a brittle blue, his lips a thin line.

"Yep, but you're forgetting one thing."

He cocked an eyebrow.

"Tracy could have refused the honor. She still can. But she's as stubborn as you are and I'm betting she won't." Emma saw her grandmother wave at her. "Encourage her to do it. Sometimes the hardest challenges are the best therapy."

CHAPTER EIGHTEEN

EMMA OPENED THE door that night to Agnes, Mildred, Larry and Will.

"Hello." Will lifted a stack of three small pizza boxes, looking extremely unhappy to be on her porch, if Emma could judge anything through the rising steam. "We're having an intervention."

Perplexed, she moved back to let them all in. "Intervention?"

"A result of the ceremony this morning." Will edged by in his pressed slacks and navy polo, leaving a trace of pepperoni and woodsy aftershave in his wake.

"Is this about Granny Rose?" Emma whispered fiercely. "Is she losing her seat on the town council?" Was Will replacing her? He wasn't even a permanent resident.

Will moved closer to her, speaking softly as the others went into the dining room. "This isn't for Rose. This intervention is for us."

Emma drew back. "There is no us."

His eyes darkened as his gaze dropped to her lips. "Not today."

"And not tomorrow." Emma shut the door firmly, wishing Will was on the other side.

"Did I forget someone's birthday?" Granny Rose came out of her bedroom in a red Mandarin-collared tunic and matching silk pants. Despite it being Saturday, at Emma's request, she'd been performing *The King and I*. There was currently an intermission for a costume change.

"No birthday, Rose." Mayor Larry led the group into the dining room. "It's an intervention, remember? We talked about it earlier."

"Of course I remember." Granny touched her temple, fooling no one.

Emma hurried to the kitchen for plates, napkins and drinks. Upon her return she found that the only seat left was between Granny Rose and Will. She discreetly pulled her chair as far away from Will as she could. Which wasn't very far.

Once she was settled, Mayor Larry pinned Emma with a firm gaze. "This stops today." He turned to Will. "The bickering. The harassment. The bother."

"I'm confused," Emma said, talking over

Will, who was trying to shush her. "We haven't done anything to warrant a citation or—"

Will shushed her again and spread his hand on her thigh.

Emma froze. The warmth of his hand penetrated her thin yoga pants. She glanced around to see if anyone had noticed, but no one's frown deepened, not even Rose's.

"See what I mean?" Larry used his fist like a gavel. "Bickering."

"Harmony Valley is a peaceful place." Agnes took over. An aging Tinker Bell on a serious mission. "We pride ourselves on our decorum, which was conspicuously absent at the Grand Marshal ceremony."

It took superhuman willpower not to point her finger at Granny Rose.

Larry and Agnes turned expectantly to Mildred. Clearly, this was going to be a tag-team intervention.

Lips pursed, Mildred wasn't saying anything.

"Mildred," Agnes prompted.

Was Mildred afraid Emma and Will might start an intervention of their own about driving when legally blind if she spoke up? Emma hoped so.

When Mildred remained mum, Agnes continued, "We all realize the dire predicament the town's in. Normally, we'd encourage discussion and debate. But we're old and you can see firsthand how upsetting that can be." She gestured toward Granny Rose.

All heads swiveled to the head of the table. Granny Rose was humming and seemed to have drifted somewhere else.

Point taken.

Agnes sighed. "This issue is upsetting not only to members of this house but other residents, as well. Mae nearly gave Phil a heart attack arguing about the situation. Sam got so annoyed with Felix, he almost stabbed him with a deer antler. You've created chaos. So we're here to intervene in this project and propose a compromise."

"We'll rezone the property and raise funds to help supporting businesses get off the ground." Mayor Larry took up the banner. "But in return, we want a guarantee the winery will stay under your ownership, Will. At the very least, you'll have to prove that you won't abandon us, like the grain mill did, or sell out."

To his credit, Will kept his cool and spoke respectfully. "I've told everyone repeatedly that we won't sell. How do we prove our commitment?"

"They could sign a contract," Emma pointed out.

Will squeezed her thigh.

He would not control her like some dollar-store puppet!

Emma shoved at him as inconspicuously as she could. He flipped his palm up and appropriated her hand with his. They fit, those hands, as if they belonged to a long-married couple.

"We can understand your reluctance to sign a contract given the way wineries have a habit of failing," Agnes said reasonably. "But we feel a further display of commitment and community involvement is critical. And so we've decided we want you to enter a float in the Spring Festival. Show the town your vision." Agnes was calm. "And to make sure Rose's interests are represented, we want Emma to help you. We feel her input is important."

"A float?" Emma sucked in a breath. She'd worked on festival floats in her time. Usually there was scenery to be painted. She'd be fine if she could color it all in with crayons.

"That's two weekends away." Will frowned, holding Emma's hand immobile when she tried to free herself. "We're coming up on some hard deadlines for the winery. If we don't set things in motion soon, it'll put us back a year."

"A float," Emma murmured, gaze dropping to their joined hands. A dangerous corkscrew of desire spun slowly up Emma's arm, encouraging her to forget her dreams. She lifted her gaze to the picture she'd painted of Yosemite's Half Dome that was hanging in the hall. She tugged on her hand.

"You have two weeks to convince us." Larry leaned forward. "If your float wins at the festival, you'll be able to speak your piece during closing ceremonies. But more important, we'll have a bargaining chip. If you feed us to the wolves, we'll have pictures and video and witnesses to whatever you promise. We'll put our foot in any future business dealings you have and make anyone who tries to deal with you think twice about taking you at your word."

"I'll have to check with my business partners." Will rubbed their hands against his thigh as if he'd forgotten where he ended and Emma began. "Before I agree."

"You have a day to decide. Your property has buildings on it we should have condemned ten years ago," Larry pointed out. "You want to restore them, right?"

"So we have no choice." Will's voice hardened. He pressed their hands deeper into the flesh of his thigh.

"It's settled, then." When neither Will nor Emma added further protest, Larry filled his plate with pizza. "You start tomorrow morning at eight. That's when Felix will deliver a flatbed trailer out to the Henderson property for you to use in your build."

"Blackmail stole my appetite." Will released Emma's hand. "Excuse us. Emma and I have plans to make."

"THAT'S IT," SLADE said later at Edwin's house after Will told his partners and Edwin about the intervention. He straightened the ends of his mud-colored paisley tie. "Nobody puts puppet strings on me. I say we cut our losses."

"I'm worried the town's input will never end." Flynn tossed his Giants cap on the coffee table next to an open laptop. "How can we show them we're committed? And then get them to butt out of our business?"

"Boys, this is not as dire as you make it." Flynn's grandfather sat on the couch, hands resting on his cane.

"Even if we build a kick-butt float, that's no guarantee of winning," Will pointed out. Failure to provide for Tracy loomed over him like an overcaffeinated grim reaper. "It's not like votes count. Mayor Larry could pull something like Emma did at the Grand Marshal ceremony and knock our feet out from under us at the last minute."

"Boys—"

"You can't bail now," Emma said from her seat on the low hearth, interrupting Edwin. "These are your parents and grandparents, your schoolteachers and doctors." She'd been silent since they'd left Rose's house. Not that Will could blame her. He didn't want to talk about what happened under the table, either. He'd held on to her like she was his partner against them.

He should have kissed Emma out of his system days ago. Now he'd have that tension buzzing between them as they worked out their differences for the town's future. That take-my-time kiss he'd taunted Emma with was going to be an empty threat, something he'd think about on his deathbed, pondering if it was his biggest regret or his greatest triumph.

"Why can't you present the town with a

contract saying you won't sell?" Emma demanded, gaining steam. "Is making a buck at the expense of this place that important to you?"

Slade shook his head. "Not good business."

"Boys!"

Everyone looked at Flynn's grandfather.

"Boys, you're forgetting our strategic advantages." Edwin pounded his cane on the carpet. "You've already commissioned plans to renovate the buildings while keeping their charm. You've already decided to scale back production. You've got a talented artist at your disposal. She can design the float to showcase these things."

Will wasn't convinced. "And the vote? How can we control the vote?"

"There will be three floats in addition to yours—one from the Ladies Auxiliary, one from the Lions Club and one from the veterans." Edwin pounded his cane again. "Those three floats don't change from year to year. Our residents are too old to crawl around on a trailer and risk breaking a hip. Your float doesn't have to be good enough to enter in Pasadena's Rose Parade to win."

"That's all?" Flynn asked dubiously.

Edwin's smile widened until it looked to

be cradling his rather large nose. "No. We have one more advantage. In case of a tie, the Grand Marshal casts a vote."

"And Tracy's the Grand Marshal." Slade smiled slyly at Will.

"You can't cheat," Emma said.

"They won't need to." Edwin gestured toward Emma. "Your talent is enough to win it for them."

Emma exchanged stares with Will. His dared her to paint. Hers dared him to admit she couldn't.

"So we're agreed. We have two weeks to prove our case," Flynn said.

"And we walk away if we don't get approval by then," Slade added.

They both turned to Will, who tore his gaze away from Emma and agreed.

"Forget for a moment that Slade can't be trusted not to bail on the town if a bigger winery makes you an offer," Emma said later, as Will walked her home along the fragrant riverbank. "I didn't agree to help."

"You could have refused at any time, just like Tracy could have refused your Grand Marshal nomination."

"You could have told them," Emma complained, wrapping her arms tightly around herself as if that was the only thing holding her together. "I can't do this."

"The Emma of old would have at least tried." Will put an arm over her shoulder. She smelled of roses and fresh air and felt like a tightly wound clock whose springs were about to snap. Every muscle beneath his arm was tense.

"Like you've tried to reassure the town with anything other than your word?"

"Slade is my business partner. I can't guarantee anything but my intent."

She made a frustrating noise. "You shouldn't put your arm around me."

"I'm not going to kiss you." Not that the idea was far from his mind. "You looked cold."

"I'm not cold. I'm upset. I'm backed into a corner I can't get out of, even if I wanted to."

"You'll figure it out."

She made that frustrated sound again.

They veered off a side path toward Rose's Victorian, walking in silence until they got to the porch steps. Emma turned to face him, sliding from beneath his arm.

"This is going to be a disaster. We'll both be free to leave in two weeks." She sounded relieved. "We'll go about our separate lives, me to pursue my art and you to do whatever it is you'll do next. My mother's trial will probably be over. She'll swoop in and bully my grandmother into a safer environment with people who'll watch over her. It'll be for the best, but it'll break her heart." She turned toward the stairs.

"Wait." He reached for her hand. "You want Rose to live here forever?"

Her brows furrowed. "If it was possible, yes. I can't see her living anywhere else. Can you?"

"I can." He tugged her closer until their feet were almost touching. Not because he intended to kiss her, but because upheaval in a family was hard. She might need a supportive hug. One friend to another. "I can see her staging a production of *South Pacific* in a retirement center."

Emma's grin was reward enough for not kissing her. His hands were only sliding up her arms to make their good-night hug quicker.

Emma's grin faded. "Will?" A whisper.

His hands reached her shoulders. His fingers traced along her collarbone, coming to rest on her neck. All he had to do was drop his arms around her shoulders to give her that friendly hug.

Instead, his fingers reached upward until his palms cupped her cheeks.

"Will?" Emma whispered again, her dark eyes luminous in the porch light.

He leaned closer. A hug and a kiss on the cheek. An appropriate good-night between friends.

Her eyes drifted closed and he experienced his first twinge of trouble.

His lips brushed hers. A light caress. Still chaste. Still friendly.

Except he couldn't seem to draw his mouth away from hers.

And Emma's arms slid tentatively around his waist.

Their kiss danced on the edge of exploration. On a sigh and the hint of a dream he'd once had.

The front door opened, dousing them in light. "Emma?"

Emma sprang back and darted up the stairs. She called good-night over her shoulder, her footsteps echoing on wood, echoing in his heart.

Now he had his answer.

If he never kissed Emma again, it'd be one of his great regrets on his deathbed.

WHEN WILL GOT home, the heat of Emma's kiss a fresh memory on his lips, his father was ensconced in his recliner reading the paper as if everything was normal. As if Will's world hadn't been tilted even further off its axis.

"Where's Tracy?" Will asked.

"Where else? In her room."

"What's she decided about being the Grand Marshal?" He wasn't going to force her to do it, as if he could force her to do anything, but it would help ease his mind about the winery if she accepted. Will knocked on Tracy's bedroom door. "Tracy, can I come in?"

"She's been in there for hours," Ben said from the living room.

Tracy didn't answer when he knocked and called for her again. Worry tightened the knots in Will's stomach and respect for privacy flew out the window. He retrieved the L-shaped master key from above the bathroom door frame and unlocked Tracy's bedroom door.

The fact that he had to shoulder the door open didn't calm him. She'd shoved a pile of clothes against it.

"What the…?" Will froze.

Tracy had her back to him. Earphones blared music he could hear ten feet away, explaining why she hadn't answered his knock. She was painting a dandelion the size of her head on the wall in the corner. Her window was flung open and her furniture was shoved in the middle of the room. A mosaic of paint spills created a trail around the perimeter, ruining the carpet.

Tracy had painted everything—from the walls to the ceiling—in black, then added neon color—oversize blades of grass, a red barn with out-of-proportion doors hanging askew, cows with pink spots in a field. Her enthusiasm for painting far outmatched her skill.

Ben appeared at his shoulder. "So this is what she's been doing with all that paint."

"We should call someone, shouldn't we? Her doctor? Her therapist?" Will stepped farther into the room, trying to put his feet on firm ground instead of clumps of paint-encrusted carpet.

What kind of person hid this kind of activity? Had she lost her grip on reality? Or was this Tracy's way of coping? She'd been better since she'd locked herself away.

Perhaps sensing she was no longer alone, Tracy turned, her face a textbook illustration of happiness—easy smile, rosy cheeks, relaxed gaze. All that changed at the sight of them. Her mouth pinched downward. Her face paled. Her eyes narrowed. "Get out!"

"Tracy, we need to talk." What did this mean? Was this compulsion of hers another negative side effect of her injury?

"Get out!" Tracy's shriek was laced with pain. Her eyes darted everywhere, her expression reminiscent of Rose's at the town council meeting.

Will had new respect for what Emma was going through.

His father tugged Will's arm. "Let's regroup in the kitchen. Tracy, that means you, too."

Tracy stomped out after them, breathing in ragged gasps that threatened to morph into sobs the likes of which Will hadn't seen since Carl Quedoba had dumped her in high school.

The family took up their customary defense positions—Will in the archway between the kitchen and the living room, Ben leaning on the counter by the sink, Tracy short pacing in front of the refrigerator. There was a moment or two of preargument silence as they each played out scenarios in their heads.

"Honey," Ben began. "About the paint—"

"Explain it to us." Will extended his arms. "Explain why you felt the need to hide what you were doing from us."

"I knew...*you*...wouldn't. Understand." She nailed Will with a glare so laser-like intense he felt he might disintegrate. Her paint-stained hands fisted like a boxer's, ready for a fight.

"I'm trying to."

Tracy jabbed the air in his direction. "You. Do not. Own me."

"I'm trying to build a winery so you'll have a job and a life here."

"Don't do. Me any. Favors."

"I only want you to be safe. And happy." But it was clear now that he was smothering her. Emma was right. He charged in and plowed the field the way he saw it, without consideration for the feelings of others—Rose, Tracy, even Emma.

Arms up in surrender, Ben stepped between them. "Can I get a word in here? After all, I am your father and this is my house." He spared a glance at the family portrait above the fireplace, as if silently asking his wife for help.

Will had lost his mother without warning. After almost losing Tracy, he wouldn't surrender her to some problem they hadn't seen coming without a fight.

Crossing her arms over her too-thin chest, Tracy backed up until she was leaning against the sink. Will held his position, held himself so still he almost wasn't breathing. When had things fallen apart? And why hadn't he realized it sooner?

Ben washed his hands over his face. "First off, Tracy, that's your room. I don't care what you do in there as long as you don't burn the place down."

"Dad." Tracy nearly bowled him over with a hug. "Oh, Dad."

"However, that doesn't mean you don't have some explaining to do, young lady." Ben released his daughter. "We care about you. We've sat at your hospital bedside and made decisions that we thought were best for you until you were at a point where you were capable of making them yourself." Ben looked at his son. "Now, Will… He likes to set boundaries and throw money at the problem."

Will had heard enough of his faults recently not to argue. That didn't mean his father's opinion didn't sting.

Ben's gaze drifted back to Tracy. "If you agree, I'm sure he'll pick another fancy rehab hospital for you to go to."

Eyes suddenly brimming with tears, Tracy shook her head vehemently.

Will's throat thickened until his voice sounded

rusty. "She's not going to another facility. She's fine right here."

Tracy's mouth began to form a battle cry, making Will quickly amend his statement. "If she wants to stay."

Ben stroked Tracy's short blond curls twice before letting his hand fall to her shoulder. "I'm a believer in giving people a chance to work through the bad stuff in their own way. And lately, you seem to be doing better. Is it because of the painting?"

Tracy hesitated a moment before nodding.

"You hated painting in the hospital," Will pointed out.

She tossed her hands in the air. "They tell. Me to. Paint. E-emotions. So stupid."

Will wasn't sure he understood the difference with what she was doing in her room, but if it made Tracy happy...

"They told you to paint out anger." Ben watched Tracy closely. "You plopped a big red glob of paint on the paper and went back to your room."

"I was. Angry."

Will chuckled. "You got Mom's temper."

"As if you didn't," Ben teased.

"The painting makes you feel better?" Will asked.

"Yes. I control what. I paint."

Control was something Will understood. "Well, then, let's make sure you have a good supply of paint."

CHAPTER NINETEEN

EMMA HAD SPENT far too long thinking about Will's kiss last night to dwell on it this morning. She had better things to do.

Like stare at the bare, thirty-foot trailer Felix had delivered twenty minutes ago.

Not one of the men making up the three winery musketeers had shown up for its delivery. Had they decided to give up after all and not told her?

There was nothing to do but stand around, listen to some overly happy birds twitter and look at the scenery—neat rows of grapevines and an unobstructed view of Parish Hill. Emma wasn't looking at the scenery and subsequently putting herself through another panic attack while she passed the time waiting for those three prima donnas.

Nor was she going to spend any more time thinking about Will's lips on hers.

She made it as far as the corner of the barn

when she heard a truck coming down the gravel drive, horn honking.

It was Will.

She supposed she'd have to see him sometime. Reluctantly, Emma turned around. "You're late."

"Sorry. I needed a peace offering." He hopped out of the truck. "I didn't think it would take me that long to rescue this. The back rim is bent and the main sprocket broken, but with a little work, you'll be able to ride again." Will lifted her bike out of the truck bed and set out the kickstand.

"Thank you." She came closer to inspect the damage, running one hand over her cheek. "I expected it to be a lost cause."

"Nothing's ever completely lost." Will drank her in a moment before reaching into the truck cab. "I brought my laptop, too. The revised architectural designs are on it."

A cat meowed from inside the cab. Emma peeked in the open truck window. A one-eyed Siamese peeked at her through the slats of a small carrier. "You adopted one of Felix's cats?"

"Sort of." He'd moved closer to her in that way he had, lowering his voice as if afraid someone else might hear. "I got Ping for you. I thought you could paint with him."

Emma stared from Will to the cat and back.

"He's kind of impossible to ignore," Will added when the cat meowed again. "But it's nice to have someone around to keep you company when you're struggling with something."

"I can't have a cat in my apartment."

"You can have one here. And you said you'd be moving. Maybe your next place will allow cats."

"It's an impractical gift." Impractical, but thoughtful. She was touched. "What if it doesn't work out?"

"I'll take him."

The cat's fur was the color of faded sandstone with rich dark-chocolate highlights. "But how did you convince Felix to let you have him? He wasn't about to let you adopt one of his cats yesterday."

"Ping can be very persuasive."

On cue, Ping meowed, confirming Will's story.

"Now, about the new vision for the winery." Will set a laptop on the driver's seat and keyed in his password. "I got these this morning."

Emma leaned in to look. This architectural design salvaged the existing red barn, and the welcome center was the original farmhouse. "Felix will be thrilled." Never mind how Will got architectural plans on a Sunday. "This is why he let you have Ping."

Will grinned. "We all have our secrets."

Like good-night kisses. Emma desperately needed to back away. Her feet remained firmly planted near his fire. "This is exactly the kind of idea I can get behind, except..." Emma looked up at Will. "If you want my full support, I have a couple of conditions."

"The oak tree stays," Will said solemnly, his gaze dropping briefly to her hand; the one he'd held the night Granny Rose had handcuffed herself in the town square, the hand he'd clung to beneath the table last night.

"Thank you. That takes care of condition number one." Condition number two was a stickier subject. "I can be an extra pair of hands on the float, but don't ask me to draw or paint anything for you. I can't do it."

It was Will's turn to study Emma. But instead of arguing, his gaze softened. "I may have a solution to that. Are you sure you can't sketch? Because if you can rough out our plans for a revitalized town square, we can use that for the theme of the float. I think I found a painter. I figured this would be a 3-D diorama and—"

Emma's hands had started to tremble at the word *sketch*. "No."

"Emma…"

"We'll need someone else to draw *and* paint." She thrust her palms in the back pockets of her jeans. "You know I'm beyond blocked. I'm lucky I can edit print ads with someone else's photos and artwork."

There wasn't enough distance between them. He was looking at her too intensely. Her feet moved this time. "I'm going to get over this, but I can't do it overnight."

He kept staring. She could almost see his brain working. "I give you permission to sketch this out."

Not forgiveness. Permission. Emma wanted to scream. "Your permission doesn't matter. I don't have permission here." She tapped her heart, suddenly realizing the truth. "It's about forgiving myself. In order to create, I have to lose myself in the moment. I lost myself when I was driving Tracy. And the other night after bowling when Granny Rose slipped away, I was trying to sketch and didn't hear her leave. I'm not ready to forgive myself. My grandmother's safety is at risk, as well as the safety of others. Don't ask me to do this."

His stare probed. He considered. After a moment, he nodded. "Get in. You need to see something."

"Why?"

"For once in your life, Emma, do something I tell you without asking."

"You're assuming you know what's good for me. Throw me a bone and I'll go with you."

He nodded. "We're going to my house. Now get in."

A few minutes later, Emma ascended the steps to the Jackson home. "Why are we here?"

"You'll see." Will led her inside and down the hall to Tracy's room.

The smell of fresh paint increased as they moved deeper into the house, but the walls she saw were a dingy white that hadn't felt a brush or roller since Will's mother died.

Will took a master key from above the door frame.

"Whoa." Emma backed up. "If Tracy locked the door, we shouldn't go inside."

Ignoring her, Will opened the door. "Okay, don't go inside. You can look from the hall-way."

Emma stood firm. "It's not right."

"Look." Will tugged her forward, until she bumped into his solid chest.

She kept her face averted, but the smell of paint was intense, calling to her artistic curiosity.

Emma turned her head. "Oh." So much black. A bold statement as a backdrop to the colorful murals on every wall. Emma almost didn't notice the disarray of Tracy's furniture. Or the canvas with a flying worm on the dresser. She recognized the squiggly line as the worm she'd tried painting days ago, but Tracy had filled the rest in.

"Tracy's been painting her walls for a week now. And she's been more confident, happier even." Will ran his hand down the slope of her back. "Art heals, Emma. It heals and it forgives. You can't just stop creating."

"But I have stopped. In my case, art doesn't heal, it disables. It puts those I love at risk."

Will shook his head. "You don't get it. Tracy—"

The back door opened and Tracy charged down the hall. "What are. You doing? My room. Mine!"

"I'm sorry." Emma held up her hands and stepped out of the room. Why hadn't she left when Will took down the key? She and Tracy would never rebuild their friendship now.

"I wanted Emma to see this," Will started to explain. "I brought her here. I made her come inside."

"It's beautiful," Emma said gently.

"Get out! Get out! Get out! Get out!" Tracy slammed the bedroom door and locked herself in.

"What's going on in here?" Ben stood at the back door.

"I was trying to help Emma and I messed up. I'm sorry, Tracy." The pain in Will's voice was wrenching.

Without thinking, Emma put her arms around him and rested her head on his chest.

"I SCREWED UP, Dad." Will sat on the living room couch, his head in his hands. Emma had left and already he missed the feel of her arms around him. "How am I going to make this right?"

"It's my fault."

Will raised his head and stared at his father, who stood across from him. "You didn't invade Tracy's privacy."

"No, but you're my firstborn. I raised you to take on responsibility from an early age. And now you take on too much. You can't make things right for everyone. People need to find their own way." His sigh carried the weariness of years as a single dad. "People will still ask for your help from time to time, but you have to put the brakes on your impulse to fix everything for everybody."

"Hard habit to break." He felt so defeated. "It's apparently what I think I do best."

"We're all a work in progress. You're ahead of most people in this world by just knowing what your faults are." Ben glanced up at the family portrait. "I'm sorry I didn't do better by you after your mom died."

"You don't have to apologize to me," Will said gruffly.

His father stood and patted Will's knee. "Apologies are part of every relationship, along with forgiveness." He headed toward the front door.

"But what am I going to do? About Tracy and the float and…everything."

Ben paused. "You have to give things up, son. The responsibility, the control, the judging. Life's mountains are high. Let someone else carry the load for a while."

Impossible. If he let things go, his life would be chaos.

His dad opened the door.

"Wait." Will stood, closing the distance between them. "Wait."

And then they were hugging as they hadn't hugged since learning about Tracy's accident.

"I love you, Dad."

"I love you, too, son." Ben's voice was husky. He thumped Will's shoulder. "Remember, the way to get to the top of life's most challenging mountains is easy. Just take one step at a time."

"THAT CAT'S GOING to be more trouble than he's worth," Granny Rose said, watching Emma release Ping from his carrier.

She had taken the cat when she'd left Will, along with the small bag of kitty litter and cat food she'd noticed on his floorboards. Granted, it was an armful, but she hadn't had far to walk. And Ping's cries had helped drown out the memory of Tracy's anger.

With a tentative meow, the one-eyed cat crept out of the carrier, sniffed at the bowls of food and water then proceeded toward the makeshift litter box. He gave it a sniff before slinking over to Emma with a superior look.

Emma leaned down and stroked his short,

silky fur. "Do you want to stay in Harmony Valley, Granny Rose?"

"I'm going to die here, come earthquake or high water." She crossed her arms over her chest. "What's this about?"

"I'm going to need you to sit here with me and Ping. And sing."

"What on earth for?"

"Because I don't like the soundtrack that plays in my head when I try to paint." Emma met her grandmother's clear gaze. "Because if you want to stay here, you need emergency services restored, not to mention a doctor's exam for those mood swings of yours."

Her grandmother huffed. "I have never had mood swings in my life."

"Call them whatever you like. As soon as Mom's trial is over, she's going to show up on your doorstep with a brochure for a retirement home in Sacramento. You know how stubborn she can be. You need to reassure her you'll be safe here."

"How does me sitting here and singing with a cat do that?"

"It won't. Unless I can paint." Emma faced the easel.

Granny Rose started to sing "A Spoonful of Sugar" from *Mary Poppins*.

At Emma's feet, Ping meowed pitifully.

Emma reminded herself this was important. Being able to paint the float wasn't about her lifelong dream. It was about helping others. Painting as volunteer work. She liked that angle.

But when she picked up a brush, her hands didn't like that angle, or any other one she could think of.

The diesel engine roared louder than the voices of Ping and Granny Rose.

ONE STEP AT a time.

After lunch, Will surveyed his team and tried to quell the nervous beat of his heart.

Flynn and Slade had assembled tools on the old barn's workbench. Tracy stood at the barn door, arms crossed and scowling. Facing the bare trailer, Emma sat on an old milk crate, looking as closed off as she had that day beneath the willow.

Will put his hands in his jeans pockets, took them out, put them back in again.

One step at a time.

"Here's the thing." Will recited the words he'd been practicing all morning, words that were humbling because they were an admission that he wasn't perfect. "My name is Will, and I'm a control freak."

They all stared at him as if he'd lost his mind. All except Emma. She tilted her head expectantly.

Her consideration gave him strength. "I need to step back and let you lead."

Emma began to smile.

"Why do you want me to lead?" Flynn deadpanned.

"No, idiot." Slade pushed his shoulder. "The collective you, as in all of us."

Flynn rubbed his shoulder, grinning. "I knew that. The question is, why is our fearless leader stepping back?"

"It's come to my attention that I can be an overbearing jerk, trying to force what I feel is right on other people. I tend to think I know what's best for everyone, which isn't the way to be a good brother." He nodded at Tracy. "Or a friend." He nodded at Slade and Flynn, and then turned to Emma. "Or a…friend." That was awkward.

Will pressed on. "I jumped at the chance to start a winery without telling my business partners all the reasons why. I considered my sister's challenges a disability and tried to plan her life accordingly. And I set the boundaries of her friendship when I had no right to interfere. I could go on, but at this point, I'll apologize."

Slade cleared his throat. "There's no need to apologize to me."

"Or me," Flynn chimed in.

The jury was still out with Tracy. She stared at the rows of grapevines, silent.

"I have one question." Emma stood, her hands in her back pockets as she stared at Will. "Do you forgive me for the accident?"

CHAPTER TWENTY

TRACY HADN'T FELT this good since before the accident.

Nearly two weeks into the project, she loved working on the float. Emma wanted no part of the painting, so Tracy did everything. She loved the smooth regularity of the stroke of the brush. She loved the banter between Flynn and Slade, and the *pop, pop, pop* of Emma working the nail gun.

The float took form when Emma worked. Will, Flynn and Slade mostly argued about the length of boards and the size of cardboard they were cutting. It seemed like they had to double cut everything. Things would have gone smoother if Will had taken charge. They made decisions by committee and sometimes they didn't agree.

But not everything was perfect.

Tracy hated the way Will looked at Emma when he thought no one was watching, as if Emma had stomped on his heart. What did he expect when he hadn't said that he'd forgiven her for the accident? And she hated how awkward it was in the barn when she and Emma worked alone, or when Will and Emma were working on something together.

Finding Emma in her bedroom that day was like being back in the rehabilitation hospital where anyone could walk in while Tracy was changing. No one respected your privacy. But for Will to have let Emma in her room was the worst of betrayals. She hadn't talked to either of them since. She'd drawn out her hurt until it seemed too late to accept their apologies. Instead, Tracy poured herself into painting as her own form of recovery.

When her work was done, she snuck off to visit different residents in Harmony Valley. She never went back to the same house twice. Nope, she visited a different person each time and carefully told them her story. A therapist had once said that the more you spoke about a tragedy out loud, the easier it was to bear.

Tracy didn't know about easier. She just knew that it felt good to talk about the accident. She told Felix about the rescue workers while she held a fuzzy white kitten. She told Agnes about the wild and crazy Mediflight ride over a cup of tea. She traded walker war stories with Mildred as she baked cookies. And every day her speech felt smoother, easier. Who needed shock therapy? She could control aphasia all by herself.

Just not in time to be the town's Grand Marshal. The thought still made her feel sick.

And then one afternoon, while she was painting, alone for once since Emma had print ad work to do and the men had gone into town, an SUV pulled into the barn doorway.

"Excuse me." A handsome man with the slick smile of a salesman got out of the passenger side.

Tracy felt a moment of panic. This stranger would expect her speech to be smooth. "Yes?"

"I'm looking for Will Jackson."

He was checking out her legs. No one had looked at her legs like that since Las Vegas. A tiny thrill raced up her spine. "He's…uh… not here."

"Can I wait?"

Tracy opened her mouth to say yes, but realized if she did, she'd have to make polite conversation. "Who. Are you?" *Not now. Don't start talking like an idiot now.*

"I'm Quinn Yardley, Action News in Santa Rosa. I was hoping to do an interview with Will Jackson about a winery he's starting." He closed the gap between them and reached up, extending his hand. "And you are?"

"Tracy." Her hand felt like a limp noodle in his. "Jackson." And then her hand convulsed, capturing his. *Idiot, idiot, idiot.* Play it cool. She released his fingers.

"Will's sister?" Quinn's smile broadened like a snake's mouth right before it unhinged its jaws to swallow its prey. "It's always great to have additional insight on a story. You don't mind if we ask you a few questions."

The driver of the SUV had been standing near the car door. He retrieved a camera from the backseat.

"I…uh…" Tracy drew back, nearly tumbling on to the gelato parlor she'd been painting.

"I didn't think you'd mind." Quinn turned to his cameraman, pulling a microphone out of his pocket. "Is there enough light in here?"

Tracy could feel her throat closing up and her tongue thickening. The air lodged inside her lungs.

"There's enough light, but she'll need to come down off that trailer."

"No," Tracy croaked.

Quinn looked at her as if she was refusing

the highest of honors. "No? It'll only take a few minutes. What is it you're painting?"

"You need...to go."

"Now, Tracy," he said in a cajoling voice, the same tone of voice her therapists used when they wanted to make her feel guilty for not completing an exercise when she was too tired, too demoralized or too angry.

"I will. Not. Be on. Camera." Tracy drew a breath. "You. Need to...to leave."

Quinn looked at her as if she were a curious lab specimen.

She hated herself for being imperfect. She hated aphasia.

"What's all this?" Emma appeared in the doorway wearing her old paint-splattered overall shorts and a messy ponytail. "Who are you?"

Quinn stepped forward and introduced himself.

Emma took one look at Tracy's face and ignored his outstretched hand. "Gentlemen, you're trespassing."

"We didn't mean to upset anyone," Quinn said smoothly, lowering his voice. "What's wrong with her?"

"Nothing is *wrong* with her," Emma said in icy tones that matched the temperature of Tracy's insides. She walked over to the nail-gun compressor, turned it on and took aim at the tire of their SUV. "Now leave, before walking becomes your only option out of here."

"We won't come back," Quinn said, as if that meant something to either one of them.

Emma stood guard until the SUV disappeared down the driveway. She shut off the compressor but remained facing the driveway. "I'm so sorry, Tracy."

Tracy barely heard her as she ran out the back door.

No one was working on the float.

Flynn and Slade had bought groceries in Cloverdale. After dropping them off at their respective houses, Will had driven to the barn. The women were nowhere to be seen.

"Tracy? Emma?" He unloaded the lumber and additional cardboard he'd picked up. They'd underestimated their need for materials since they'd overestimated their skill at carpentry. Well, Flynn was skilled, but Will and Slade didn't like to let him have all the fun. Hence the wasted supplies.

"Tracy? Emma?" Will walked around to the back of the barn, calling for them again. He followed the trail to the river. When he reached the trees he found Emma sitting on the bank tossing pebbles. "Hey. What's going on? Where's Tracy?"

Emma didn't say a word. She just kept winding up and pitching stones.

Will sat down next to her. She hadn't talked to him during the entire build other than to ask him for a hand. He'd missed their sparring. He'd missed her superior grin. He'd missed her.

Emma's cheeks were streaked with tears. Her breathing was ragged. "I've lost Tracy," she said in a small voice.

He slipped an arm around her and pulled her close, as he'd been wanting to do since the night he'd kissed her.

Emma turned her face into his shoulder and sobbed once. Just once. And then with a huge, shuddering sigh, she sat up and lifted her dark, watery gaze to his.

"People think she's broken," she whispered.

Will used to be among them. Now he viewed her aphasia more like a handicap in a horse race. Tracy carried more weight than the rest of them. Life would be harder for her, but that didn't mean she wouldn't run.

"She's not broken." Emma straightened, but kept her gaze locked on his. "She's so much smarter than I am. And quicker at putting things together up here." She tapped her temple. "How could anyone look at her and think there's something wrong with her?" She disengaged herself, grabbed a sizable rock and threw it into the river. A line drive. He remembered teaching her and Tracy how to throw a baseball. Emma had been awkwardly enthusiastic, determined to conquer the skill in her own way.

She drew a deep breath. "Do you know what I see when I look at this river?"

"Water?" His attempt at humor fell flat.

"I see browns and greens, eddies and currents, the sparkle of a fish beneath the surface." She scooted away and angled herself to face him. "I see motion and calm, slowness and speed."

"I get it. You see depth when you look at Tracy. So do I."

"But you see her with conditions. You don't see the total beauty of her. You don't hear the emotion when she talks. It comes out in spurts, but it's there. She's there, multilayered and beautiful." Emma stood up. "Exactly as she's always been."

She was right. Will couldn't see beyond the

challenges Tracy faced and the limited tools she had to meet them. It was like the first day they'd raced up Parish Hill when he'd realized Emma was a dreamer and he was a realist. The distance between their outlooks was vast and unbridgeable.

"The world sees her the same way you do, as if she can't get as far in life as anyone else." Emma looked out on the river, her face drawn in sadness. "I'm the reason the world sees her that way. And she knows it." Her gaze dropped to his as she stepped back. "And now I know why you can never forgive me."

Will sat on the bank, watching Emma leave him.

It hit home then, in a way it hadn't before, not in all the times she'd told him or the way his dad had warned him. This wasn't a situation where she'd eventually come around to his way of thinking or things would miraculously become easier between them without any change of heart on his part.

Forget her fear that she couldn't have both close relationships and be an artist.

He and Emma had no future if he couldn't find it in himself to forgive her and she couldn't find a way to forgive herself.

THE FLOAT WAS close to completion. It was rudimentary, but it didn't matter. Emma thought it was perfect. The float represented the past she loved and the future she hoped was in store for her hometown. And in two days they'd win the contest at the Spring Festival.

Emma had come back after dinner to admire the float alone. She sat cross-legged on the workbench so she could have a better view.

"It turned out pretty well, didn't it?" Will walked into the barn holding a water bottle. The day had been warm, but was giving way to the chill of an incoming fog bank. He'd changed from cargo shorts to jeans and had thrown on a Stanford sweatshirt.

She'd been working next to him earlier and had almost laughed out loud when she'd caught him humming the chorus from *Oklahoma!* She was sure he'd been struggling not to jump in and tell Flynn and Slade what they should be doing.

"I like it." Emma slid down, wiping sawdust from her shorts. "I'm going to miss working on it. I enjoyed getting to know Slade. I don't believe his threats that he'd take the money and run anymore. And I'd forgotten how fun Flynn can be." She went over and shifted a grapevine in a five-gallon container so the vines hung off the front of the trailer. "Flynn still hates the barber chair, though, doesn't he?"

"You braided his hair." There was something odd in Will's tone, but Emma was paying more attention to the float than him. "Who braids a man's hair?"

Emma laughed. That had been the highlight of her day. "His hair has grown past his shoulders. He's got great bone structure, but who could see it beneath that baseball cap and hair?" She and Tracy had exchanged a rare grin while she'd worked on Flynn.

She stood on a step stool and fiddled with the ribbon on the sheep Slade had found online. It had arrived today. The sheep was life size, with a pink bow and dark eyes that begged for a hug. After the festival they'd decided to donate it to the nearest children's hospital.

"I didn't like you touching Flynn's hair." Will was behind her, his breath wafting gently across the shell of her ear.

Emma's heart slowed to a limb-freezing halt. Other than the day that nosy reporter had showed up, she'd successfully avoided being alone with Will for more than a week. She'd tucked away crushes, infatuations and fascinations. She'd parted ways with what-ifs and

what-could-have-beens. She was on the path
of recovery, not discovery.

"Turn around, Emma." Suddenly she recognized that tone of voice. It was the same deep
rumble he'd used to tell her he was going to
kiss her that day in her bedroom.

"I can't." To turn around meant she'd kiss
him. And a kiss would only reignite feelings
she'd been doing her best to ignore. A kiss
could break her hold on the precipice of love,
sending her tumbling down where she'd be
vulnerable and lost.

"Emma." His voice sounded weary. "I don't
like it when you braid Flynn's hair."

"You don't?"

"No." His hands settled on her shoulders,
warm and heavy and full of want. "And I don't
like it when you tease Slade about his ties."
His hands circled her shoulders slowly, as if
learning their shape.

"I almost nailed Slade's tie to the gelato
shop. You can't not tease a man about that.

"Turn around, Emma."

"I can't." Her voice dropped to a whisper,
as featherlight as her hold on her control. Will
might want her, but he could never forgive

her. She knew because she hadn't forgiven herself.

His hands glided down her arms until they came to rest over her hands. His fingers tangled with hers. He moved closer, the heat of his body begging her to turn around and close the distance between them, begging her to let him claim her.

"I can't." An answer to a question he hadn't verbalized, her voice barely a whisper. She was so close to giving in, so close to crossing a line she wanted desperately to honor. Her integrity.

"Emma." His lips pressed against the back of her neck just above the collar of her T-shirt, soft as dandelion fluff, but heavy with need.

Despite her best intentions, Emma tilted her head to one side, inviting his lips upward. He accepted the invitation, pressing his mouth beneath her ear, advancing to her jawline. She turned her head slightly, giving him better access. He accepted the invitation, the press of his lips against her flesh more urgent now, demanding she turn, demanding she accept, demanding she submit.

And then he stopped. The absence of his kisses drew a moan from deep within her.

His stubbled cheek rested against her smooth one. He spoke with aching tenderness. "Emma."

Her grip slipped. And she was lost.

WILL LEANED AGAINST the wall of the barn, cradling Emma in his arms as he watched the moon rise above the crown of her dark hair.

She turned and lifted her face. "One last kiss."

Will couldn't resist. One last kiss to end a perfect evening.

Emma arched against him; her lips claimed his, her hunger met his need.

Not enough. Not nearly enough.

Will pressed her closer, deepened the kiss. Together their bodies generated enough heat to cocoon them from the nip of the brisk night air.

"One last kiss," Emma murmured against his mouth.

The way she said it, as if this was goodbye, had Will pulling back. "I'll walk you home."

She covered his lips with her fingers before he could say any more. "No. Here at the barn, it's only the two of us, without pasts, without futures. I know you can't forgive me and I don't expect you to. But out there—" she sighed "—out there, we have baggage and responsibilities, to ourselves as well as to others. I knew when I turned around that you and I only had this one moment."

Her words created a void in his chest where his heart used to be. "Don't say that."

She stared at him expectantly. "Does that mean…?"

He hadn't forgiven her and he was sure she could see it in his face. He'd hoped they could forget about it, put the issue in a corner and not discuss it. He was stupid and naive, but he'd been hopeful that the attraction between them would make her forget.

The evening chill nipped at him. "But Emma, we can—"

"No. We can't." Emma stiffened, then pushed her way free of his arms. Her eyes were filled with hurt. In his need to hold her, he hadn't meant to hurt her. Her pain seeped into him, making him feel emptier than before. "I can't. I have more respect for myself than that. You should never have promised to kiss me. You should never have asked me to turn around."

He reached for her, but she backed away. What was he going to do? He knew the texture of her skin, the taste of her mouth, the urgency of her embrace. He knew when something would make her laugh. Keeping his distance, pretending he didn't know those things about her would be agony.

"You can forgive Mildred a deliberate mistake that almost cost me my life and yours, but you can't forgive me an *accident*." It wasn't a question.

"I can't. I told you." Despite what his father had said, despite how much he wanted to. Anger and frustration pierced him, prodding words he didn't want to say. "And you don't forgive yourself, either. It's why you can't paint."

"True," she whispered, her gaze dropping to her hands. And then she raised her chin, raised her liquid gaze to meet his. "Promise me…" Emma winced, swallowed. Started again. "Promise me you'll never look at me like you want to hold me. Promise me you'll never touch me like you have tonight. And promise me you'll never kiss me again."

The weight of her request clawed at him, threatening to bring him to his knees. How could that be? He liked Emma. He wanted Emma. But he didn't understand the meaning of those powerful emotions.

"You owe me that much. I know you'll

honor a promise." Her eyes were luminous in the moonlight.

The words she wanted to hear hung bitterly on his lips, reluctant to take form.

In the end, he could only nod his head.

ROSE WAS WAITING for Emma on the porch swing. She had a piece of paper in her hand that looked like a letter and a grim set to her mouth that didn't bode well for a man who'd been making out with her granddaughter twenty minutes ago.

He'd insisted on walking Emma home. She'd kept a half step ahead of him the entire time. Their time, their moment, was over. Will felt broken and numb. He wanted to gather her in his arms and tell her everything would be all right. But he couldn't promise her anything.

"There you are." Rose stood, still gripping the paper. "I should have known you'd be with him after receiving this."

"What is it?" Emma trotted up the stairs. Will admired her concern for her grandmother's well-being. It matched his for Tracy.

"Someone—" Rose's stare was icy "—requested an arborist's report on the oak tree in the town square. I'm sure the big corporation that's going to give Will his next few millions doesn't like oak trees."

"It wasn't me." Will climbed the stairs, holding up his hands.

"What does it say?" Emma reached for the report, but Rose yanked it away.

"It says my tree has a fungus." Rose peered at the page. "Anthracnose. What does it matter what it's called? It's obviously Latin for death." She clutched the page to her breast in a dramatic turn worthy of a stage production. Then Will came into her line of vision and she drew herself up like an avenging goddess. "You killed my tree. You killed it so you could put your *hot spot* there."

"Granny Rose, you know that's not true. People don't infect trees with fungus. And besides, Will's changed the plans so that the communications tower will go on Parish Hill."

For a moment, Rose seemed to drift back into reality. She blinked, casting her gaze about the worn porch floorboards.

"May I see it?" Will reached for the paper. "There might be something on there that tells us who requested the test."

Fury flared in Rose's eyes. "Don't you touch it. Don't you touch it or my tree."

"It's okay, Granny," Emma said softly. "Give me the report. Please."

Rose handed over the page.

"Come inside." Emma took her grandmother's arm. "We'll put on *South Pacific*. Bali Hai is calling."

"Is the computer nerd coming inside?" Rose glanced up at Will as if he were an ogre.

"No. He's going home to Ben and Tracy," Emma said, pain lacing her words.

She'd done nothing to earn such pain. Emma was right. He had to stay away or risk hurting her even more.

CHAPTER TWENTY-ONE

"GRANNY ROSE?" IT was an hour past sunrise when Emma trudged downstairs the next morning. Her footsteps echoed hollowly on the wood floor, as hollow as she felt inside.

Last night she'd fallen in love. She'd tiptoed around the feeling for years, always finding excuses not to fall, finding other men wanting. Then along came Will, reminding her of her hero-worshipping crush and brushing aside her common sense. Will had pushed her off the edge of reason with the same calculated zeal he approached everything else. She'd taken the plunge toward love, but she'd taken it alone.

It was her own fault for not being strong. But he'd been too much of a temptation. And then he couldn't even lie to her!

She'd wanted to double over. She'd wanted to crawl off into the darkness. Instead, she'd demanded he promise to leave her alone. Will kept his promises. Always.

But just in case, she was calling in reinforcements. She needed her mother here to take care of Granny Rose so she could leave Harmony Valley and Will behind.

Before she'd gone to bed last night, Emma had made sure Granny went to her room, lending her a paperback romance she was reading. Then she'd dragged herself upstairs, forcing herself to attack a canvas with harsh, raw colors on a too-wide brush. Ping had watched her critically, as silent as the missing soundtrack in her head. She'd told him if she was going to be heartbroken, she was determined to conquer the shakes and the uncertainty. In the end, she'd conquered nothing and fallen asleep with Ping curled against her side.

It was the wrong solution for the wrong problem. The story of Emma's life lately. Will was right. Just because she knew she had to forgive herself for the accident didn't mean she could do it.

This morning, there was no coffee brewing. No bustle of activity. No to-do list on the kitchen table.

"Granny Rose?"

Silence.

"Granny?" Emma headed toward the first floor bedroom. She knocked. When she received no answer, she pushed the door open slowly, trying to respect her grandmother's privacy. "Granny?"

The room was empty. Her grandmother's bed was made. The romance novel was on the quilt where Emma had left it. Granny's work boots weren't paired neatly in front of the closet. Emma called louder, moved faster. A check of the bathroom revealed her towels were dry. Granny Rose hadn't showered this morning. Emma ran to the front door. Her grandmother's coat was missing from its hook.

Emma breathed in guilt-laden, panicked gasps. She'd tried painting again. And again, disaster. But she had to think, not feel sorry for herself. Her grandmother needed her.

Maybe Granny Rose had gone out. She was a notorious early bird and kept up an active schedule. She could have slept in or decided not to shower this morning.

Granny Rose left without her coffee? Not likely.

What if she'd left the house after Emma had said good-night?

With trembling fingers, Emma called Agnes and confirmed that her grandmother hadn't come by or spent the night.

By now, Emma's entire body was shaking. She ran toward the town square, rounded the corner of El Rosal and stopped. The town was empty. Her grandmother wasn't handcuffed under the oak tree. Emma hadn't realized how much she'd been counting on that possibility.

She ran over to the ancient tree and looked into its branches. After all, her grandmother had been a trapeze artist. It was possible. But the tree was empty.

A noise from the north end of the square had Emma turning.

Will jogged along East Street on nearly silent feet.

Emotions and powerful physical sensations washed over Emma. The strength of his arms around her. The heat of his lips on hers. And the agonizing disappointment.

Emma couldn't deal with him now. She had to think of Granny Rose. Or *like* Granny Rose. Her grandmother was convinced Will wanted to sell out the town and she knew all Will's hopes rode on their float.

Understanding dawned. Spinning away, Emma jogged quickly across the square in the opposite direction from Will and Parish Hill.

"Emma?"

She sprinted down Main Street. Past Snarky

Sam's. She ran despite the stitch in her side and the choking sob in her throat. Cutting over on Jefferson she continued until she was at the turn into the gravel driveway to the Henderson property. From there, she could see the barn doors were open.

Emma ran faster.

The closer she got to the barn, the more of the float she could see. The cardboard buildings were crushed. The gallon containers with corn and grapevines had been tipped over, dirt spilling onto the ground. And at the far end of the float, the red barn that represented the winery was demolished. A pair of spindly human legs hung over the edge, unmoving.

"Granny Rose!" Emma faltered. Her breath hitched.

Will sprinted past.

Her grandmother hadn't come home last night. Was she dead?

Emma slowed to a walk, hugging herself in an attempt to keep it together. Despite what happened between them last night, Emma was grateful Will was there.

By the time she reached the float, Will was standing on it, leaning over Granny Rose. "She's alive and breathing, but I think she hit her head."

Emma climbed up next to him, her own legs threatening to buckle.

"Don't panic." Will steadied Emma. "There's blood, but her pulse is strong."

Her grandmother was bent at the middle like a broken matchstick, her head on one wooden frame, knees over the other. Blood stained one shoulder of her blue windbreaker and the wood beneath her neck. Her white hair was in disarray.

"Granny, are you okay?" Emma placed her hands on her grandmother's cheeks. Her skin was soft, yet chilled by the morning air, sprinkled with the scent of rose water and blood. She pulled off her thin pink jacket and draped it over Granny Rose's torso.

"Don't move her," Will cautioned. "She may have injured her neck or back."

"She needs an ambulance." And it would take at least thirty minutes for one to arrive from Cloverdale. Emma felt sick.

"Your house is closer," Will said. "Go. Call."

She shook her head. "Run to my house. If she comes to, the sight of your face will upset her."

After a moment's hesitation, Will nodded. "But sit down, before you keel over, too."

Emma's knees folded beneath her quickly. "Hurry."

The wait for the ambulance was excruciating. Emma kept up a steady stream of one-sided conversation, holding Granny Rose's cold hand, her gaze never leaving her face. Her grandmother looked peaceful, as if she was sleeping. Or not.

Terror vibrated through Emma's body in convulsive tremors that kept her upright. All the while, her brain kept repeating: *my fault, my fault, my fault.* She'd never paint again. She'd never so much as try.

Will returned, keeping silent watch at the door.

A siren finally sounded in the distance. The louder it got, the more Emma felt as if the tension in her body would break her into pieces.

As the ambulance pulled in front of the barn, Granny Rose blinked her eyes open. "Emma? Where am I?"

Relief softened her grip on her grandmother's hand. "You're safe."

Granny Rose squirmed.

"Stay still," Emma ordered. "You've had a fall, and we need to make sure you're all right before you move."

Flynn and Slade appeared, right on time to

finish working on the float. They surveyed the damage without a word. Will pulled them aside and explained what had happened.

Tracy showed up, took one look at Granny Rose's blood and retreated to the door of the barn, crossing her arms and staring down the driveway.

The emergency crew seemed to take forever to amble over, asking for her grandmother's name and a situation update. There were two men. One looked like he'd graduated early from high school and the other looked like he was ready for retirement. Both frowned when Emma couldn't tell them how long Granny Rose had been lying there.

The older EMT did all the talking. "Rose, how many fingers am I holding up?"

"You're giving me the Boy Scout pledge."

Emma patted the back of her grandmother's cold hand. He was indeed holding up three fingers.

"What year is it?"

Granny Rose told him.

"Who's the president?"

Granny Rose answered correctly.

"Can you feel me squeezing your toes?"

"I think you're impertinent. The last person to touch my tootsies was my husband."

"But can you feel me squeezing?"

"Yes." Granny Rose kicked out the foot he was holding. "I'd like to get up now. I'm not sure how I got here, but I'd like to start my day. I have a dress rehearsal of *The Music Man* before lunch."

"Ma'am, I need you to hold still."

"I said—"

"Ma'am, we'll get you out of here as quickly as we can, but your safety is our first concern. I see nails and sharp wood splinters. You don't want to be cut, do you?"

"No," Granny Rose grumbled.

It took a few more minutes for them to determine her grandmother could be moved. They put a brace on her neck as a precaution before they lifted her onto a stretcher and loaded her into the back of the ambulance.

When Emma started to climb in with her, the older tech stopped her. "No one's allowed to ride with us, ma'am."

"But she's my grandmother."

"It's policy. We're taking her to the Healdsburg District Hospital. If you check in at the emergency room desk when you arrive, they'll take you to her."

They started an IV on Granny Rose and then drove off.

Emma turned around to face everyone and the devastation her grandmother had caused. Granny Rose had sabotaged the best chance for a stable future the town had.

"This is my fault. I should have heard her leave last night." Somehow, Emma managed to hold her head up, but she couldn't look at Will. "I've let you all down. Since the accident I've been of little use to anyone. And whenever I try to paint or sketch someone gets hurt. I hurt Tracy and I haven't been able to take care of my grandmother. I don't know who I am or where I fit in. I'm just so…lost."

No one looked her in the eye.

Not even Will when he weakly tried to argue. "You shouldn't blame yourself for something Rose did."

Emma swallowed back tears. Tears would help no one. "But I do. The float is ruined. There's no way we can recreate it in time for the festival." She hauled in air. "A few weeks ago, I couldn't believe anyone would feel so low they'd call themselves worthless. But that's how I feel. Worthless."

FLYNN KICKED AT a torn piece of cardboard. Slade stroked his gray tie.

Will registered the pain on Emma's face,

but it was a distant feeling. His chance to speak to the entire town and convince them that this new vision of Harmony Valley was good for everyone had been lost. Frustration built like a firestorm in his gut, burning away any hope he'd felt these past few weeks.

"We can rebuild," Flynn said optimistically, righting a planter with a grapevine in it.

"No," Will said. "There's no point trying to fix anything. Rose demolished any hope we had." The fire inside raged, demanding someone suffer as much as he was. He met Emma's gaze. "It was all a dream, like one of those dandelion wishes kids make that never come true."

Choking back a sob, Emma ran out of the barn.

"Dude, that's harsh." Flynn frowned.

The lid on Will's temper blew. "I may be a control freak, but I'm a realist. I know when to cut my losses. I can't fix this any more than I can fix Tracy."

Tracy gasped and stalked out.

Will bit back a curse.

"I know this is a surprise, coming from me," Slade said, "but I stand with Flynn. We can rebuild. But we'll need to duct tape your mouth shut, because if you start in on me or Flynn, like you did with the girls, we're gone."

"What's the point of rebuilding?" Will gestured to the destruction in front of him. "Tracy doesn't want anything to do with the winery. Maybe it was stupid for me to think I could create a life for her here. Half the town hates the idea. How many more setbacks do we need before we realize this wasn't meant to be? It's time we turned our attention to developing our next app. We can brainstorm ideas this afternoon." When Will didn't feel as if his heart had been ripped from his chest.

He'd driven away the two women who were most important to him in the world. The only thing left to do was move on.

"Rose looks good," Mildred said, wheeling her walker down the hospital hallway next to Emma and Agnes. "And she's in good spirits."

"She won't be once she realizes they shaved off her hair in back," Agnes said, touching her pixie cut. "She was awfully proud of that hair."

"I bet we can get Phil to shave off the rest of it. Then Rose would look like one of those punk rockers." Mildred paused to let an attendant with a wheelchair move past them.

"Even if she let Phil near her hair, she won't be happy about it." Agnes waved to a nurse behind a counter. "Nor will she be happy that we're suspending her from the town council, at least until her doctor approves her for activity again."

"Do you have to do that?" Emma asked. "It's so important to her."

Agnes nodded.

"Every time I think of her outside all night I feel sick." If Emma had needed any more proof as to why she couldn't have both an artist's career and a family, she'd gotten it.

Mildred stopped wheeling and looked squarely at Emma. "It wasn't your fault. If anything, we're to blame. We've seen the signs for some time, but we didn't want to mention it to her or to your family."

"No, it's my fault," Emma persisted. "She's always been there for me and last night…last night Will walked me home and she didn't like it. I knew she'd focused her fears on Will and still I let him walk me home." Because she'd been hopeful that he'd change his mind. She should have known better.

"Ah." Mildred chuckled. "So you've found a compromise after all."

"We haven't. At least, not like that. Will can't forgive me for the accident." Emma sighed.

"The question is, honey," Mildred said, "can you forgive yourself? I've seen the way you mope around. Take it from me. Life is too short to carry remorse and regret."

"I agree," Agnes said. "If you wait for someone's forgiveness to move on with your life, you might be waiting a long time. It's what's inside you that matters."

Emma knew that what they said was true. It was convincing herself that was the hard part. "Enough about me. What about the float? Is there any way the council will let Will speak at the festival without it?"

"If we allowed him to speak at our festivities, we'd have to grant the microphone to anyone who wanted to speak about anything. He's been given time at our council meetings. Fair is fair. Rules are meant to keep order. It's bad enough Larry bent them at the Grand Marshal ceremony." Agnes hugged Emma. "Even though I support Will's efforts to revitalize Harmony Valley, if he can't convince enough residents to stand with him, Larry will never vote his way."

CHAPTER TWENTY-TWO

IT WAS LATE when Emma flopped onto her bed at Granny Rose's. Her grandmother was being kept overnight for observation in Healdsburg and her mother had come down from Sacramento to stay in the room with Granny.

That left Emma alone with her guilt. She'd messed up royally, starting with the accident and ending with Granny Rose being in the hospital.

After trying unsuccessfully to sleep for several hours, she dragged herself out of bed before dawn. Ping yawned, stretched, protested and then went back to sleep. Emma pulled on an old pair of jeans and a sweatshirt and returned to the scene of her grandmother's crime.

The float hadn't been touched since they'd rescued Granny Rose. It was still a wreck. If she was going to make things right, she had to start here. She considered approaching Flynn, Slade and Tracy to help her, but it hadn't been their inattentiveness that caused this disaster. No. Emma had to do this on her own.

Emma lifted the five-gallon planters off the trailer. That left the buildings they'd created with wood frames and cardboard. They'd had to special order enough cardboard to complete the float and only had one sheet left, so the salvaged float would need to be simple in design.

She climbed onto the platform and began tearing off the ripped cardboard. With the help of a crowbar, she pried off the two-by-fours that framed the buildings. It was hard work. By the time she was through, Emma regretted doing such a thorough job with the nail gun.

She stepped back and looked at what she had to work with. Tracy had painted rolling green hills on the bottom half of the plywood backdrop and a blue sky on the top half. There was only an inch left of the paint Tracy had used to depict the red brick buildings in town and nothing of the gray.

She'd need paint. And her sketch pencil.

Emma's hands started to tremble. Her heart thudded. And her ears reverberated with the screech and rumble of a big diesel.

She curled her fingers into tight fists, forced herself to breathe slowly.

She could do this. It didn't matter if it looked like a kindergartner painted the float. She had to do it.

"So you're giving up." Edwin leaned forward in his recliner to shake Will's hand. The older man's skin looked pale. His eyes weren't their usual bright blue. Edwin glanced at Flynn, removing flags from the Harmony Valley map in the kitchen. "I had hoped… But you can still help. If you meet anyone looking to get off the beaten path, tell them about our town."

"I'll do that." Although it was unlikely he'd find any takers in Silicon Valley, where making your next brilliant career move was more important than sitting with friends and watching the river go by.

"People tend to get lost in the day-to-day out there," Edwin added.

Will had been lost in his own pain when the ambulance had taken Rose away, so much so he hadn't gathered his partners for a brainstorming session. It wasn't until the middle of the night, when he couldn't sleep, that he'd recalled Emma's words.

I'm worthless.

Her words had struck like a blow to the head, shuddering down his spine. Emma wasn't worthless. She was intelligent and caring. She made people laugh. She made him laugh. She was talented. She had an artist's touch.

And when she touched Will, he felt stronger and more alive. He loved the way she sighed when he nibbled her neck. He loved the way her eyes turned nearly black and slumberous when he kissed her deeply. He loved the determination that straightened her backbone when he told her what to do. That was probably why he ordered her around so much. He loved doing it. He loved…Emma.

Will slumped deeper into the couch, thrusting his fingers into his hair. Could he have screwed up his life any worse? He'd been so callous to her, so idiotic. There was no way she felt the same and no way she'd ever forgive him. He slumped farther, staring at the ceiling.

"Hey." Flynn pulled a small canvas painting out from under the map. "I remember this."

"Is that one of Emma's?" Will stood, needing to touch something she had created. His biggest fear was to lose someone—or something, in the case of the float—for inexplicable reasons, and yet he'd thrown a chance at love away because he couldn't forgive Emma for things beyond her control. His father was right. Accidents had no clear line of blame. And he'd realized his misperception too late.

"This is horrible." Will forced levity into his tone as he looked at the painting and tried to forget the pain in Emma's eyes. "You've got a big butt."

"I was big boned," Flynn said.

Will clasped his friend's shoulder, needing an anchor. "And I was good at basketball."

"How. Is Rose?" Tracy stepped into the barn, one hand clenched tightly at her side.

Emma was happy to see her friend. It was late morning. She stood in front of the float, staring at it as if it was going to be her next great work of art.

As if. She'd been contemplating it for too long. There was no inspirational music playing in her head. Only the distant, disapproving rumble of a diesel engine.

She smiled gently at Tracy. "She'll be all right. One more night in the hospital. Which is probably as much time as she can take with my mom."

Tracy rolled her eyes sympathetically. They both knew how militant Emma's mother could be. "I decided. To suck. It up. And be. Grand Marshal."

"I'm sorry I got you into that. But I know you'll do a great job."

"Knock wood." Tracy rapped on the barn door. "What are. You doing?"

Emma turned back to the float, clenching and unclenching her fingers as if they'd cramped. "I'm going to fix the float. Somehow."

"But you can't. Paint."

Emma laughed, but it was an empty, sad sound. "Thanks for reminding me."

Tracy walked inside and stood next to Emma. "I heard what. You said. About. Worthless."

Emma fisted her hands tighter, knowing she deserved Tracy's censure, but nonetheless feeling the stab of hurt.

"I agree," Tracy said.

Emma imagined herself crumpling to the ground, beaten by life's obstacles and the loss of her best friend. The smell of dirt and defeat were so sharp, so real, she was surprised she was still standing.

"No, no. I am. Worthless." Tracy sucked in a breath, blew it out forcefully. "Too."

"You're not," Emma whispered. "You're not broken or disabled."

"But—"

"I don't care what anyone says. I know

you." She poked Tracy's shoulder. "I see the anger when Will finishes your sentences. The joy when you paint. You aren't broken. And I should know." She laughed, this time bitterly. "I see the way you hide your laughter when Flynn and Will talk in movie quotes. I hear your frustration when the words don't come fast enough. And I feel your pain when you hold words in rather than try to join a conversation. If anyone ever tells you you're disabled, you tell them they don't speak your language. You are not broken."

Tracy grabbed Emma and hugged her tight. "I'm sorry. I'm a big B."

"Me, too." Emma knew Tracy wanted to say more, but she didn't need to hear her friend's words. Because Emma knew. She knew that today she'd finally had her apology accepted and forgiveness offered. Today was the day she'd been waiting for since the accident.

After a brief episode of tears on both their parts, Tracy sniffed. "Do you. Forgive me?"

Emma wiped at her eyes. "Shouldn't I be saying that?"

"No. I've been. Letting people. Boss me around," Tracy said. "Should have. Insisted. To see you. And said. I forgive."

Emma couldn't work words past the tightness in her throat.

"I brought you. Something." Tracy opened her fist to reveal an artist Carina Career doll.

Emma plucked the doll from her hand and looked at Carina's paint-stained coveralls and perky ponytail. "Carina looks confident no matter what her career." Emma could use some of her chutzpah.

"You draw." She pointed at the float. "I'll paint. We'll fix it. Together."

Emma's pulse beat so loud it drowned out all the sounds of the accident in her brain. And yet, above the pounding, she heard her grandmother's high-pitched singing, Ping's distinctive meow, Tracy's ripple of laughter and Will's deep voice telling her most fears were silly.

"I know people believe in me." Emma drew a deep breath and stared at her hands. "The question is…do I believe in me?"

"WHAT ARE. YOU doing?" Tracy appeared in Will's bedroom doorway the morning of the Spring Festival.

Without looking at Tracy, Will transferred another stack of shirts from his dresser to his suitcase. "I'm leaving."

"Because of E-Emma?"

"Among other things."

Tracy sat down on the bottom bunk, slouching so she wouldn't hit her head on the one above. "You like her."

"I do." He looked at Tracy, expecting to see the frail woman he'd taken home from the hospital. But there was color to her cheeks now, even if there were circles under her eyes. Harmony Valley was good for her. "I realized something in the past day or so. You can't blame people for accidents. I...I forgive Emma. I'm going to tell her before I leave." But he wouldn't tell her he loved her. He couldn't stand to see her disdain when she rejected him. And she had many reasons to reject him.

"You like her," Tracy repeated, wonder in her voice.

"Do we have to have this conversation?"

"Yes." Tracy snorted. "You don't...know best. For anyone...not even. You."

Will stopped packing and sat on the bed next to her. "Am I really that much of a mess?"

"Yes." But she was grinning. "A friend. Called me. About a. Job in. Santa Rosa. I want. To take it. When I. Can drive."

Will hugged her. "That's wonderful. But

you realize I'm going to call you every day when you're gone."

"Call?" She pulled back to look at him, her blue eyes sparkling with laughter. Talking on the phone was definitely not the best way to stay in touch with her, at least for now.

"You're right. I'll text or email."

"Okay. Now. Come to…the festival."

"No."

"I have. A surprise…for you there."

"I can't. Rose will be there. And you know how I upset Rose." And Emma. She'd be there. He didn't think he could stand to see Emma in front of everyone. He had to see her alone.

Tracy stood up and held out her hand. "Come on. Y-you'll like. My surprise. And I'm the… Grand Marshal."

Will relented, letting his sister lead him out to the living room.

She let go of his hand and walked over to their dad, who was reading the newspaper in his recliner. "Dad. Time to go."

Ben lowered his paper and looked at his two children. "I think I'll skip the festival this year."

"Grand Marshal." Tracy tapped her chest and walked to the door without looking back.

Shrugging, Will went out after her, followed by Ben.

Tracy led them to the far side of East Street, where the floats were hitched to trucks and lined up for the festival's parade behind Mayor Larry's white convertible.

"Do I really need to see them?" Will muttered, meaning the floats from the Ladies Auxiliary, the Lions Club and the Veterans.

Tracy turned around and shook her finger at him.

Ben laughed.

And then Will realized that there was a fourth float hitched to Flynn's black truck. It was their float, stripped down to nothing but the plywood backdrop and painted with the delicate lines and brushstrokes of a true artist—Emma. Oh, there were still thick strokes that had Tracy's magic on them, but the buildings, the oak tree in the town square, the communications tower on top of Parish Hill, all had Emma's finesse.

A group of kids from Rose's production of *The Music Man,* complete with their T-shirts painted to look like band jackets, started swarming the float.

"Careful." Tracy helped some of the smaller kids up.

"I'm going to go really slow." Flynn hopped over the hitch, a grin splitting his face beneath his ball cap. "Nobody's going to fall off. Uncle Will is going to walk next to the float to make sure of it."

"But—"

"It was all Emma," Slade said, leaning out the window of Flynn's truck, his bright red tie a signal flare of hope.

"Hey!" Tracy protested.

"And Tracy," Slade amended with a salute her way.

"Together?" Will couldn't believe it.

"She's my…best friend." Tracy grinned. "She said she…painted this…because of. Rose and. Me…and you."

This was the heart of Harmony Valley—people pulling together and creating everyday miracles, helping each other heal, giving and receiving forgiveness. Will could see it now in the smiles of his friends and family. He could feel it in their energy and enthusiasm. With a community like Harmony Valley behind him, he could do anything.

And then he saw something else. The kernel of an idea for a new app.

"Where is this best friend of yours?" Will

had to talk to Emma. He had many things to say to her.

But no one had seen her.

"AND FIRST PLACE in our float competition goes to..." Mayor Larry's gaze ranged over the crowd.

Most people in the town square were sitting on folding chairs. A few were taking a little midmorning snooze, waiting for the ceremony to end and the barbecue to begin.

Will held his breath and Tracy's hand. She'd done a spectacular job making announcements throughout the morning. Her speech was halting, but heartfelt.

Mayor Larry put an end to the suspense. "A New Future for Harmony Valley! By Will Jackson, Emma Willoughby and friends."

Will didn't hear anything for a few minutes but enthusiastic shouts followed by slaps on the back from Flynn, Slade and his father.

"Speech! Speech!" his father yelled, pulling him in for a hug. "I'm proud of you, son."

"Me. Too." Tracy made it a group hug.

Will thought he might collapse from sheer happiness.

Mayor Larry was waving at him. "Will, come on up here. And bring Emma with you."

He looked around, but Will didn't see Emma. He climbed onto the podium solo with a grin that he felt down to his very toes. "I need to say that this town has taught me a lot. Building a winery here means so much to me, more now than when my partners and I started talking about it. It means so much to me that I've decided to make my home here."

On the grass below him, Flynn and Slade exchanged surprised looks.

"It means that fire and medical services will return to town. Where's Rose?" He found her sitting behind him on stage. "No one should have to wait thirty minutes for emergency services, right?"

"Right-o!" Rose wore a pink hat worthy of the Kentucky Derby, but it still failed to cover the big white bandage at the back of her head.

"And I promise, if we can't save the old oak tree, we'll plant a new one."

Rose grinned. "The winery's got my vote, once they let me vote again."

"You don't know how much your support means to me. You were a strong advocate for what was right in this town." Will scanned the crowd, but still didn't see Emma. He experienced a moment of panic. Maybe she'd left already, taking Ping with her. "This winery means that my sister or your niece or your granddaughter can find a job in town if she wants it. Or go searching for her place in the world if she doesn't."

"That's me!" Tracy waved at him and then pointed to the oak tree, where he finally found Emma, leaning against the trunk. Her hair was in a messy ponytail, her jeans were paint stained and her pink T-shirt looked slept in, and yet she couldn't be more beautiful to him.

But he had the podium and he was going to use his few minutes to make a difference. "A winery here means that our traditions, crazy as some of them are, will be passed on to our children and grandchildren. But only if we embrace change, not only in town, but here, in our hearts." Will tapped his chest lightly, sparing a glance toward the grain silo, knowing his mother would approve.

The crowd applauded with more enthusiasm.

"It looks as if you boys are going to get your rezoning permit." Mayor Larry gave him a thumbs-up.

"But none of this would have been possible without my great business partners, my wonderful sister and one very special woman." Will's eyes locked on to Emma's. "She's an amazing, talented person. A woman who reminded me that you have to let people choose what's best for them, and that you have to keep reaching deep until you find forgiveness."

"Who is he talking about?" Rose asked.

Will turned, but kept the microphone close so that everyone could hear. "I'm talking about Emma. She makes me a better man."

"Oh." Rose fluttered her hands. "Proceed."

Will turned around. Emma had her hand over her mouth. But she wasn't running and she wasn't frowning. It was hard to tell from this distance, but the look in her eyes seemed almost...hopeful.

"I forgive you, Emma," Will said. "In my heart I forgave you long before I realized it in my head. But more important, I'm asking you to forgive me. I wasn't ready for you. Not the way you make me look at life or the way you make me feel. I may look rich on paper, but I'm poor without you." And he'd be destitute if she never forgave him. "Over the years, I've tried to keep every promise I've made, at least, the ones that counted. But I've made you a promise I don't think I can keep—the one about never kissing you again."

"You do realize you're saying all that into the microphone?" Rose asked.

"Yes, Rose, I want everyone to hear, because in keeping with Harmony Valley tradition, I have something to say to Emma underneath the oak tree." He abandoned the podium and walked down the steps, never taking his eyes off Emma.

The crowd began to murmur, and those who were standing parted to let him pass. In his wake, Flynn, Slade, Tracy, Rose and Ben followed.

"When did they fall in love?" Rose asked behind him. "If she says yes, I'm going to have to get her a pair of handcuffs sooner than I expected."

Will chuckled. Something in the grass caught his eye and he knelt to pick it up. When he reached Emma, he took one of her hands in his. "Life put you in my path again for a reason. And now I find it difficult to contemplate going through life without you."

Will dropped to one knee. In his free hand was a dandelion. He twirled it, made a wish and blew.

He ignored his father's mutter about weeds.

He did not ignore Emma's intake of breath or the sparkle in her dark chocolate eyes.

"I won't tell you what I wished for. I think you know." He'd wished for forgiveness and everything that went along with it. Patience and kindness. Love that was everlasting. "I love you, Emma. I think I've loved you for years without ever knowing it."

"You'll recognize it now," Mr. Mionetti said. "She'll never let you forget it."

The trouble with public proposals, Will realized belatedly as the crowd laughed, was that your audience considered the experience interactive. The object of Will's affection had yet to speak.

Tracy exchanged a soft smile with Emma. It was approving, not that they needed it.

"Emma Willoughby, I love you. Please do me the honor of becoming my wife."

And then Emma was in his arms, tumbling them to the grass with a kiss that said *yes,* and one that said *I love you,* and another that said *forever.*

* * * * *

REQUEST YOUR FREE BOOKS!
2 FREE WHOLESOME ROMANCE NOVELS IN LARGER PRINT
PLUS 2
FREE
MYSTERY GIFTS

✻✻✻✻✻✻✻✻✻✻✻✻✻✻✻✻✻✻✻✻✻✻✻✻✻✻

HEARTWARMING™

❋❋❋❋❋❋❋❋❋❋❋❋❋❋❋❋❋❋❋❋❋❋❋❋❋

Wholesome, tender romances

YES! Please send me 2 FREE Harlequin® Heartwarming Larger-Print novels and my 2 FREE mystery gifts (gifts worth about $10). After receiving them, if I don't wish to receive any more books, I can return the shipping statement marked "cancel." If I don't cancel, I will receive 4 brand-new larger-print novels every month and be billed just $4.99 per book in the U.S. or $5.74 per book in Canada. That's a savings of at least 23% off the cover price. It's quite a bargain! Shipping and handling is just 50¢ per book in the U.S. and 75¢ per book in Canada.* I understand that accepting the 2 free books and gifts places me under no obligation to buy anything. I can always return a shipment and cancel at any time. Even if I never buy another book, the two free books and gifts are mine to keep forever.

161/361 IDN F47N

Name _____ (PLEASE PRINT)

Address _____ Apt. #

City _____ State/Prov. _____ Zip/Postal Code

Signature (if under 18, a parent or guardian must sign)

Mail to the **Harlequin® Reader Service:**
IN U.S.A.: P.O. Box 1867, Buffalo, NY 14240-1867
IN CANADA: P.O. Box 609, Fort Erie, Ontario L2A 5X3

* Terms and prices subject to change without notice. Prices do not include applicable taxes. Sales tax applicable in N.Y. Canadian residents will be charged applicable taxes. Offer not valid in Quebec. This offer is limited to one order per household. Not valid for current subscribers to Harlequin Heartwarming larger-print books. All orders subject to credit approval. Credit or debit balances in a customer's account(s) may be offset by any other outstanding balance owed by or to the customer. Please allow 4 to 6 weeks for delivery. Offer available while quantities last.

Your Privacy—The Harlequin® Reader Service is committed to protecting your privacy. Our Privacy Policy is available online at www.ReaderService.com or upon request from the Harlequin Reader Service.

We make a portion of our mailing list available to reputable third parties that offer products we believe may interest you. If you prefer that we not exchange your name with third parties, or if you wish to clarify or modify your communication preferences, please visit us at www.ReaderService.com/consumerchoice or write to us at Harlequin Reader Service Preference Service, P.O. Box 9062, Buffalo, NY 14269. Include your complete name and address.

HWDIR13R

ReaderService.com

Manage your account online!
- Review your order history
- Manage your payments
- Update your address

*We've designed
the Harlequin® Reader Service
website just for you.*

Enjoy all the features!
- Reader excerpts from any series
- Respond to mailings and special monthly offers
- Discover new series available to you
- Browse the Bonus Bucks catalog
- Share your feedback

Visit us at:
ReaderService.com

LARGER-PRINT BOOKS!

GET 2 FREE
LARGER-PRINT NOVELS
PLUS 2 FREE
MYSTERY GIFTS

Love Inspired

Larger-print novels are now available...